To Suzanne and Mace,

THE TIDES
OF CECIL COVE

Life on our cove is good!

Shannon O'Barr Sausville

Shannon

This is a work of fiction. Any resemblance to actual
persons or events is coincidental.

LARKINGTON COVE BOOKS

ISBN-13: 978-0692093207
ISBN-10: 0692093206

For everyone who loves the magnificent Chesapeake

CHAPTER ONE

Julie has moved back to Cecil Cove. Contractors had been working on her grandmother's cottage for months preparing it for her return, although Julie herself had been absent during all the construction. When I heard tires crunching on the gravel road, I looked up from doing the dishes to see an unfamiliar SUV pull into the garage next door and knew that the day of her return had finally arrived.

Most people wouldn't expect to encounter a gravel road only thirty miles from Washington, D.C. For me, that throwback feature engendered some of the visceral appeal of the waterfront community on the Western Shore of the Chesapeake Bay. Originally my community consisted of a collection of modest vacation cottages dating from the era before construction of the Bay Bridge made the Eastern Shore a viable weekend getaway. Now, however, those little cottages had been renovated, expanded, and winterized, with roofs raised and modern amenities added; these changes allow my generation to live full-time on the estuarine fingers of the Chesapeake Bay and commute in and out like the tides to professional jobs in D.C. or Baltimore. Almost all of the roads in the community had started as dirt or gravel or even oyster shell. Over the five or six decades since the cottages were originally plunked down on the most minimal foundations, various groups of neighbors had pitched in to asphalt the majority of the roads until only the last dozen or so houses remained unpaved. I hadn't realized how integral the sound of car tires crunching on gravel was to my memories of living here until I'd moved back just over ten years ago; the sound induces a mental downshift when my tires hit rock at the end of a work day leaving the outside world back on the asphalt.

Julie's husband died somewhat more than a year ago. The neighbors had told me about Bobby's death. In this small community everyone eventually heard almost any piece of news about anyone tied to our little set of homes.

I hadn't gone to the funeral. As much as I had once loved Julie, as much as I had once considered her my sister, I had mentally tried to cut her and Bobby out of my life so completely that they may as well have been dead for the last thirty years. How could I go to the funeral of someone I hadn't treated as living? I had left my anger at Julie herself behind quite some time ago. If forgiveness from either of us was going to be expressed though, I didn't think her husband's funeral was the place for that to happen.

Julie had sent cards for seminal life events over the years, presumably as a way of letting me know that she had let go of her anger and possibly as a way of reaching out to me. Even after I had started to let go of my anger though, I hadn't know how to respond to her efforts, so I hadn't.

Now she was going to be living back in the cove where our friendship had started more than thirty years ago.

SIOBHAN MAY 1971

Dad stood waist deep in the rising mid-tide next to our dock behind the stern of a small fishing boat. With his T-shirt in a heap on the dock, he was wearing only a bathing suit. He had the cover of the boat's outboard engine off, grumbling a bit to himself about how he needed to finish up before he left for Texas tomorrow. Brian was sitting on the dock next to Dad's toolbox, handing down tools like nurses hand surgeons their instruments. I had brought down a coloring book and a box of crayons but had left them strewn on the picnic table. I was sitting on the dock next to Brian swinging my legs over the water.

A handful of one to two foot swells rolled through and rocked the boat right when Dad was putting some part or another in place. His wrench and the part fell, fortunately, in the boat, not in the water. Dad cursed anyway, "These assholes that don't slow down at no wake zones."

I teased him, "Daddy said a bad wooorrd…. But there aren't any boats out there right now. Where did the waves come from?"

Dad walked along the outside edge of the boat to a point where he could reach in to grab the dropped tool. He looked up at me and answered, "The boat passed into the creek a minute ago. It takes about a minute for the waves to reach us."

Brian chimed in, "Count alligators the next time a big boat comes in without slowing down."

"Count alligators?" I questioned. "What do you mean?"

Pointing with his wrench toward the buoy marking the entrance from the river into the creek, Dad answered, "When a big boat passes the no wake buoy without slowing down start counting one alligator, two alligator, three alligator….. until the waves from the boat start slapping up against our shore."

"Oh, you mean seconds. We do Miss-i-ssipp-is in school," I sing-songed.

"Well, you can do Mississippis if you want. I'd rather count alligators though."

Of course it seemed like forever before another big boat came into Lord's Creek from the river without slowing down. As soon as one did, I started chanting alligators, walking up and down the dock. Dad had been right. The waves from the boat took over a minute to reach our shore. "Seventy-two alligator, seventy-three alligator." I stopped counting as the waves started to slap our dock.

A slightly worried voice at my elbow asked, "There aren't really alligators, are there?"

I spun my head around quickly. Julie had appeared on the dock. I had played with her a couple times last summer when she was visiting her grandmother, but I hadn't seen her since. She was wearing a purple jumper and sandals with white straps. Her long brown hair was a little messy the whole way down to her waist.

"No, I'm just seeing how long the waves of a boat take to get here," I answered.

"Oh." Julie didn't seem interested.

A slightly alarmed disembodied female voice yelled, "Julie, where are you?"

Dad, whose yelling started at stentorian and got louder from there, bellowed out, "She's on our dock, Mrs. Marconi."

A few seconds later, wearing a cotton housedress and slippers, Mrs. Marconi walked out onto her dock and looked over at ours. "Julie, tell me you did not climb the fence in your jumper and sandals, did you?"

"No, of course not. I walked on the rocks." Julie pointed to the riprap that protected both of our shores. Some of the neighbors had expensive wooden bulkheads. Dad, however, had put in the piles of stone known as riprap on both our and Mrs. Marconi's shoreline earlier in the spring, borrowing equipment from friends at the marina to move the piles of rock. The riprap was not only cheaper, according to Dad, but I liked it because it made great homes for water creatures. I often saw blue crabs do the sideways crawl named for them into holes in between the rocks. I was never sure whether the crabs were looking for food or trying not to become someone else's food. Water snakes also seemed to view the riprap as a waterfront apartment complex and could often be seen slithering into various crevices or sunning themselves on the portions of the rock above the tide.

Mrs. Marconi shook her head. "Oh, much better to walk on wet rocks in sandals. Julie is going to be staying with me this summer because both of her parents will be traveling for work. I reckon this won't be the last time she appears on your dock, Jack."

Dad dismissed her concern with, "I'm sure there will be mutual invasions." He pointed at me and Brian with his wrench. "I'm just about done with this boat. I was going to ride my kids over to the marina, park this money pit, and get my pickup. There're enough life jackets for Julie if you want her out of your hair for a little while."

Julie's grandmom said, "If you're sure she's not in your way." Julie was jumping up and down on the dock with her hands folded together as if in prayer, leaving her grandmother no doubt as to what Julie wanted.

Julie and I colored until Dad was done. Brian grabbed the green crayon and drew alligators on the inside cover of my coloring book. When it was time to go, we each sat on the edge of the dock, where Dad grabbed us each by the waist and lowered us one by one into the boat. He climbed out of the water and up the ladder at the back of the boat, handing us each a life jacket as he moved forward to the wheel. "Put it on or you don't go," Dad commanded.

Brian asked, "How come you don't have to wear one then?"

"Because I can swim a heck of a lot better than you," Dad answered. He started up the engine, which as far as I could tell sounded like he'd fixed it. He undid the lines from the dock and spat some tobacco over the side of the boat as he was backing out.

"Oooohhh, gross Dad." I made a squished up face.

He turned around and grinning looked back at me "Gross, maybe, but a lot safer than lighting a cigarette when you're working on a gas engine. You wouldn't want me to get blown up, would you?"

"Noooo." I hadn't been paying attention, but I then realized that Dad had been without the usual cigarette perched in the corner of his mouth all afternoon.

He took the boat slowly out of Cecil Cove and into Lord's Creek, pointing out to us that he was observing the no wake zone. When he left the creek and got out into the river, he pushed the throttle forward and picked up speed. A couple times he deliberately crossed some small wakes from other boats to bounce us around a bit. The ride to the marina, one creek up from us, was unfortunately only a few short minutes.

Brian asked, "Why don't we get a boat of our own, Dad?"

"Because boats are money pits, son." Dad answered. "They are always breaking down, just like this one. Then it costs a fortune to fix them. Particularly if you pay for the marina to do it. I told my buddy I could fix this for one-third of what the marina would have charged him. But the marina won't let me do the work at their place, so I told my buddy to have it towed to our dock."

"Why do boats break down so much? And why do so many people have them anyway?" Brian continued.

"Salt water is bad for engines, Brian. That's why I've got such a great job out on the oil rigs and the tanker ships. Something is always going wrong with that much water and wind around equipment. They've got mechanics for the small stuff, but for the big stuff, they need engineers too."

Dad maneuvered the boat into its slip at the marina. He stowed our life jackets back under the seats of the boat and lifted each of us up onto the dock. He left the keys to the boat in the office. We went into the marina store to see if Grandpa was working. He wasn't, but I loved the little store at the water's edge anyway, even though it wasn't much more than a small shack with a dingy cracked linoleum floor. Boaters could buy soda, bait, and oil for their boat, all in one spot.

What I loved most about the store was the one-armed bandit hiding in the back corner with a big "Out of Order" sign on it. Dad had told me that right around when I was learning to walk Anne Arundel County had banned slot machine gambling. According to Dad, the marina owner had been friends with an owner of one of the slot machine halls. To keep federal agents from seizing all of his equipment, the casino owner had conspired with friends to sneak a few of the machines out hoping that the ban would be lifted after a few months. The marina owner hid the slot machine in the back of the marina store and put an out of order sign on it, although he would tell people he trusted with a wink and a nod that it worked just fine. The bandit had stopped with a martini glass, an olive and a bunch of cherries in its windows. The arm was secured in place with a rope that went around to the back of the machine that I assumed was to keep people from pulling on the arm for fun.

Although we pleaded for sodas, Dad shooshed us out of the store after he chatted with the teenager who was working the register and headed us to the gravel parking lot. Dad opened the passenger door to his pickup truck and told me and Julie to get in. Then he told Brian to climb in the back.

"How come we can't ride in the back if Brian gets to? I always ride in the back going home from the marina." I whined.

"Because I didn't ask Mrs. Marconi if it was ok for Julie to ride in the back, and Julie's not my kid. So, you can stay up here with her." Dad answered.

"Awww man." I knew arguing further was pointless, but I told Julie that we needed to make sure that we asked her grandmother about riding in the back for next time. Julie nodded intently.

Julie and I spent almost every day together that summer. As soon as we were dressed and had eaten breakfast, Mom would push me and Brian outside, with Mrs. Marconi doing the same with Julie. We had no shortage of outdoor activities. Some days Brian would abandon us to play with other boys, other days he would play with us, and on some days every prepubescent kid male or female on the cove joined forces for some game or another.

Mrs. Marconi's yard had exactly enough room for a croquet course that she left up the whole summer, although Mrs. Marconi's bright aqua bird bath with seahorses spouting water out the top was smack in the middle of the course. Brian was the best at croquet, and since I could never beat him, I mostly tried to knock his balls out of position with mine.

Julie and I also liked to set up a pretend restaurant on whichever dock we were playing that day. I took Frisbees and filled them with oyster shells from the yard, acting like I was serving plates of raw oysters. Sometimes I would add the black walnuts that fell all over our entire lane as an appetizer. The neighbors on the opposite side of our house from Julie's grandmother only used the house for occasional vacations, leaving me free to pick the wild raspberries that proliferated in their unkempt yard and add them to the menu. Julie preferred to play bartender, filling up Styrofoam cups with water from the cove, decorating the cups and pretending they were cocktails with fancy names.

Brian, this other boy Bobby who lived on the creek, and Jim, who lived on the other side of the cove, were into playing Indians that summer. They weren't allowed to take the canoes out by themselves yet, but they were allowed to sit in them and beat on some cheap drums Jim's parents had bought him. One day when we were on our side of the cove, Brian let me and Julie help him put a bunch of Baltimore Colts stickers all over our canoe, which he named *The Colt*. He told us that having the stickers meant the Big Horse God would protect us when we were in the canoe. I wasn't sure what a horse god could do on the water, but I had fun putting the stickers on.

If Mom, Mrs. Marconi or some other parent was willing to sit on a dock, every kid on the cove could be found swimming. Every family had at least a few rafts or inner tubes, all of which ended up shared in the middle of the cove.

As long as the weather was decent, Julie, Brian and I were outside from the time we got pushed out the door in the morning until dinnertime. Even for lunch, we were expected to stay outside, with Mom or Mrs. Marconi bringing sandwiches and Kool-Aid down to the dock. When Dad was out of town, Mom and Mrs. Marconi often combined efforts for dinner meaning Julie and I got dinner together too. We separated at bath time, only to start all over again the next day.

On rainy days, Mrs. Marconi taught us to make peanut butter cookies from scratch and brownies from the box mix. Mom occasionally brought home some leftover arts and crafts from the church's vacation bible school. She didn't teach the bible school, as she didn't have the patience for that many kids. She did, however, help clean up the rooms after the kids were all gone. If the leftover materials weren't enough to save for a future class, she got to bring them home for us. If we had been allowed to stay inside, Julie would have been content to work on those projects all day every day; her projects always turned out better than mine.

Dad was gone almost the whole summer except for a couple weekends, and Julie only saw her parents one weekend the whole summer. The best day of the whole summer came one day in mid-July when Dad was home. Julie and I were playing Chutes & Ladders in our living room when Dad came in grinning. Dad announced that we needed to come out to the garage, and we followed willingly enough. The big doors were open with Mom and

Mrs. Marconi standing in the entry way. They moved aside, and Julie and I saw two brand new three-speed bikes, identical except for color. The one for me was candy apple red, and the one for Julie was a vivid purple. Each bike had a small white wicker basket on the handlebar with somewhat tacky plastic flowers the color of the bike glued to the basket.

Mrs. Marconi admonished, "Julie, you need to thank Mr. Barrett for putting your new bike together for you." We both came out of our awed trance to give excited hugs to Mom, Dad, and Mrs. Marconi. Mrs. Marconi had gone to the store the day before and had the store load the boxes in the back of her station wagon. Dad got up early and put them together for us.

I had been learning on Brian's ugly old brown baby bike, onto which Dad had put the training wheels back. I had been trying to convince Dad to take off the training wheels and let me try to ride by myself. Julie had a bike at her parents' house that still had its training wheels too but she had not had any sort of bike at her grandmother's.

We both jumped on our new bikes and managed to wobble for a few feet before ending up in an undignified half-tilt with one leg on the ground that was better than completely falling over but not by much. Dad grabbed the back end of Julie's bike and helped her to make her first tentative loop around the driveway. I was impatiently waiting for Dad to help me when Brian came up behind me eager to emulate Dad. With Brian's help, I started to make my first loop around the driveway, but lost my balance when the loud grunt of a heron directly overhead startled me. Dad showed us where we were allowed to go on the bikes, which was disappointingly only our gravel road as it wrapped around the cove. The whole road was gravel forcing us to work a little harder for stability. To ride on asphalt roads, someone had to take us to the park, and we seldom convinced either my Mom or Julie's grandmother to do so.

Up until we had the bikes, Julie would occasionally try to wheedle some arts and crafts time even when it wasn't raining. Once we had the bikes though, Mom and Mrs. Marconi had to threaten not to let us have dinner if we were late coming inside.

No other girls our age lived on our road. However, since Brian often played with his friend Jim on the far side of the cove we peddled over there regularly, despite the fact that Jim clearly didn't like playing with girls around most of the time. "Tell your sisters to go away," Jim said to Brian one of the first times we came over on our bikes, beating on the drum. "The gods of the Great Shellfish Bay do not like girls."

Brian unintentionally deflected the insult by saying, "Julie's not my sister. Just Siobhan."

"Really," Bobby asked incredulously. "They act like Siamese twins. You never see one without the other." He then pulled the corners of his eyes out with his fingers and broke into a bad version of "We Are Siamese" from *The Lady and the Tramp*. The rest of the summer, whenever the boys saw us coming, they would start singing that song. Julie and I protested, but we were secretly pleased that people considered us sisters.

Julie's parents had enrolled her in a private school closer to their house, forcing her to move back there at the end of the summer. The last day of the summer when her grandmother was packing up some of her stuff into the station wagon to return to her parents', Julie and I hid in the linen closet at my house, burying ourselves under piles of sheets and towels hoping that the adults couldn't find us. Then she wouldn't be able to leave. Of course, we couldn't stop giggling at the brilliance of our plan, and Mom dug us right out. When her grandmother was leading a tearful Julie to her car, she tried to console us by saying that Julie's parents were still likely to travel during the school year, and she expected to have Julie over on some weekends. We knew seeing each other only on the weekends wouldn't be the same as during the summer though.

I told Julie I hoped that her parents had to work all next summer so we could have another summer like this one. Julie was already crying because she had to leave, but she seemed to cry harder when I said this, although I didn't understand why.

CHAPTER TWO

Bobby's death ripped out all the north-south threads of the tapestry of my life, leaving behind only a sad tangle of my east-west running threads. Bobby had been my north and south for thirty years. He was the logical, practical, orderly one, always cutting straight through my seat-of-the-pants emotional reactions. We had woven our lives together with children, grandchildren, extended family, hopes, dreams and hard work. Now all of those years of work were in a jumbled mess at my feet.

I woke up over and over again every night after Bobby died, sweating and panting. When my body succumbed to sleep, my mind leaped on the opportunity to reshuffle all the decisions of the last several months of Bobby's life, as if desperate to find some sequence of choices I or the doctors or Bobby could have made that would have made the outcome different. Details of his illness that I didn't even realized I'd noticed at the time had been recorded somewhere by my mind and were now nocturnally broken apart and endlessly reassembled. I was so tired some mornings that I could barely sift through what was real and what my mind had invented during the fitful tossings I called sleep.

13

As the weeks of widowhood started to play out, I felt choked by our home just outside of Washington, D.C. This despite the fact that our neighbors and friends had been as helpful as Santa's elves on Christmas Eve. When Bobby had been in the hospital, the holiday decorations for Halloween, Thanksgiving and Christmas had magically popped out of our garage and onto our lawn. I would come home at the end of visiting hours to find plates of lasagna in the fridge. The dog had had more play dates than most of the urban toddlers of this affluent Chevy Chase neighborhood. The support had been critical for coping with the illness and the first few days after Bobby died. Once the initial wave of visitors and pity had abated though, coping with my loss seemed to get harder not easier.

Our social life since the kids had moved on to college and beyond had been about couples. Couples hanging out drinking wine, talking about jobs, and complaining about their almost grown kids who nevertheless still needed cash. I was no longer a couple. No overt pity nor any lack of welcome emanated from our group of friends. But when I was with them now, both they and I were pretending things were the same when nothing would ever be the same.

In the house itself, memories launched themselves at me out of inanimate objects. I ruthlessly collected all of Bobby's things and crammed them into his walk-in closet so that I wouldn't be continually battered when I saw them while microwaving a meal or watching TV or taking a shower. I wandered through our 3,500 square foot house wondering what the hell I needed all that space for. I jammed clothes in bags that I intended to set out for some charity or other and piled them in one of the kids' old bedrooms. On some evenings I would be so dizzied by wandering through the house that I would jump in the SUV and drive to the mall, wandering through shops without buying anything, watching a movie, all ensuring that I stayed until the mall closed to avoid facing the house.

Then a few months after Bobby died, when I was utterly losing my mind trying to cope, I got the news that my grandmother's nephew Bill had passed away. He had been living in her cottage since 1981. Shortly after Grandmom's death in 1989, her lawyer had told me and Bobby that she had left the cottage in a trust with Bill as the beneficiary.

Bill had been a little slow. He had worked steadily at his job as a stock person in an auto parts store for his whole adult life with a slightly lopsided grin perpetually plastered on his face. As far as anyone knew, he hadn't drank alcohol or done drugs or in any way caused trouble. He bought frozen dinners by the dozen and ate alone at home. He hadn't seemed to need a social life outside of the store, all the better since he couldn't get much beyond, "Hi, how are you?" I guess Grandmom had wanted to make sure he could live comfortably, and setting him up in the cottage was her way of assuring his lifestyle.

I found out now though that the lawyer had been under strict instructions not to divulge until Bill's death that I was the ultimate beneficiary; Grandmom's trust had only left Bill the right to live in the cottage. Hence now that Bill was gone, the cottage was mine. A little ray of clarifying sunlight crept into my brain, and my plan started to form as the possibilities afforded by Grandmom's bequest sank in. I doubted myself and chewed over and re-worked my plan, wondering if I was making the apparently common mistake of the recently aggrieved widow trying to make changes too soon. When I put my plan in front of the kids though, they were all supportive, at least in the broad strokes.

Bobby Jr was attending law school in Los Angeles on the premise that a California law school would set him up better for his ultimate dream of being an attorney for the entertainment industry. Bobby's old firm had offices in L.A., and even if they didn't have a position for him, Bobby's colleagues would be able to help him get into a firm. David had enrolled in ROTC practically the second he got to college, and he was heading toward a career in the Navy as soon as he graduated in May. Caitlin had recently turned 27, married to a 35-year-old man with a good solid federal job. She and her husband had a five-year-old, a three-year-old and, if Caitlin had her way, another one would be coming soon. She needed the four bedroom colonial in a solid school district more than I did; despite a good solid income, she could never afford to buy a house in this Chevy Chase neighborhood now.

Bobby had always done the heavy lifting for our estate planning, so I was fairly naïve about how to handle the legal aspects of my plan. I contacted Bobby's former partner who did our prior wills to help me with the paperwork. The broad outline of my plan was that I would move to Grandmom's cottage, Caitlin would end up with title to the Chevy Chase house, after selling her current house to provide her share of the funds to assure that over time the other two kids would end up with the monetary equivalent of their share of the house. Neither of the boys ever anticipated wanting to settle in the D.C. area and would not begrudge Caitlin the house itself as long as they were otherwise fairly compensated. Ever the provider, Bobby had left a substantial life insurance policy leaving me liquid assets to help make the plan work.

I hadn't been to Grandmom's cottage in more than two decades, but I knew the house would be in need of repair and update. I hired a decorator and a contractor to check out the cottage to see what needed to be done and how much renovations would cost. Fortunately, the attorney for Grandmom's trust had been responsible for handling Bill's possessions, and by the time my team got there the cottage was a shell empty of possessions.

The contractor confirmed that the 1,200 square foot cottage did need a lot of work. They reported that the kitchen cabinets were falling apart. The decorator was horrified as she showed me pictures of the bathroom that still had the pink fixtures of the 1960s with tiny black and white tiles on the floor. To add space the contractor raised the roof and put on a partial second floor. I had initially envisioned a more expansive addition, but the contractor told me that I would probably have a few more grandchildren before getting the permits to expand the footprint of a home in a Critical Area. I stared somewhat cluelessly at him when he first mentioned Critical Area. He then launched into a diatribe on the 1984 Critical Area Act that protected with various rules and regulations all land within 1,000 feet of the mean high water line of tidal waters of the Chesapeake Bay and the ongoing difficulties this Act presented to his business. When I interrupted the discourse to ask him what my options were, he stated succinctly that going up is easier than going out and recommended raising the roof.

I didn't want to see the cottage in its dilapidated state and didn't want to be reminded too much of what the place had looked like when Grandmom had lived there; I therefore told the decorator and contractor in broad strokes what I wanted and left the rest to them. The decorator would periodically come by with a narrow set of choices from which I picked out cabinets, countertops, and colors. Then the contractor executed the plans. The decorator ordered new furniture that blended in with her grand schemes for a modern beach bungalow, allowing me to leave Caitlin most of my more traditionally styled furniture, which fit better in the colonial anyway. The contractor and decorator sent me pictures periodically to show me progress, but when I parked my car in the garage the first time, I stepped into my new beginning and in some ways back into a life I left thirty years ago.

I wasn't entirely admitting my real reasons to myself, but I knew that Siobhan was one reason that I was avoiding the cottage up until the moment of move in. I had long since realized how wrong I had been thirty years ago, but I had never apologized, and I didn't know whether she would want anything to do with me. I had occasional fantasies about the friendship I could have with the woman I once viewed as my sister, now that the two most important people in the world to me, Bobby and my grandmother, were gone. I was afraid that if I saw Siobhan during the renovations, and she told me to go to hell that I would chicken out and give up on my whole plan to move back. I wanted to move in and then do my best to make things work between the two of us. And if I couldn't repair the relationship, then I could act like tons of people who never even knew who their next door neighbors were. Siobhan was not the sort to wage war. If she wanted nothing to do with me, she would simply shut me out.

Months after I set my reinvent-my-life-plan into action, the cottage was ready and moving day had arrived. Inauspiciously, the first step I took out of the Jeep onto the garage floor wrenched my ankle painfully. I looked down to see what I had tripped over and had to pick up the object to see what it was. The surface was gritty and dusty, but when I turned the object over I saw the faded purple wax. It was a sand candle I'd made as a kid. Grandmom used to archive my arts and crafts projects on the shelves that ran around the garage at head height. She had always displayed the most current one on the kitchen fridge or the mantel, but as new masterpieces arrived, older items transferred to the garage storage space. She would tell me that she wanted to keep my treasured artwork in a special spot, but in reality she hadn't wanted to clutter up her small house with every creation I dragged home. The garage shelves appeared to otherwise be cleaned off of all my childhood masterpieces, but this one had survived by blending in with the dusty shelves and cobwebs.

CHAPTER THREE

The dogs brought about our first conversation. When I am home during congenial weather, I often let my two chocolate labs out unattended into the fenced part of my yard. They usually spend the bulk of those times chasing squirrels and running up to the road side of the fence to bark at any strange cars going by. Back when Bill had been feeding the feral cats next door, they also spent much time charging the fence on that side in the vain hope that it would magically disappear. Now my dogs were too old and a bit too overweight to get over the fence, leaving the feral cats completely safe if they stayed in Bill's yard.

Unexpectedly one day three dogs were cavorting in my yard, already friends by the time I noticed the addition outside my kitchen window. I realized from looking at the rather spindly younger dog that just because my fence was an impediment to my dogs, it wasn't a barrier to a more ambitious canine. Since the strange dog drooling with delight all over my two clearly didn't have a mean bone in its body, I walked outside and asked it, "Where'd you come from, fella?"

Julie appeared around the side of her garage and leaned against the fence common to our yards. "Guilty. Literally, he's Guilty. Bobby named him that. I think he made a self-fulfilling prophecy for mischief." She was smiling warmly, but tentatively. Her smile was as it had always been, two rows of perfect white teeth that had not needed the four years of braces mine had. Her straight thick long brown hair that she had always worn as long as it would grow was now cut to shoulder length, expensively coiffed and highlighted. She was a little plump but in a normal middle-aged mother sort of way.

I smiled back. "I believe I was usually the one guilty of letting dogs run amok. Guilty is a great name though. These are Godiva and Hershey," pointing at each of mine in turn. "And I wouldn't have let them out unattended if I had known there was a new dog in town."

Julie nodded and waved her hand in dismissal.

"Welcome back, Jules. I'm so sorry you're back because Bobby's gone though." Such a lame sentence when someone's whole life has been upended, but nothing better had come to mind.

"Thanks. I hope I'm not making a big mistake moving so soon, I mean, they tell you not to make big decisions too quickly after something like this happens, but I was going crazy every time I opened a drawer in the office and saw his handwriting on the files or in the checkbook and then cousin Bill died and ..." She trailed off abruptly and looked abashed. "Sorry, I shouldn't be babbling when my dog is destroying your flower beds." She pointed behind me.

Indeed, Guilty was rolling on his back, all four legs splayed out above his body, twisting his back from side-to-side on top of the pansies and new mulch that had gone down last week. Despite the destruction of several hours of work, nothing but laughter would do. I smacked him playfully on the rump releasing an earthy smelling puff of mulch dust and told him, "C'mon, get up and go back to your momma. You can hang out with your new friends later."

While I was doing this, Julie had come around the fence and in my yard to retrieve him. She looked up somewhat shyly at me and said, "I hope he can." Then she hurried back over to her place, Guilty in tow.

When I realized that Julie was coming back to the cove, I'd obsessed over how our first meeting after all these years would go. Should I bring one of my infamous soups to the front door? Should I stick to my stubbornness and wait for her to approach me? Would we flat out ignore each other? Would she talk to me? All in all, I was just as happy the dogs took the first meeting out of my hands.

SIOBHAN SEPTEMBER 1974

Our big black lab King was true to his breed. At every opportunity, King would try to sneak into the water side of the yard, where he had a free path to fly off the end of the dock in a hopeless attempt to catch a duck. He also loved to dogpaddle out to us when we were swimming. Wet dog didn't bother me, and I delighted in watching dogs swimming, making me the worst culprit in "accidentally" not latching the gate well enough. Mom's response was to shake her head when the soaking wet lab pressed his nose up against the door and leave King outside until he dried out. Dad found dripping canine distinctly offensive and usually started swearing at the sight of wet dog so accidental gate openings were fewer when he was home.

Usually by September too many sea nettles were in the water to continue swimming in the cove. This year though, the end of August had seen so many thunderstorms that the water didn't have enough salt for the nettles. Brian, Julie, King and I therefore kept swimming right up to the first day of school. I was not looking forward to the start of school. First of all, Julie had to spend most of her time back at her parents' house in order to attend her private school. Second, Brian was now in junior high school, leaving me all by myself waiting for the bus. Mom had at least decided that I was old enough to go to the bus stop by myself. I had been afraid that since Brian would not be with me, she would insist on humiliating me by walking me to the stop and waiting with me.

"Seee-ba-han Barrett?"

The latest in what would be a long line of teachers who had no idea how to pronounce the traditional Irish name with which my mother had fallen in love made a worse attempt than average. The name may have given me God's grace, but it didn't spare me from endless teasing from the still somewhat provincial schoolboys when the teacher butchered that name.

I heard the boys all snickering behind me as I raised my hand and informed my new fourth grade teacher "I'm Shi-vawn." The teacher looked somewhat abashed and scribbled something on her attendance list, presumably some pronunciation guide.

After school, I told my Mom and Brian I hated all the boys, hated how they'd made fun of my name. The whole time at recess they had run around the swing set screaming, "Seee-ba-han, Seee-ba-han...." "Everyone knows how to pronounce Brian. Why did you give him such an easy name and me such a horrible one?"

Mom shrugged and seemed generally disinterested. To distract me from my tirade, Brian offered to go swimming with me. "C'mon, we won't have many days left where the water's still warm enough for swimming." We changed into our suits and ran down to the dock. Brian had learned the butterfly stroke in camp this summer. He had been trying to teach me ever since he got back, but my feet willfully refused to stay together for that kick. Since Brian was one of my main swim teachers, and he was now in junior high, Mom had recently relented on her rule that an adult had to be on the dock for me to swim provided Brian was in the water with me and we didn't go further out than the end of the dock. Julie's grandmother was still pretty uptight about unsupervised swimming but since Julie was back with her parents, Mrs. Marconi had to leave us Barrett children to our fate. She was probably looking out her living room window shaking her head though.

While I was still trying unsuccessfully to master the butterfly kick, Brian walked along the shoreline with his arms up like wings and his head bobbing like one of the herons looking for fish. I started laughing too hard to concentrate on kicking.

As we continued to paddle around, I asked Brian, "D'ya wanna play chess after dinner?" Chess was my newest passion, although I didn't quite have the different moves of the different pieces down pat. But I would drag whomever I could to play with me at any point.

Brian was usually a good sport. He never just let me win but he would ask, "Are you sure?" if the move I had made was a bad one. Mom and Dad both knew how to play, but Mom was usually busy with dinner, cleaning up, heading over to the church for some volunteer work or more often these days heading to her room to read before bed. If Dad were home from the oil rig, I could occasionally wheedle him into playing. He never seemed resentful, but I knew if he had the choice he would rather have been reading his newspaper or working on some project out in the garage.

I was a board game freak right from my first game of Chutes and Ladders. Mom and Dad usually got me a new game for my birthday and for Christmas. I would then plague everyone with requests to play the newest game over and over again. Julie was ok with games of chance or checkers, but she didn't have much use for chess or Risk. I liked strategy games that lasted as long as possible. Brian was the one to indulge me no matter what my latest fad was, and his reaction to my chess craze was no more or less enthusiastic than it had been to Sorry! or The Game of Life or Monopoly.

Aside from the rough start with the teasing boys, fourth grade was hands down my favorite year of elementary school. Every afternoon during the first period after recess we learned about Maryland history. Since most of our class lived in the local waterfront communities, our teacher placed a special emphasis on Chesapeake Bay-related facts. She mimeographed maps of different parts of Maryland, and the map she gave us of the South River stayed up on our refrigerator at home until it fell apart years later. The day I brought that map home, I put it on the kitchen counter, proudly showing Mom and Brian that I knew where Cecil Cove was.

"Did you know that Cecil Cove was named after Cecil Calvert, first proprietor of Maryland and the second Lord Baltimore?" I asked, trying not to let proprietor get twisted on my tongue.

Brian questioned, "What's a proprietor?"

"I don't know," I said, somewhat deflated that he had focused on a fact I didn't really understand. "But Cecil was one."

On the map, I ran my finger over where our little Cecil Cove connected up to Lord's Creek, which then joined the South River. "And guess what else," I continued, not giving Mom or Brian enough time to answer. "Lord's Creek was named after Cecil too because he was Lord Baltimore."

I remember Mom harrumphing a little bit. I would find out years later that Mom had always supposed that Lord's Creek had a more celestial connotation, and was somewhat annoyed with my news that the appellation was just another reference to Cecil.

CHAPTER FOUR

JULIE AUGUST 2014

Regular sleep again escaped me when I moved back to the cottage. During the first week I was so exhausted from unpacking that I crashed. After that, although I slept better than I did in the first few months after Bobby died, I had difficulty falling asleep because every unfamiliar creaking of the cottage would startle me back into wakefulness. I took to allowing myself a glass of wine at night to make sure that I could get to sleep. Once I got to sleep though, I started having some variant of the same dream repeatedly, and I would wake up clammy with sweat. Bobby was actually still alive. The ICU had made some terrible mistake and declared him dead, but he came back out of a coma. Then either he finds me at the cottage wondering why I left our house in Chevy Chase or he's wandering around Chevy Chase looking for me confused as to why I left him.

Unable to stay asleep, however, I came to appreciate dawn on Cecil Cove. My designer had assured me that in my bedroom overlooking the water I didn't want the room-darkening shades Bobby required in our Chevy Chase bedroom. The first morning that I awoke in the cottage at dawn to a fuchsia scoop of ice cream filtering through the gossamer sheers on my bedroom window I understood my designer's rationale. I walked to the window to get a better view of the spectacular sunrise but the light was so intense I had to look down, and then I noticed that intense pink color was reflected in the glassy surface of the water below.

Never having been an early riser before Bobby's death I don't have any specific memories of sunrises from childhood at Grandmom's. My parents' waterfront had faced the west such that even if I had been awake for sunrises I wouldn't have seen them there. As I now discovered, the colored cloud shows at dawn were never the same twice. Even on rainy, gloomy days, the play of shadows and shades of gray that appeared were mesmerizing. My favorite sunrises became those where, like the first time I was awakened by one, the enormous scoop of fuchsia ice cream would start to appear over the trees on the opposite side of the creek. I loved how as the sun rose and tightened into a smaller ball in the thick atmosphere of dawn, the light would scatter into the clouds in pinks, yellows, oranges and reds. On a calm day before any boat traffic had disturbed the absolutely flat surface of the water, the usually nondescript blue-brown water perfectly reflected the array of colors. On cloudier days, the orb of the sun itself might be obscured, but a variably intense peach to yellow light would creep out of the clouds and start to show in the water, with the shadows of the trees showing as black outlines in water the color of a child's melted sherbet.

Bobby and I had made a number of trips to the Caribbean over the years, and I had never seen the sunrise reflected in the sparkling clear turquoise water through which one could see to the bottom. The waters of the Chesapeake were nowhere near that clear because the nature of an estuary is to move sediment back and forth with the tides. The suspended silt meant that the water appeared somewhat brownish from up close. At sunrise though, that suspended silt turned the water into a mirror of the cloud show in the sky as effectively as if someone had silvered the back of a piece of glass.

I had a reasonable view of the sunrises from my bedroom window, where I had first noticed them, but the best view to be had was on the dock. I took to setting the timer on the coffee-maker the night before and heading out with the morning French Roast to enjoy the show.

Since the weather was still warm, I bought a kayak, a life jacket and an air horn equipping me to paddle out to where Lord's Creek opened up into the river and I could have a wider horizon to view the dawn. A fraction of the weight of the heavy aluminum canoes we used as kids, the kayak could be slid into the water by even a single middle-aged woman. But this slightly plump slightly out-of-shape middle-aged woman was rather clumsy getting herself in and out of the kayak. After some particularly graceless exits where I rolled myself like a beaching whale onto the surface of the dock, I fantasized either about some dock ladders or a Jet Ski that I could drive up on a boat lift attached to the dock.

After a few viewing sessions with the kayak, I reminded myself that I had taken photography classes in college, and that with a little practice I could probably create some terrific series of sunrises. Maybe I could even use some of them as more personalized art for the walls of the cottage.

Following the sunrise exercises, I would head back in for another round of coffee, a shower and my makeup.

JULIE SUMMER 1978

Since I knew the boys were climbing on Grandmom's woodpile when I went in to the bathroom to put my makeup on, I guess not pulling the curtains was stupid. And sure enough bozo Bobby and ingrate Jim showed up doing a Kilroy imitation at the bathroom window. Once I saw them, they started pretending to put mascara on, opening their eyes and mouth wide and using a finger as a fake brush. I shrieked "Freaks" at them and ran out of the bathroom.

Maybe just maybe if Brian had been at the window, having a boy spying on me wouldn't be that bad. But even if Brian noticed how much I'd developed over the last year, I don't think he'd stop seeing me as his kid sister's best friend. I couldn't even fit in a training bra anymore. No AAA cups for me. But I probably could have had watermelons stuffed under my rainbow t-shirt and Brian wouldn't have paid attention.

Brian had thick black hair that almost touched his shoulders, feathering away from his face. He had his dad's slightly swarthy complexion, unlike Siobhan with her unruly auburn hair and freckled pale complexion that she got from her mom. And Brian's eyes were that smoldering dark brown that I believe is the sexiest eye color possible. Brian wasn't that tall yet, but I would bet that he was going to end up as tall as his dad. If I told Siobhan that her brother was the one I'd developed the massive crush on, she would be appalled. She could only see Brian as a brother.

I was mortified at the idea that anyone would guess that I had a crush on Brian though. Since Jim was the one whose family had the Jet Ski, he was the one I flirted with endlessly to get rides. Jet Skis were still relatively new and not many people had them, at least not on this side of the river. Around my parents' neighborhood, Jet Skis were more prevalent. My parents were gone for most of the summer again though. If I wanted to ride one, I had no option other than to convince Jim.

As we often did when we wanted to hang out with the boys, Siobhan and I pedaled our bikes around the gravel road to Jim's side of the cove after I finished my makeup. Thank God Grandmom had finally gotten me a full-size grown-up ten-speed instead of the purple baby bike with the white flower basket I'd been using since I was about six or seven. Siobhan and I had put cutoff jean shorts on over our bathing suits and rat tail combs in the back pockets to fix our hair before the boys saw us. I was vain about my hair, which was thick, medium brown and perfectly straight reaching almost to my waist. The only time I wore a braid was for swimming. Any other time I had the chance I would let my whole mane loose. Siobhan's hair was a little wiry and since it tended to curl in odd directions, she usually pulled it into a somewhat haphazard pony tail secured with a rubber band. Siobhan's hair could be gorgeous when she would let me blow dry it straight, but she never wanted to be indoors that long in the summer. In the sun its beautiful auburn color matched her eyes perfectly. She hated the accompanying freckles though. As soon as her mom would let her wear makeup, she and I had gone through the makeup aisle at the drug store looking for foundations to cover them up.

Siobhan and I ditched our bikes in Jim's parents' yard and ran out onto their dock. None of us kids had any particular respect for property lines. We ran or biked from yard to yard or swam from dock to dock without ever asking parents whether they wanted us in their yards. At any given time, one lucky set of parents around the cove could look out to see a half dozen or more kids on their dock, while the rest of the parents reckoned the kids would be home by dinner time.

By the time we got around the cove by road and onto the dock, Bobby and Jim had swum across the cove from Grandmom's cottage to Jim's dock towing some logs from the woodpile on the raft. I don't think anyone knew who owned the raft. The base was some lumber fastened together, on top of which someone had attached some corrugated tin. We had loaded sand on the flat surface of the tin. Then we would pile some wood in the center with some old newspapers stuffed underneath for a fire starter. As darkness came, we would push our impromptu bonfire out into the cove with a line attached. If the fire needed more wood, we would pull the raft in, add another log or two and float our fire back out. The next day, one of us would sweep the ashes into the water. The raft would get tied up next to whichever dock was closest until the next bonfire.

"It's too early to light the bonfire," I said. "Aren't you going to take us out on the Jet Ski, Jim?" I tossed some of my hair forward in what I was sure was an alluring maneuver.

"No chance," he replied, not even looking up from where they were arranging logs on the raft. "We ran out of gas yesterday."

"Someone must have a can of gas for their lawnmower around here." I wasn't giving up on a Jet Ski ride that easily.

"Don't be stupid," he chided. "You don't use straight gas. You have to add oil. Dad doesn't let anyone do the fuel mix but him. If you don't get it right, you'll blow the engine up."

I didn't have any comeback for that.

Having set up the bonfire for the night, the boys headed off to play with Jim's car. Jim was only fifteen and didn't have his driver's license yet, but his dad had bought him some beat up old Chevy to fix up. His dad challenged him to get the jalopy working by the time he got his license, but I seriously doubted that Jim would succeed unless Brian worked some miracle. Brian and Siobhan's dad could fix just about anything. When Mr. Barrett was in town, he and Brian were often out in the yard working on a bike, a lawnmower, a boat motor, you name it.

I gave up on the Jet Ski ride, for the moment. Watching boys slobber over car engines was boring, so Siobhan and I took our bikes back to our houses. We spent the rest of the afternoon sunbathing on the dock.

"I'm roasting. Perfect time for to jump in. The tide is full." I knew my statement would re-start our ongoing debate over whether high or low tide was best. I loved the high tides for the swimming. I would complain on those afternoons where the dead low came smack in the middle of the afternoon because I would hit bottom if I jumped off the end of the dock.

Siobhan, however, loved to watch wildlife. In between our cool off swims, she could often be found lying on her stomach on the lawn chair, hanging her head over the dock to spot some form of wildlife doing something she found interesting. Whenever I would complain about a low tide, she would come back at me with how at low tide she could more easily see the crabs that we both loved to eat scuttling around the bottom. She was also not shy about pointing out that when I wasn't babbling incessantly, the birds came closer to the shore at low tide to fish or to pull up the sea grasses from the bottom. I didn't care much about birds though so I stuck to my position favoring high tide and left Siobhan to her birdwatching.

When dusk settled in, we pulled sweatshirts over our bathing suits. The boys lit the bonfire and pushed the raft out into the cove, tying it to Jim's dock. Whenever the fire started to die down, they would pull the raft back in and add more wood to the fire.

We used to try to light sparklers on the raft even though my grandmother went hysterical. She swore someone was going to lose a finger or an eye if we kids played with fireworks. However we reasoned that if Jim's dad bought the sparklers for him, then Jim's dad trumped my grandmother as long as Jim was doing the lighting. Then Jim's next door neighbor had a hissy because we weren't getting the raft far enough away from the docks and houses to set off the sparklers safely. Since all the moms adamantly banned swimming and canoeing after dark, which would be the only way to get the raft out far enough for safe sparkler lighting, we gave up on fireworks completely and just lit bonfires.

CHAPTER FIVE

SIOBHAN JULY 1979

The dead baby blue crab was tangled in the cordgrass, claws pointing downward, its apron almost a translucent white. The tide was coming down from full, waves from the Jet Skiers who were cavorting out in the main body of the river finally lapping up to the riprap on the shore of our isolated little cove, tossing the crab but not enough to release it from the vegetation.

I felt like the crab, snarled in the environment supposed to protect me.

Brian died on the Fourth of July. I was left stuck in this cottage, stuck in this little cove. Always the cove had been our sanctuary from all the petty tragedies of childhood. When the kids teased me about my name, I could come home and read my fantasy novels on the dock. When one Greg Parker didn't know I was alive last summer, Julie and I could practice our crawl stroke racing to the other side of the cove. But Brian was an inseparable part of the landscape, teaching me how to swim, handing Dad tools as he worked on some engine, playing endless board games with me, throwing crab guts into the water as we feasted on the dock. How could I be forced to stay in this house looking out on those waters when Brian would never be part of the picture again?

And I hated the endless procession of casseroles that showed up at our door in the days and weeks following his death with some kind, neighborly face hiding behind it, saying how they weren't trying to intrude but they wanted to be of some help. Most people knew the broad strokes of what had happened, but I know some of the neighbors were hoping to hear the details and were using the casseroles as an excuse to see if we would tell them more of the story.

Bobby and Jim had been almost incoherent with fatigue and grief by the time the police let them come home to the cove the night of the accident. Brian, Bobby and Jim had taken the canoe out to the river to get a better view of the Independence Day fireworks. Except the river at night in a canoe was dangerous, especially on the Fourth of July. Everyone who had a boat poured out of marinas, coves and creeks onto the larger fingers of the Chesapeake to watch fireworks. Most of these people had been drinking Schlitz and eating crabs all afternoon to boot. And just as inevitably, once the fireworks were over, they were all hell-bent on getting home, especially this year since most people still had to work on the next day, a Thursday.

The water was choppy that evening from all the boat traffic, not choppy enough to be a problem to a motor boat. But to a canoe with three rowdy teenaged boys, the water was choppy enough to flip them in water in which none of them could stand. The two boys told the police that the rope we used to tie the canoe to the dock got tangled up with something, and they couldn't get the boat flipped back upright. They gave up on the canoe and started to swim to the closest shore.

When Bobby and Jim hauled themselves on the shore in somebody's yard, they believed Brian was right behind them. He wasn't. They started screaming Brian's name, which brought the owners of the place out. The boys started to go back in the water looking for Brian, but the owners held them back trying to determine what caused the two teenaged boys' hysterics. The owners of the places on either side heard the commotion and came outside as well. Once the adults figured out that a third boy was out there, a couple of the neighborhood men hopped in someone's little john boat, fired up its outboard, and went back out looking with some big flashlights. Someone else called the police, probably one of the wives. Another neighbor who knew Mom from church drove over to our neighborhood to find my parents. In the cerebriform way of all these little creeks off the estuarine rivers off the Chesapeake, the spot where Bobby and Jim had hauled themselves up on shore was not much more than a football field away from our little cove by water, but the distance was almost four miles by road back to our street.

The canoe was found no more than an hour after the boys crawled on shore, drifting upside down, no rope attached, a large dent near the bow. The rope was found early the next morning by a fisherman pulling his crab pots; the rope was tangled up with a pot that had broken free from its mooring, but otherwise not cut or torn. The authorities didn't retrieve Brian's body until the middle of the afternoon when an incoming high tide washed him up on the opposite side of the river where some unlucky homeowner spotted him. The back of his head was matted with blood.

Although everyone calls the large bodies of water directly off the Chesapeake "rivers," they aren't rivers as defined in a geography class. They have no current as most people think of currents, and they don't flow in a single direction. Their waters take their momentum from the tides and to a certain extent the wind. In an actual river searchers would look downstream using the strength of the current to estimate how far a body might move; here the searchers had to look up the tides and find out the direction of the wind. In the late hours of this particular morning, a strong wind from the southeast began pushing up the greater Chesapeake Bay, pushing more water into our river with the tide, but also pushing more water toward the creeks and coves on the northern side of the river.

On finding Brian with the head wound, the police, Department of Natural Resources and Coast Guard concluded that Brian must have untied the rope from the canoe to free it from the crab pot on which it had snagged, tried to pull the canoe back to shore with him, and that most likely some boat had crashed into him and the canoe in the darkness.

Of course, the authorities looked for a boat with damage to its bow over the succeeding days, but on the western side of the Chesapeake alone, there are thousands and thousands of boats, hundreds and hundreds of private docks, and dozens and dozens of marinas, not to mention garages where people store their boats when they're pulled out of the water. Hence, the likelihood of finding a single boat with a ding on its bow was extraordinarily low.

As word spread about the accident, the casseroles started to land like cannonballs pushing me down. Even though many of the drop-ins were from her church, Mom started to hide from the constant string of visitors who just happened to stop by to see if we needed anything, to just make sure we were ok. After a couple days of being polite, I would run to my room when the doorbell rang. Dad had been excused by his company from going back to the Gulf for a few weeks, and since he took refuge in working on engines in the garage, he ended up being the front line for the visitors that would show up at the house.

Brian's memorial service was on the flat grassy field between the community clubhouse and the sands of the community beach. Ashes can't legally be spread in the water within three miles of shore, but the funeral home had given Mom and Dad a tiny box with about a thimbleful worth of ashes in it that they could throw in the creek. After the pastor intoned, "Ashes to ashes, dust to dust..." finishing his part of the service, the whole choir of our local church with its best soprano Abby a few steps in front started singing:

Come to the water
Stand by my side

The pastor took Mom's hand and with the other reached back toward the rest of those gathered, beckoning all to walk toward the water. Dad took Mom's other hand and mine on his other side. We walked to the water. Mom stepped forward with the box from the funeral home, took the lid off and flung the ashes into the water.

I know you are thirsty
You won't be denied

I'd never focused on the words of this hymn when we belted it out around the campfire at summer camp. All we'd tried to do was stretch de-n-i-e-i-e-d into about a twenty-syllable word. I know that Mom picked out the hymns for the service, but I didn't want to think about coming to the waters knowing that Brian wasn't ever going to be out there with me.

After flinging the ashes, my mother stood with her fists clenched staring out at the water as the choir continued to sing. My Dad had moved behind me and wrapped his arms around me. I fixated on a great blue heron standing absolutely still in front of the rushes on the far side of the beach.

Your goodness so great I can't understand,
And, dear Lord, I know that this all was planned.

But now I lost it. What numskull in the choir wasn't smart enough to skip that verse, even if Mom had picked the hymn? How was Brian getting hit by some drunk driving his boat too fast on the Fourth of July all part of God's plan? What a crock. I broke out of my father's embrace and started running back toward the house, cutting through yards and parks. Some of the adults stared at me but neither Mom nor Dad tried to follow. They knew I would retreat back to the house where I'd been hiding since the accident, and they knew I'd safely run between the beach and our house hundreds of times before.

Julie followed me a few minutes later though. She didn't bother knocking on the door to the house. She just came into my bedroom, sat on the edge of the bed where I had thrown myself facedown, and rubbed my back gently. "I used to love singing that hymn at camp," Julie said. "That verse would not have been in my Top 40 countdown for a funeral though."

I could almost laugh at that, but my nose was so stuffed from crying that I just sort of snuffled. Julie and I always tried to listen to the *American Top 40* countdowns, and if we couldn't listen to them, Julie had a subscription to *Billboard*. Sometime in the last few days, she had brought over some recent ones to my room for times when she couldn't get me out of there. Since I didn't immediately turn over, she started reading out the list from the latest issue, adding her own commentary about the hairstyle of this artist and the love life of that artist. About halfway through her recitation of some countdown, she paused and noted, "You know we have to show up at the fellowship hall at some point. Before I came after you, I told Grandmom to try to buy us a little time but we're probably about out."

The church had organized a potluck affair in the fellowship hall for after the service. Mom and Dad would have headed straight there leaving me to my grief, but Julie was correct that if I didn't make an appearance at some point, some adult would come get me.

I knew she was right about getting over there, but I viscerally resented this requirement to put my grief on display to allow spectators to feel good about their exhibitions of kindness. I washed up my face. Julie insisted on playing makeup artist saying that my eyes were too red to see whether I was getting the blush on even or not.

We would normally have ridden our bikes, but we were both still wearing dresses. We knew we couldn't get away with changing into jeans or shorts. Besides, walking over to the church took longer, and the longer getting there took, the less time I had to spend having people compete to bring me to tears with their condolences.

Despite the deluge of casseroles that had been dropped off, I hadn't been eating much in the last few days. For some reason though, I became wildly hungry when I smelled all of the food in the fellowship hall. I dragged Julie directly to the buffet tables, avoiding talking to anyone on the way through the hall, and piled a plate high with beef stroganoff and macaroni and cheese. The food not only tasted heavenly enough to be in a church, but the more I kept my mouth full, the less I had to say. Julie stayed right next to me, picking at the plate of food she'd made. Various church members sat down next to me and told me how sorry they were. I mumbled thanks, continued eating and clenched my toes as tight as I could hoping to keep my eyes from leaking. A few of the kids from the neighborhood came by, looking as awkward as I felt, most not getting out much more than "Sorry" before moving on.

The worst was probably when Bobby Owen and his parents sat down across from me at the table. Bobby looked miserable and also like his parents had forced him to come over and talk to me. I tried to do the looking down at my plate trick, but I'd eaten everything on it, leaving me with no choice but to meet their gazes. Bobby stuttered out something about how sorry he was that they hadn't had better sense than to go out in the canoe. The Owens offered the standard "if there's anything we can do to help your family through this time" lines. I caught a glance of Bobby's father looking at Bobby with a steely look that made me think Bobby's parents were livid with him for having been out in that boat. Although it seemed to me they should have just been thankful they weren't the ones having casseroles shoved down their throats.

On a day in late August, when I was still moping in my room, Mom and Julie's grandmom made me go over to Julie's house. Julie's parents lived on a creek on the other side of the river from us, the expensive Annapolis side of the river. Julie was often at her grandmother's even during the school year because both her parents were civilian defense contractors who were sent all over the world by the Navy for some sort of consulting. This day, however, was one of the rare occasions when Julie's parents were both in town.

"C'mon let's float on the rafts. We can't swim, there's sea nettles everywhere this year but if we climb on the rafts right off the dock we won't get stung." Julie pleaded.

I didn't care about doing much of anything, but I'd been dropped off at her house, so I followed her to their dock. We lounged on the floats keeping our arms and legs up out of the water. Julie's mom appeared after a couple hours. "C'mon you two. Siobhan's mother will be here any minute, and I want those rafts and all that water stuff away. School starts next week, and your dad and I are headed back out of town, so you won't need them anymore this year. Get them packed up in the garage. And put them away neatly in the storage cabinets, don't just pile them in the first place you see."

Julie grumbled about what the use was of having a dock and a boat her parents wouldn't take out of the garage and rafts that had to be put away before summer was even over. Nevertheless, we got out of the water and dragged the rafts up with us. We threw our T-shirts and jean shorts on right over our bathing suits and slid on our flip flops to avoid getting splinters from the dock. As we were walking to the garage we opened the air valves on the rafts and pressed the air out. Their garage was almost full to the brim. We had to climb around the back of the boat up on its trailer, as well as some boxes and piles of miscellaneous stuff to get to the storage cabinets at the back. When we had crammed the deflated rafts in as best we could, we turned around to make our way back out.

And then we saw the front of the boat. We saw it at the same time. The small hole and the cracking of the fiberglass, and a little chunk of bright blue right at the edge of the hole. Words started pouring out of Julie's mouth. "No, no, it couldn't have been…. I mean lots of boats might have dings in the bow so it might not even have been….. No, no, no…." But I knew what that blue was from. It was from our canoe *The Colt*, specifically the stickers with which Brian and I had covered the hull. While Julie was gibbering, I wasn't saying anything. I stared stupefied, and then I tried to run out of the garage, knocking over boxes and bruising my shins as I struggled to get past all the junk. Julie was trying to follow me, sobbing "No, no, no, you can't tell….. it's my parents….."

But I did tell, how could I not?

When I got out of the garage, Mom had pulled up in the driveway and was standing next to the car with the driver's side door open. Julie's mom was a few feet away, and they were exchanging so-called pleasantries. They obviously didn't like each other much. I know my Mom frowned on how Julie's mom dumped care of Julie on Julie's grandmother. Julie's mom was a career-focused woman who rated herself above the stay-at-home mom crowd.

I ran straight to the car and threw myself in the passenger seat, yelling to my Mom, "Let's go!" Julie came out of the garage crying and I heard her mother saying "Jules, what the hell?"

Julie's mom tossed back at my mother, "Looks like we've had some early pubescent disagreement."

I was crying in the front seat at this point and kept repeating, "Go, go, go, Mom."

After pausing for what seemed like an eternity, wondering if it was worth trying to figure out what was going on, Mom shrugged her shoulders at Julie's mom, sat down, put the car in reverse, backed out of the driveway, and headed out.

Once we were off their street, I howled, "Mom, Mom, Mom, you've got to call the police. It was them, it was them."

Mom wasn't sure what to make of the outburst as I'd had so many of them over the last month or so. "It was them, what. What do you mean?"

"Mom, it was their boat. We went to put the rafts away, and I saw it. The front of their boat has a hole in it. The Johnsons were the ones who hit Brian."

"Siobhan," Mom's tone was shocked and admonishing. "You can't just say things like that about your best friend's parents. Boats get dinged up all the time if people aren't careful pulling them out of the...."

"No, Mom, I saw it. A Baltimore Colts sticker. Part of one was stuck on the fiberglass. "

At a stop sign Mom grabbed a cigarette out of the ashtray with shaking hands and was silent while she fumbled with the car lighter. "Siobhan, are you sure of what you saw? This is a very serious accusation."

"Mom, it couldn't have been anything else. You have to hurry and call the police. Julie saw it too and she'll take the sticker off so they can't prove anything."

"Now Siobhan, you don't know what Julie will do."

Thankfully Dad was home when we got there. Mom's hands were still shaking on the wheel as she pulled into the driveway, and her lips were trembling. As we got out of the car, Dad looked back and forth at us perplexedly. He finally coaxed out our respective stories. Mom retreated to their bedroom as soon as she had related what she had to say, and Dad shooed me upstairs while he called a friend of his at the police without my listening in. I tried to listen from upstairs anyway but only caught a few phrases: "My daughter saw something suspicious...... my son did have very distinctive stickers on the canoe....."

I never knew what Julie told her mom or whether they had tried to do anything to the boat before the police got there or how long the police took to go out there and investigate.

I doubt the police were supposed to tell us what they learned. However, one of the investigating officers kept his boat at the marina where my grandfather worked and had known Dad for years, and he probably decided Dad had the right to know what had happened to his son.

According to what the Johnsons told the police, they had gotten home from separate assignments late on July 3rd. Julie was already at her grandmother's. They figured she'd want to hang out with me anyway, and they decided to have a day of alone time instead of picking Julie up for the Fourth. After having watched the fireworks on their boat out on the river, they claim they felt guilty that they weren't spending time with their daughter on one of the rare occasions when they were both home. Deciding to surprise Julie, they started across the river to Mrs. Marconi's and take her home in the boat.

Their story was that in the dark they couldn't see the canoe and they never saw Brian at all. They acknowledged that they hit an overturned canoe, but they said that since they didn't see anyone they assumed the canoe had been abandoned and was adrift. Their boat had a fairly serious ding though, and they decided they shouldn't risk going all the way to Julie's grandmother's and then back. Instead they went home.

If Julie's parents had gone to the police with that story as soon as they found out Brian had been killed, things probably would have gone better for them. The police believe that, although their story was probably mostly true, the Johnsons also knew that the ding in the boat itself wouldn't have been definitive enough proof to convict them of any crime. They therefore kept their mouth shut after they found out Brian had died rather than take a chance that the police would disbelieve some aspect of their story. The Johnsons would have had no way to know what the blue sticky stuff was on the front of their boat until Julie went into hysterics after my visit. Once they knew about the Baltimore Colts bumper stickers, they also knew that the police could send samples from their boat and from our canoe to a lab for testing and establish definitive proof that the two vessels had collided. That's why the police think that Mr. Johnson collapsed as soon as the police showed up at their door and told the police everything, but the time when honesty would have halted prosecution had passed more than a month ago.

Julie's grandmother picked up Julie when they came to arrest her parents. I'm pretty sure her grandmother didn't know how the police had found out about the boat. Unfortunately, Mom had insisted that I help her with the gardening right as Mrs. Marconi pulled up and Julie got out of the car. Julie ran up to the fence and started screaming at me. "I hate you. This is all your fault. Why couldn't you keep your mouth shut about the boat? My parents are in jail and all because of you." At this point, Julie's grandmother was moving as quickly as she could toward Julie.

Mom got up and threw her arms around me, moving me toward the house. Even as Mom was hustling me in, I yelled over my shoulder, "Jail is where murderers belong. I hate you too!"

Mom was completely unsuccessful in calming me down. I don't even know what she tried to say. Eventually she left me sobbing on my bed face down where I stayed for hours.

And that is how we left the matter. Julie wouldn't speak to me. I wouldn't speak to her. She blamed me for her parents being arrested. I blamed her for her parents killing Brian. Mom and Julie's grandmother did not like the fact that Julie and I had become estranged because of the accident, but neither one of them was able to overcome our stubbornness. I don't know what Julie's grandmother tried on her end, but I know I got to the point that I would stick my fingers in my ears and walk out of the room when Mom brought up the subject of Julie. Mom threatened to send me to a counselor once but I knew she wouldn't. She herself spent more and more time in her room in the months after Brian died, and she certainly wouldn't want some counselor asking her how she was coping or suggesting group sessions.

The prosecutor's office asked if my parents wanted to testify at the sentencing about the effect on our lives. My Mom threw them out of the house. "Isn't it bad enough already? You want to make the wounds deeper by having us stand up in front of our former friends and neighbors and talk about just how bad it is to have lost our son."

JULIE JUNE 30, 1979 ET SEQ.

A great blue heron took off from the other side of the creek with a grunty protest when some of the kids at the party encroached on his space by jumping off the dock. One of the boys asked with a leer at the girls on the dock, "Did you know that herons' legs change colors when they're ready to mate?"

I decided that was enough of the outside. Siobhan stayed outside hanging out with some of the other kids while I went into the kitchen and got another cup of the spiked punch. I had never had much chance to drink before, and starting my second cup I was already feeling a little tipsy.

I had wrangled an invitation to one of the high school seniors' parties for me and Siobhan. The party was supposed to be outside because the girl's parents weren't home and she didn't want the house to get trashed. Then she realized that the neighbors would see all the alcohol in the yard, and she came up with the brilliant idea of moving all the beer and punch to the kitchen, effectively moving the bulk of the party indoors.

I headed into the living room to see who else was there. A guy's arm slipped around my waist and pulled me toward him. "Jules, how are you?" The arm belonged to Brian, and he was more than a little tipsy. He held a beer in the hand opposite the one that had grabbed me.

I had had a secret crush on Brian for years, but I never told anyone. The one person to whom I could tell secrets was Siobhan, and I certainly couldn't tell her this one. In fact, I went out of my way to flirt with Jim or anyone else that was around in the fervent hope that no one would catch on. Even if Brian was drunk, I was going to enjoy this moment with his arm around me.

A handful of other kids were hanging out in the living room talking about nothing in particular. A big console stereo was in one corner of the living room. One of the kids grabbed a record and started playing a Bee Gees album. Someone else turned out the overhead lights. Only the light from the kitchen and the remaining light from outside streaming in through the front window illuminated the living room.

Brian kept his arm around me and was swaying us to the music. He leaned down to ask me a question, and I summoned all of the bravery that could be imparted by alcohol and kissed him right as he was starting his question. He kissed me back at first, his other hand coming around to grab me, the beer can pressing against my back. Then he pulled back, "Siobhan will kill me."

"I don't care. She'll get over it." I replied, still pressing myself toward him.

The lights came back on. The girl whose house it was and whose parents were away for the weekend had finally started to worry about the damage a few dozen teenagers could do to the gold-carpeted living room with the fancy velour sofas.

"Please go outside," the girl pleaded. She should have thought of that before she invited all these people over. And in this neighborhood where everyone knew everyone else, parents in the adjacent houses were sure to have noticed. In a fleeting malicious twinkle I pictured a bunch of teenagers sloshing beer on my Mom's perfectly white couches. At least then she'd have to pay attention to the fact that she had a daughter.

Then my mind jumped back to the fact that I had just kissed Brian Barrett! But Brian was slipping away in the group of kids being herded outside. I wanted to find him again, but Siobhan was the first person I ran into when I walked down the back steps out into the yard.

Over the next few days, I was dying to find a chance to be alone with Brian, but Siobhan was seemingly everywhere. Brian was also always surrounded by other guys from the neighborhood.

On July 4th, Siobhan and I were stretched out tanning on lawn chairs on her dock. Brian came down to take the canoe over to

Bobby's house. I tried to get him to take me and Siobhan to give us the chance to watch the fireworks with the guys.

"No road," he said. "Just us guys hanging out."

Siobhan ran up toward the house to use the bathroom, and I was finally alone with Brian even though he was in the canoe already.

"Hey Jules," Brian started to say. My heart started pounding. I was so hopeful that he would admit that he had had a massive crush on me the way I had had a massive crush on him, but that he'd been too afraid to say so.

My hopes didn't last long though. "I was really drunk the other night," he went on. "You're like my second kid sister. I had no business kissing you. I hope you're not going to say anything to Siobhan." He was already paddling off as he finished his last sentence, and Siobhan was coming out of the house.

The worst. His kid sister. I would have been less disappointed if he had said he hated brunettes or hazel eyes or thought my boobs were too big or too small. I was in a funk the whole rest of the evening. Siobhan and I watched the fireworks on her dock, but then I went to Grandmom's house pretty much right after that complaining of a headache. I shut myself in my room and went through my teen romance magazines hoping they had some articles about how to make your best friend's brother find you irresistible.

I was so absorbed in my own petty tragedy that I didn't pay much attention to the commotion outside. Grandmom came up and knocked on my door quite late. "Jules, your light is on, I know you're awake."

I told her to come in, expecting her to try to find out what was wrong with me. Instead I was surprised to see she had been crying.

Then she told me that Brian was missing. At that point, that's all anyone knew. The police had come over to talk to the Barretts. They knew that Bobby and Jim had swum ashore after the canoe capsized, and Brian hadn't been behind them. People were out looking still, but it was dark and late.

I started sobbing. Grandmom sat down on the bed next to me and rubbed my hair back from my forehead. "Can I go over to Siobhan's?" I asked.

"No, not right now, honey. We can't intrude. If they're getting any sleep, God help them, but most likely they'll be up all night. We'll go over in the morning."

First thing in the morning, Grandmom pulled a bunch of Sara Lee cinnamon rolls out of the freezer and baked them up. She and I carried them plus some thermoses of coffee next door. She told me that if the Barretts didn't want company we would drop off the food and leave. Mr. Barrett looked awful when he opened the door. He hadn't shaved, and he was still in the clothes he was wearing last night during the fireworks.

Grandmom started, "We're not trying to intrude Jack. We just wanted to bring you some breakfast."

He stepped back to let us in. "No, please. Julie, Siobhan's in her room. She could really use you."

I went upstairs and let myself in to Siobhan's room without waiting for a response to my knocking. Siobhan was sitting up in bed in her pink old lady pajamas that she hated but that were all her mom would buy her. She had one of her weird science fiction books open on her legs, but she wasn't reading. I sat down next to her, hugged her, and told her over and over again that they'd find Brian this morning, that he's ok, that he's a great swimmer, and there'd be some silly reason why he couldn't get back last night like maybe he swam to the far side of the river and couldn't find anyone to take him home.

I went downstairs at some point and got us some cinnamon rolls, but we both barely picked at them. We hardly talked at all. Talking about any of our normal stuff seemed too weird, but talking about what might have happened to Brian was too awful.

I don't know how long we were there like that, but suddenly Grandmom and Mr. Barrett were in the doorway. I knew by looking at Grandmom's face that the news was bad. She said, "Jules, it's time for us to get out of their hair."

I didn't protest. I gave Siobhan one last squeeze and headed out. Mr. Barrett went into Siobhan's room and closed the door. Mrs. Barrett was nowhere to be seen when we went downstairs.

Grandmom didn't tell me until we got back in her house that Brian's body had been found that afternoon. I kept crying and crying. Siobhan had to be even more crushed that I was. I realized that in one way Brian had been right. He had been the closest thing I'd ever had to a brother.

Compared to what Siobhan must be feeling, I felt selfish when I found my mind wandering back to kissing Brian at the party and wishing I'd had the chance to convince him to feel differently about me. It wasn't just that Brian had been good-looking. Unlike most of the good-looking boys, Brian hadn't seemed to know it and didn't try to act cool and aloof. Sure, he had acted a little macho when other guys were around, but he had also joined me and Siobhan as we rode bikes around the neighborhood, set up pretend restaurants on the dock and played endless board games on rainy days.

Grandmom made me come downstairs to eat a sandwich at some point. I sobbed, "How can this happen? We all know better than that. Only the idiots who buy boats without knowing anything about the water have accidents like that."

Grandmom surprised me with her disagreement. "What do you mean? My father fished from the day he was born, but that didn't stop him from falling off his fishing boat when the water was about 45 degrees. He went out alone in early November. It was about 60 degrees in the air but the water had already started to chill down."

Grandmom's words were enough to briefly pull me out of my sobbing state. I had never heard this story about her dad and raised my gaze hoping she would continue.

"Yes, dear. He knew enough not to go out alone. And even being from Georgia, he knew enough not to go out when the water is so cold your system goes into shock so fast you can't possibly get yourself out. But he still reckoned he could catch a few more fish for the freezer. His little boat was adrift right outside Shady Side with its fishing lines all tangled up in some trash that was on the bottom of the river. He must have been trying to free up the lines and fell out somehow. The *Emma Giles* darn near ran into his boat, but some people on board saw the boat and then they saw Dad. "

"What's the *Emma* what's-er-name?" I asked.

"She was one of the ferries that used to run between Baltimore and a bunch of places on this side of the Chesapeake. She shut down in the thirties I think."

"Wow, they had ferries here?"

"This part of the world had a lot more ferries than roads at first. Once the roads got better and the Bay Bridge got built all the ferries started to go out of business. But, boy the people on the *Emma* that day were shocked. Dad wasn't dead yet when they pulled him out, just unconscious, but they couldn't save him. They pulled him out of the water onto the ferry. People on board pulled his wet clothes off him and covered him with blankets right away. They couldn't revive him, and the hospital couldn't do anything for him either."

"Where were you when this happened?"

"I was at work. I was 16. I worked at a restaurant, same one as my mother did. I started busing tables and then got promoted to waiting on them. That's where I met your grandfather. He had inherited his dad's skipjack, and he tried making a living as a waterman because that was what was expected of him. But he hated the work, and he saw how hard the life of a waterman was. When he sold the boat, we got enough money to get into our first house. Then he got oh so lucky. He had met some Navy guy at the marina when he was selling the boat, and through him he got a job on some construction crew working at the Naval Academy. They were still working on Preble Hall and expanding Bancroft way back then. The bottom fell out of work at my restaurant once the depression hit. Nobody had money to go to restaurants any more. I did whatever I could do cleaning houses or watching people's babies. "

Grandmom had never volunteered this sort of family history before, and I hadn't known to ask. I found her story a welcome distraction from persistently dwelling on Brian's death. "When did you move into this house?" I queried.

"Oh, quite a bit later. After the war was over, people started vacationing again and some developers started to throw these cottages up using military surplus material. Your grandfather saw that this community would become a full-time place eventually. Most people who bought these places were buying a summer home, but he decided to buy this place and make it our permanent home. For one thing, these places were dirt cheap compared to some other homes. These really were just little cottages. They weren't insulated. The kitchens were tiny. But your grandfather reckoned that after all his years doing construction he could make this a full time house. Your mother was horrified."

We both smiled at that. Despite the fact that Mom was seldom home these days, she was absurdly vain about having a home that a decorator magazine would want to highlight. I guess that trait had displayed itself early.

"She didn't want to leave her friends at our old neighborhood. She also hated the idea that everyone else that came here was rich enough to buy a second house, and we were one of the few full-time residents. Plus the house was quite basic. Your grandfather had to do a lot of work to make this into even what it is now. He did the work all pretty much himself, with the help of some friends here and there.

"My parents never had two spare dimes to rub together, so my older sister and I both got jobs as soon as we could to have our own spending money. But until I got with your grandfather, I never dreamed I could ever live on the water like this. I had to pinch myself when I would wake up every morning and look out at the cove. I liked our nest even better in the winter when not as many people were around.

"Your mother never came around to liking this house. As soon as she finished high school she moved off to college and never even came back for the summers. Of course, she could only do that because your grandfather saved every penny he could along the way.

"She had a holy hissy fit when I told her I was bringing you here for the summer that first time too. I know you were upset that you had to leave your princess bedroom, but if possible your mom was angrier at me than you were at her. I guess she thought I'd give up my house to move to her fancy place. But leaving here seemed like leaving your grandfather, and I still missed him way too much then to do that." Grandmom paused with some inner deliberation. "Now I'm not trying to criticize your mom for wanting more for herself. If your grandfather hadn't wanted more for himself, he'd have been a dirt poor waterman freezing his fingers and toes off every winter trying to scrape enough oysters off the bottom of the bay to feed us. Your mom has the same ambitious streak he did. She wanted more than what she started with, she just started a little higher up than we did."

I know that Grandmom tried not to complain or criticize my mother in front of me. I often came across her and Mrs. Barrett in mid-conversation, and they both made great effort to pretend they weren't talking about my Mom, but I would overhear enough to know they were. Every now and then Grandmom slipped when talking to me, and her real opinions would slip out. Her backtracking today was more elaborate than usual. I didn't disagree with her about Mom's ambition, but as far as I could tell the difference between her ambition and my grandfather's was that Mom's ambition was personal while my grandfather's had focused on his whole family. And Mom let her personal ambition get in the way of her family life.

Later that evening, I overheard Grandmom on the phone with my Mom. "You mean, you were home all day yesterday and you didn't even consider spending the Fourth with your own daughter." Obviously I couldn't hear the other side of the conversation, but as Mom didn't like being criticized, Grandmom's remark probably wasn't received well.

I then heard Grandmom telling her about the accident and Brian being found. Grandmom was mentioning things like needing funeral clothes for me and not knowing when the service would be. I could tell they were arguing over where I was going to be staying for the next few days. As events played out, Grandmom and I went to the funeral without my parents. They were both back off to some new assignment.

Mom was finally back in town sometime in August. I'm not sure who had the brilliant idea that bringing Siobhan out to our house might be good for her. I knew Siobhan well enough to know that a different dock would not pull her out of her funk. I had no idea that bringing her to our house that day would ruin my life though.

After Siobhan's mother drove away with Siobhan, I flung myself at my mother. "Mom, Mom, Mom, we've got to do something, what are we going to do, she saw, she saw, she saw."

Mom held me away from her like a space alien and asked me what on earth I was hysterical about.

I screeched, "The boat. She saw the marks on the boat. She saw the Colts sticker. She's going to tell her parents, I know it."

Mom's face was as stony as I had ever seen it. "She's going to tell her parents what? What are you talking about, Julie? Your dad banged the boat up pulling it out of the water. I don't know what the hell he was doing. He probably tried to put it on the trailer by himself instead of letting the marina folks do it for him. And then I couldn't believe he brought the damn thing home. Why on earth he didn't leave it to get fixed, I'll never know. Now of course he says that since we won't be home to use it the rest of the summer, he's in no hurry to fix it and he can get a better deal if he waits until the marinas are desperate for business in the cold weather."

My chest was heaving as I listened to Mom. I wanted to believe her so badly. I stared at her face and into her eyes, desperately looking for some sign of sincerity. Mom's face was a mask that I couldn't read anything from one way or another.

"But, the Colts sticker from Brian's canoe," I blubbered. "It's definitely part of a Colts sticker we saw. How could that be? And Siobhan's going to tell her parents, I know it."

"I have no idea what you mean about a Colts sticker, Julie," Mom said. "Is seeing the boat what got you two all upset? I told you I have no idea what your dad ran into at the marina pulling the boat out. I'll call Siobhan's mom a little later and try to calm things down. You know, honey, Siobhan is still distraught over Brian's death. And I'm sure you are a little bit too. It's very easy to mix things up when you're all emotional."

I longed for her story to be true. I wanted it to be true more than anything else. I listened all evening with my door cracked to hear Mom make the promised call to Mrs. Barrett, but I never heard it. I could tell she called Dad later that evening though. I couldn't tell what she was saying to him. Normally, when Mom was on the phone she spoke in her big, loud self-important voice. When she was on the phone with him this time, I could tell she was keeping her voice quiet, and I knew she'd been lying about the boat getting damaged at the marina.

I laid in bed unable to sleep. I kept flip-flopping between the undeniable evidence of the Colts sticker on the boat and the story Mom had told me. Then I thought I had it. Of course, Mom was right, I was at Grandmom's for the Fourth of July because Mom and Dad were working. Then Mom and Dad couldn't have done it.

Some of the local kids who knew we were never around must have taken our boat for a joy ride knowing Dad always left the keys under the driver's seat cushion. Dad was probably in a hurry pulling the boat out of the water at the marina, and he might not have even noticed the damage until Mom started yelling at him. I had comforted myself considerably with my ever more elaborate story of a boat-jacking, and I was even plotting how we might help the police find out who'd really hit Brian. I was drifting off to sleep with these fantasies, when I sat bolt upright in bed and knew Mom's story was all a lie. My subconscious mind pulled to the surface the memory of Grandmom berating Mom on the phone about being home for the holiday and not even trying to see me. I curled over on my side in the bed. My stomach hurt from worry and crying.

I tried to calm myself down. Siobhan was my Siamese sister, she would never tell on me. She would never ruin my life. I mean we both knew my parents were next to worthless. She would never let the whole world know how worthless they were. She just couldn't do that to me. How embarrassing if everyone suddenly learned that my parents didn't know how to do the right thing.

And then I got angry. I wasn't sure what I was angry about, but that hard spot in the pit of my stomach felt hot and red and furious. I stayed like that all through the next day, unable to calm myself down. Restless, fuming, worried.

The police came that next day, and I crawled out of my room and listened to them from the balcony over the living room talking to my Dad. The officer in charge didn't even let Mom call Grandmom herself to come pick me up and wouldn't let Mom come upstairs to talk to me, telling her they would take care of calling Grandmom. I heard them agree that they would let Grandmom come get me, and these nice officers would just sit on the couch with my parents until Grandmom and me had gone, and then they would "get on with matters" once I was out of the house.

The arrogant jerk acted like the police were doing Mom and Dad some tremendous favor by not hauling my parents out in handcuffs in front of me and throwing me in the squad car with them for good measure. I couldn't hear the officer call Grandmom from the kitchen, but I assume he did because she did come get me. She came up to my room, helped me pack a few things, told me Mom and Dad would be busy with the police, and that I needed to stay with her.

I walked out to the car with her mutely, glaring stonily at the figures perched on Mom's expensive white sofas, pressing my lips tightly together. Grandmom started to say something in the car, but I told her that I had listened to the police talking to Dad from upstairs and I knew why they were there and I was mad and I didn't want to talk to her or anyone else right now. I had probably never in my whole life told anyone that I didn't want to talk. That statement alone probably surprised Grandmom into speechlessness. We drove silently over to her house, and the blistering orb of fury in the pit of my stomach burned hotter and hotter.

I was angry. Angry at Siobhan. Yes, Siobhan. Why did she have to look at the boat? What could she really tell from some blue sticky stuff on the front of it? How could my Siamese sister ruin my life? The police had taken my parents away to jail and it was all her fault. If only she'd kept her damned mouth shut, none of this would ever have happened. And now, I was going to Grandmom's house and I'd probably have to see her. Well, I would let her know what I thought of her the first chance I got.

CHAPTER SIX

The deer were eating my pansies down by the dock again. I opened up the sliders to shoo them off. They lifted their heads up to stare at me, but they didn't move. What this area needed was some good natural predators, I reflected, as I looked down at the hopeless chocolate labs sleeping on the floor. If I let them out the deer would be scared away, but the dogs would leap in the water and then I'd have wet dog instead. I slipped on one of the pairs of flip flops that I keep by every outside door of my house and marched out into the yard to chase the deer off myself. I had to get within about ten feet of them before the deer took me seriously and bounded off along the shoreline.

For waterfront houses, the water side is technically the front yard, but I find this confusing since the main door to my house is undeniably on the road side; I therefore tend to think in terms of road side and water side rather than front and back. I do my more serious gardening on the fenced in road side, not the water side. While the larger deer might be able to jump the fence into the road side of the yard, they don't appear to do so on a regular basis. I suppose I couldn't blame the deer for foraging in the water side of my yard though. Ever since the new housing development around the high school had gotten its permits and the construction crews had started tearing down their habitat, deer were as abundant as squirrels in my yard.

I did not personally resonate with the gigantic community by the high school that was attracting so many new homebuyers. The new development didn't have the community beach and park areas that were so special to me. As a single person though I didn't need a 4,500 square foot brick and siding mini-mansion sitting on a third of an acre. For a larger family, I could see the appeal of the county's best school district, and the fact that the house sizes were more in line with what a modern family with kids expected. But for me the new houses were far less charming than my little 2,000 square foot cottage.

Part of the new community's appeal was also undoubtedly the shortage of houses for sale in our waterfront community. Houses in our community seldom went on the open market because they usually passed from one generation to the next. The house on the other side of me, the side opposite Julie, was an exception. No owner had lasted more than four or five years. The owners before the current ones had been a rich Long Island couple that showed up for two weeks per year using the place only as a vacation spot.

After I shooed off the deer, the tortured sounds of classical music started drifting out from the house next door. The current neighbors on that side kept almost completely to themselves. I wasn't even sure what the husband looked like. I knew they had a roughly teenaged daughter because I had seen her getting in and out of cars. I surmised that either she or her parents were set on some sort of musical career because, if the weather was decent, they kept their windows open, and I could hear someone practicing the piano for hours at a time. Not playing, which I might have found pleasant, but practicing. Sometimes, like now, I'd hear the same handful of measures over and over again.

I was startled out of my reflections on the neighborhood by the sirens of an emergency vehicle covering up the piano playing as the vehicle turned onto the gravel road. I jogged up to the road side of the house to see what was going on.

Guilty began woofing incessantly when the fire truck came by, bringing Julie out of her house to grab him by his collar.

One of the firemen gave us a thumbs up, and I watched as they proceeded to turn the truck around and backed up the road.

"I guess it's some sort of drill, huh?" Julie asked over top of wailing siren and barking canine.

"Thankfully yes." I replied. Guilty stopped barking as the truck moved further off. "I can only remember one time since I moved back to the cove that the emergency vehicles were actually necessary. Unfortunately, it was the day they found Bill."

Julie responded, "The lawyer told me he was found dead in the house by a co-worker. Why would they send screaming sirens?"

"Lord only knows, but they did." I said. "I was out in the yard gardening when a police car with lights flashing but no siren pulled up to your grandmother's cottage. By the way, I always thought of it as your grandmother's cottage even though Bill lived there for close to twenty years. Anyway, I pretended to garden a bit as I watched the police officer knock on the door. A pickup truck with an auto parts store logo pulled up a few minutes later. I was kind of shocked when the policeman pulled some tool out of his pocket and broke the door open. A man in a red polo shirt with the same auto parts logo got out of the truck and walked halfway to the front door but he didn't go in after the cop."

"'Sorry to be nosy,'" I had called out, 'but when a police officer breaks into your next door neighbor's house, you tend to be concerned. What's going on?'

"The man in the red shirt looked over at me, blinked, and then asked, 'Have you seen Bill lately?'

"I answered, "A couple days ago maybe, I'm not sure. I've been doing some odd work shifts lately though so I'm not on the same schedule as most people. Is something wrong?"

"'He hasn't shown up to work for the last two days, and that is just not like Bill." The man in the red shirt had looked concerned.

"He was right. When I was on a normal day shift, Bill got up regularly and went to work without fail as far as I could tell.

"The police officer came out with a grim expression. He had put a hand on the shoulder of the man with the red shirt. 'I'm sorry Fred. It's not good.' The officer then had looked over at me. 'Does he have any family? Anyone I should call?' He was at that point addressing both of us. The man in the red shirt had merely shrugged.

"I told him something about how Bill's aunt used to live here before she moved into a senior community and then ultimately passed away. And also that my Mom had told me your grandmother had a lawyer who took care of the stuff Bill couldn't handle himself. I told him I didn't know what the lawyer's name was or how to find him.

"'OK, thanks," the officer said. 'I've got to call an ambulance.' And off he went to his squad car. But, jeez, all afternoon vehicles had come through. First the ambulance, then a fire truck, then a couple more squad cars. And every single blessed one of them came through with their lights whirling and their sirens blaring. I couldn't let my dogs out of the house the whole damned day. Then a hearse pulled up.

"You know how the Thompsons on the other side of your house always knew someone on the police force, so I knew they would be able to find out what was going on. A day or two after all the cars came through, I waited until I saw them come out with their teacup dogs and went out to be nosy.

"The Thompsons of course had found out the scoop. Bill had not shown up for work for two days in a row without calling, which was absolutely out of character. At first, the store manager, the Fred who had been in the red shirt, had a hard time convincing the police to head over to the cottage yet. They tried to say that an adult not showing up for work for two days was not enough to send the police. Fred continued to insist and explained to the police that there was more reason than average to worry about Bill because he was a little slow. As he approached the house, the police officer could see Bill lying on the floor through the window of the front door, so he had enough justification to break in. According to what the Thompsons got out of their friend at the police, the medical examiner reported that Bill had a heart attack and probably died within a few minutes.

"They said the police had found a packet of paper on the fridge in a plastic sleeve with the lawyer's contact info and a full power of attorney." I concluded.

"Wow, nobody told me that part of the story." Julie shook her head. "Poor Bill. I was always a little uncomfortable being around him because it was so hard to talk to him. But it's sad that his boss at the auto parts store was the first person who noticed something was wrong."

Julie took Guilty back into the house. I went back around to resume surveying the cervine damage to my pansies.

What I hadn't had the nerve to bring up with Julie was that I had assumed that after Bill's death I would eventually see a "For sale" sign go up near the house. I remember seeing a van from a clean-up service that I assumed was taking out Bill's personal items, and I expected I'd soon be seeing real estate agents next door. But then a few months later I started seeing construction vehicles. I had wondered at first if the house was in such disrepair that the lawyer needed to organize some renovations in order to sell it. But I didn't know to whom the money would go. Bill didn't have any kids and his parents were long gone. Then I presumed the cottage would probably go to Julie's mom as his first cousin and that would certainly explain trying to get more money out of the sale.

One day though the contractors were griping as they came out of the house while I was working in my flower beds. One of them was complaining to his mates that he was heading over to Chevy Chase to meet with the "boss lady" and the designer. He said that he hoped the designer was running the show because he hated dealing with homeowners who couldn't make up their mind and who didn't have a clue what was realistic, especially rich housewives like this one.

The contractor's words started a cogitative stream flowing through my head: The appellation of housewife didn't sound like Julie's mom to me. I didn't know where Julie's mom lived but I did know that Julie lived over in Chevy Chase. Did the house go to Julie? Contemplating Julie's grandmother, such a bequest would make a lot of sense. Lotty Marconi hadn't much approved of how her daughter had raised Julie, and from what Mom had told me the only reason Mrs. Marconi spoke to her daughter at all after the accident was to maintain a relationship with Julie. So, if Mrs. Marconi was savvy enough to provide for Bill even before she died, she would have known how to bypass her daughter in favor of Julie in her will.

I had found myself worrying, almost obsessing, about the fate of the house even more. Before I realized that the house was going to Julie, I had been worried that some stranger would buy the place, and I would be stuck with some troglodyte next door. Then I tried to debate with myself as to whether I would prefer the troglodyte or Julie. But then I reasoned, surely Julie wouldn't move into the dinky little cottage when she had some big house over in Chevy Chase.

As the weeks went on, the contractor had raised the roof and put on a partial second story to the little cottage. At even the most inconvenient times, I found myself asking the same questions over and over again: If Julie intended to sell the cottage she wouldn't go to that much trouble, would she? But why would the contractor be worried that the homeowner wouldn't make up her mind? If she were just selling the house she wouldn't need to get involved in the details herself. She couldn't be moving back to the cove, could she? But then the Thompsons had gone to Bobby's funeral and told me how surprised they were that Julie's kids all looked like adults already. What if she wanted a smaller house because she was by herself? What if she couldn't afford her big Chevy Chase home without Bobby's salary?

I made sure I did a lot of gardening around the time the contractors finished up in the afternoons, hoping I could overhear what the plans were. I didn't quite have the nerve to come out and ask them. When I saw the furniture trucks bringing in brand new sofas and bedroom sets, I was certain that Julie must be moving back. I asked myself over and over how I could live next to Julie. I hadn't spoken to her since 1979. I wasn't angry anymore, I could finally honestly say that I wasn't. From what Mom learned from Julie's grandmother over the years and had forced me to hear, Julie had a miserable few years with her dad in jail and both parents out of their high paying jobs. If Julie had wrongly lashed out at me instead of them way back when she was a teenager and her life was falling apart, I was overdue to let that go. Since she had sent flowers to Mom's funeral, I assumed she'd move on as well.

After all my months of speculation, Julie was in fact back. Although I had obsessed over her return, thus far we had had occasional incidental conversations, like two old schoolmates getting reacquainted. But she and I had been like sisters. I didn't know how to recover our lost sisterhood or if trying was even wise. But I didn't know how I could keep pretending that we had never been like sisters and treat her like some casual acquaintance when we ran into each other at the fence.

We had not, in any of our chance meetings thus far, touched on that awful time following the accident and the arrest of her parents.

I supposed we would inevitably have to address the subject if we were going to live next door to each other for the foreseeable future. I hoped that when the accident finally came up, we could discuss it without ruining the relationship we were starting to build now. On my side, I believed I could, since I did know for a fact that my own life had improved immeasurably since those rage-filled teenaged years where all I could do was plot my exit from Cecil Cove.

SIOBHAN SEPTEMBER 1983

I was finally leaving Cecil Cove. Retreating into a shell all through the end of high school, I studied hard and got good grades. I saved all the money from my part-time job, using the job as an excuse to socialize as little as possible. I knew the only way out of the cove was going to college. I couldn't wait to leave, couldn't stand staying in that house. I couldn't understand why Mom wanted to stay, I questioned her, I screamed at her.

For the most part, Mom took my occasional rages in silence. Although I had noticed throughout childhood that Mom periodically retreated to her room with a book, she did so more than ever after Brian died and, if possible, even more so after Dad left. Often she would emerge from her room slightly glassy-eyed and a bit slow on the uptake. I guessed at some point that she was taking some sort of medication, but I certainly couldn't ask and didn't know enough to guess exactly what. For the most part, her silent periods meant that I was left to myself, which is what I wanted. Every now and then, however, I would be more frustrated than usual, almost itching for some sort of confrontation, and I would then try to get some response from her. Her responses were usually so laconic, however, that I didn't get much satisfaction from them.

Somewhere around Christmas my senior year of high school though, I guess I was finally too much. Mom was stringing the Christmas lights along the dock, and I had followed her more out of habit than any sense of holiday cheer. While we were down there, some nincompoops came motoring toward the cove in their floating duck blind. The hunters had tied a bunch of dried corn stalks all around the perimeter of some small flat boat, and they were hiding in the middle trying to keep their dogs quiet. They floated some decoys out. Their wake sent wavelets slapping up against the bulkheads and riprap around the cove.

"What do they think, some ducks are going to be fooled into believing a corn patch grew up overnight in the middle of the creek and come close to see if there's food? How stupid? Everything about this place is stupid? Why do we stay here? Thank God I'm leaving for college." I continued in this vein for long enough that I guess I was not ignorable.

Mom threw her cigarette in the water, glared directly at me and screamed loud enough I sat back against one of the pilings. "Why do we stay? Because everything I've ever had is right here in this cottage. Everything good. Yes, everything bad too. But I can't leave everything, because then I've got NOTHING." I stood completely still for what seemed like ages but was probably a few seconds. The tears were going to come and nothing would keep the dam from breaking. I turned and ran back up the path into the house and locked myself in my bedroom for hours.

Dad's father was in his late seventies when he passed away from lung cancer in 1980, not surprisingly since he had smoked more than two packs per day since he was a teenager. He kept on smoking right up to the end, always with a pack of cigarettes tucked up in the sleeve of the white T-shirt he wore underneath his blue marina service shirt. After Grandpa died, Dad finally left for good, although he and Mom never legally divorced.

I don't know how long my parents' marriage had been shaky, but Brian's death put paid to it. All through my childhood Dad had come and gone seemingly with no rhyme or reason for stints on the oil rigs and tankers down in the Gulf of Mexico. Somewhere after Grandpa died he simply didn't come back. Rumors flew that he was living with someone somewhere outside Pensacola, that after Brian died he may even have been there some of the time that he was supposed to be out in the Gulf. I didn't know, I didn't care, and I found that I didn't even particularly fault him for wanting to spend as little time as possible here; after all, I was dying to get away. Dad still sent Mom money routinely every month after he left. He also sent me cards on my birthday and for holidays. He would ultimately send money for my college expenses.

Dad left his beat up old pickup truck when he left. I took driver's ed at school, and I insisted that Mom take me to get my license exactly on my sixteenth birthday. I went as far as to tell her I didn't want any other present for my birthday. I went out and got a part-time job at the local drugstore within two weeks of getting my license. For one, I wanted a job in order to put spending money away for college. Second, I could always use the job as an excuse for not wanting to socialize. Mom, for her part, seemed thrilled that I had my license as, without the burden of chauffeuring me around, she was able to retreat further into herself.

At the drugstore, I did whatever tasks they needed, whether stocking shelves or doing inventory or running a register. More often than not though, I ended up at the register at the pharmacy counter. The pharmacist was an older man with a comb-over who could be fairly brusque with the teenagers on the staff when their work didn't meet his standards. I never had a problem with him. He was efficient and detail-oriented, and his prickliness came from having no patience whatsoever for any of the teenaged staff who weren't. I'm sure the manager put me on the pharmacy register because I was almost compulsively detail-oriented and was therefore least likely to arouse the porcupine's quills. When I stocked the shelves, I would make sure all the boxes and labels were perfectly lined up, which probably made me slower than some of the other staff, who would empty the cartons onto the shelves as quickly as possible.

The pharmacist seemed to truly enjoy his job. If he wasn't swamped, he would take people's prescriptions personally and ask them if they had any questions about their medicines. He checked every order at least twice. He kept the shelves of medicines meticulously neat. Once he got used to me, and he realized that I was as much of a perfectionist as he was, he would explain things to me when we weren't busy.

One night when a few of us were doing inventory, one of the other kids, Mark, said to me, "I feel sorry for you. You keep getting stuck with old man Nelson."

"I don't mind. He's just picky." I returned.

"Better you than me. He always snaps at me for anything I do when they put me back with him. I guess he thinks 'cause he makes so much money he can treat people any way he wants." Mark complained.

"What do you mean 'so much money'? How would you know?" I asked, my curiosity piqued.

"I got called into the manager's office one time when he was putting the paychecks into the envelopes. Mr. Nelson's was right on top of the pile, so I looked." After Mark told me what the salary was, I vowed to do a little research on the requirements to be a pharmacist that would allow one to command what seemed to my teenaged self to be a pretty respectable paycheck.

Mark went on to complain about other injustices at the store, most of which seemed to me to be caused by Mark's own sloppiness.

The next time I went to the library, I did some research on the qualifications to be a pharmacist. Although I could see how the job might get boring at times, I found myself attracted to the opportunity for perfectionism and also to the ubiquitous presence of the job. If I'd thought the matter though, I might have realized myself, but at the library I learned that pharmacists didn't work only in drugstores. They could also get jobs in hospitals or teaching. In fact, everywhere in the country, people needed pharmacists, unlike an oil tanker job where one had to leave one's family in order to earn one's paycheck.

I next focused my research at the library on what schools offered pharmacy degrees, with the enthusiastic support of my guidance counselor who had been dogging me to think about which colleges I might like to attend. Even with no nudging from the guidance counselor, I was determined to get out of Cecil Cove, and the pharmacy path seemed pretty attractive to me. I spent hours at the library with a Barron's guide book on colleges and universities. The book was twice as fat as the telephone book, with newsprint for paper. After I was done, I would always have to go into the ladies' room and wash the ink off my hands. By the end of junior year, I had made a list of just over a dozen places in which I was interested. I sent off postcards requesting admissions materials to the addresses listed in Barron's. Over the summer following my junior year, I rushed daily to the mailbox as soon as I heard the postman's truck crunching along the gravel road to see if any of the literature had shown up yet.

Whenever a new college's materials came in, I would sop up every detail. Every school was perfect, at least on the day when its materials arrived. Eventually, I had application packets from all of the places I had selected but wasn't sure which one I wanted most. I was also a little dismayed when I realized how much the application fees were, realizing I would spend a big chunk of the money I had saved from my job if I applied to every single place that caught my fancy. I could ask Mom for some of it, but she would never go in for applying to more than a dozen colleges. I did further pruning and narrowed the choices down to four with two backups that had slightly later application dates in case I didn't get in to my first choices.

I eventually matriculated at a mid-size campus of the State University of New York system out near the Finger Lakes in Western New York. Western New York seemed like the back of beyond, far enough away to allow me to start fresh. During orientation week at the natural sciences table set up in the athletics hall where incoming freshmen could ask questions and register, I inquired about doing the new pre-pharmacy program. Whatever unlucky assistant level chemistry professor got stuck manning the table asked me why I didn't want chemistry as a major. I replied that I liked working with the pharmacist at my part-time job and hadn't seen anything else that I liked as much. I acknowledged that I had enjoyed chemistry well enough in high school, and the math aspects came easily to me, but I wasn't inspired to study chemistry for its own sake. When he questioned why I would be content counting out pills instead of doing real chemistry, I had no answer. I was somewhat taken aback. Why would someone who obviously was supposed to encourage students toward the various programs on offer at the school be so negative, particularly as the science table was by far the least busy table in the hall; I thought they should be happy to take people who wanted any of their majors.

After seeing that I was genuinely interested in pharmacy, even if he didn't understand how that was possible, the professor explained that the college was pioneering a new six year program. For the first two years students did baccalaureate level work, and then they automatically rolled into a Pharm.D. program for the last four years. The professor also felt compelled to note that after the first two years, I would have the right coursework to revert to a more traditional science major. I pointed out that part of my attraction with a pharmacy degree was that I could be virtually assured of getting a job anywhere in the country. He didn't comment on the job possibilities but he did find a cheaply printed up flyer for the new program and was happy to have me move on. I read that as long as I declared myself in the first semester and kept a B+ average for the first two years, I couldn't be turned down for the Pharm.D.

College, and in particular my chosen pharmacy program, was a godsend. I loved the classes, I made friends, I went to parties, and I even dated in the somewhat haphazard way that college students called hooking up at parties dating. I didn't talk much about home life, but neither did plenty of other kids. Besides, talking about classes or exams or what parties would be going on during the weekend was all too easy. I wasn't around my family, wasn't around Cecil Cove, and I found that all the activity going on around me pushed the anger and bitterness into some far corner of my mind. When something would trigger my memories of Cecil Cove and home, the slurry of negative emotions at first came surging back. My solution was to surround myself with as much activity as possible leaving the negative no chance to intrude.

At first I only went home for occasional holidays. I stayed in New York for the summers after school was out as three months in a stretch at Cecil Cove would undo whatever contentment I had established during the school year. I had planned to find a summer job in a local drugstore like I had in high school, but some of the girls in my dorm told me how much money they made waitressing in the high-end tourist restaurants that boomed during the summer in the Finger Lakes. These enormous tideless defiles clawed out of the native rock by retreating glaciers thousands of years ago serve as sublime summer retreats for thousands of tourists. Armed with that knowledge I instead found a job waitressing at a waterside restaurant on Seneca Lake, rumored to be bottomless, but at least 600 feet deep in some spots.

Somewhere toward the end of my first summer, my newfound waitress friends drove us out to Keuka Lake. We got cheap wine from one of the local wineries. We went to a community beach at the south end of Keuka and surreptitiously opened the wine there. I had grown up swimming in natural bodies of water, but swimming in Keuka was nothing like the balm of swimming in the offshoots of the Chesapeake. The water was icy, frigid, breathtaking even at the end of August. My friends promised I would get used to it, and I did, to a point. But when I stayed in the water without swimming, I felt like I was in a state of suspended animation. And the bottom, well, it wasn't there. The first ten feet out from the shoreline were stony but manageable, but walking any further away from shore was literally falling off a cliff with only frigid water supporting me. And Keuka was only about 100 feet deep on average, unlike its bigger, deeper cousins Cayuga and Seneca.

As I settled into a life where I felt comfortable and to which I knew I could return, I stopped viewing home as a trap. I came to regard the drive home as merely following the natural flow of the Susquehanna to my origins in Cecil Cove. The Susquehanna begins up in Western New York where it's a fairly small river in a somewhat flat bed, prone to flooding with the slightest excess of rain. The main road from the Western Finger Lakes to Binghamton crosses over the river a few different times. The route home then picks up the Susquehanna again just inside the Pennsylvania border. By the time I would cross her in Harrisburg, she was starting to resemble a river mighty enough to be one of the major sources of fresh water for our country's largest estuary. When I got home and looked at the water out the window, I would envision the rain drops landing in New York and traveling all the way here to my home.

Over the years while I was in school I also gradually realized that, despite all her work with the church, I was Mom's only family and that she must be lonely despite her predilection for solitude. I sent more and more cards home and started to spend more holiday time with Mom. Maybe when some people go through traumatic events like an unexpected death in the family, they can point to some epiphany or seminal moment when they realize they're better. For me, healing and forgiveness and understanding dripped in to my heart one drop at a time like a plugged up drip coffee machine struggling to perform.

Once I moved up to New York for college, Dad began to invite me down to Florida as well. Eventually I accepted the invitations and made periodic visits. En route to the first visit, I was palpably nervous, grabbing the armrests of my airplane seat until my fingers hurt. My seatmate on the flight down saw my hands and asked if I was afraid to fly. I nodded rather than explain to my fellow passenger, but I laughed to myself because I was so anxious about seeing Dad that I had forgotten that I should be nervous about flying for the first time.

I knew that Dad had moved in with a woman and her two teenaged kids sometime after he stopped coming back to Cecil Cove. I wasn't expecting the chatterbox that met me at the door with Dad on that first visit though. Ana didn't stop talking from the second he introduced us until she went up to bed several hours later "to give us time to chat." Dad and I sat in the silence for a few minutes, until I got up the courage to say "I'm not sure what I was expecting, but I guess someone so different wasn't quite it." On that first visit, Dad had merely nodded in his own taciturn way.

On the next visit though, Ana left us to talk and went up to bed after what seemed more than an hour of straight chatter uninterrupted by breathing, having not allowed either of us any input into the conversation. "If you can believe it, the chatter was what drew me to Ana," Dad volunteered. I kept completely silent knowing that if I made any response he would clam right up. "I couldn't stand the silence at home. Your Mom and I couldn't find any safe subject to talk about once Brian was gone. We couldn't even talk about you because we'd end up talking about how you were dealing with Brian's death. I'm not criticizing you or your mom. None of us knew how to cope with Brian's death. When I met Ana down here at a bar near the port where my tanker was docked, she talked non-stop for the whole evening just like she did today. After I went back to the tanker that night, I realized what a relief it was not to be sitting in a vacuum with my thoughts." I'm not sure I had ever heard Dad put so many sentences about his feelings in general together, and he certainly had never shared any of his feelings about losing Brian.

Once he stopped talking, I realized I needed to say something. So I nodded and fumbled out, "Then I'm glad for you, if she's what you needed to move on." After that, we both lapsed into a somewhat embarrassed silence. On future visits, Dad stuck to more prosaic topics.

As Dad continued working on the oil rigs and tankers, we had to coordinate my visits with both his schedule and my school schedule. Dad had in enough years with his company that he probably could have retired and taken a job on shore with a more predictable schedule, but he loved nothing more than fixing something that was broken. I knew that meant that as long as he was healthy enough, he would go on working for the oil company. If they made him retire, he would probably find a job at a local marina. Anyone who knew as much as he did about boat engines could get a part-time job with no problem.

At least one night of each visit, we ate out at a waterfront restaurant. We always waited for a window or outside table to permit maximum birdwatching. While watching the pelicans fish one night, Dad popped out, "Even though the Gulf is fantastic, I still miss the Chesapeake." I was somewhat surprised. The white sand beaches and the persistent warmth of Florida were many people's idea of heaven. He continued, "Watching the pelicans fish is ok, but I miss watching the osprey all summer long. They remind me of those dragon books you were always reading on the dock."

"How is that?" I asked perplexed, but remembering that Dad referred to all my fantasy books as dragon books irrespective of whether the particular book had a dragon in it or not.

"Well, you look up and see the osprey soaring kind of calmly, but then you can tell they've spotted fish for the family dinner because they go from peacefully spread out flat to vertical and vicious. Their wings flap like one of those furious dragon gods on the cover of your books holding themselves in position directly above the same spot. Then they plummet. Most of the time they come up with dinner too."

"OK, I can see what you mean about the osprey looking like my dragons, but I don't think I ever brought home dinner off the dock." I joked.

"God, I miss the oysters I'd get from my buddies too." Dad remarked as a dozen oysters on the half shell were dropped off at our table. Dad, of course, knew a lot of the Chesapeake watermen from his time at the marina. They had learned to come to him privately for repairs that would have cost a fortune at a marina. As a kid, when the watermen were on our dock waiting for Dad to finish, I would hear them talk about how hard making ends meet was. They would grumble about the latest restriction on how many rockfish or crabs or oysters the state or county would let them take. Worried about the falling harvests, they would talk about the silt-ups and the algae blooms that were bad for the oyster beds.

Often Dad took payment for his repairs in some sort of catch, whatever was in season. In the cold months that meant oysters. Dad had a special thick leather glove in the garage he would use when he had oysters to shuck. He would put the glove on his left hand, and hold the oyster with that, while with his right hand he found the right spot to insert the oyster knife, give the knife a quick twist, and pop the oyster open.

"These oysters ain't bad though," I commented as I slurped down the last of my share.

"Nope, not at all. You weren't much for raw oysters as a kid, you know."

"I know, but I loved Mom's oyster stew." When I was a kid, Dad would periodically present Mom with big jars of oysters with the same pride as a feral cat leaving a dead mouse on the front stoop, and I knew oyster stew was in the making. I loved the oyster stew Mom would make. The stew was nothing but butter, milk and the oysters, but the salty briny taste would infuse into the fat. I didn't even want to eat the oysters in the stew, I only wanted to slurp that broth with the yellow fat bubbles floating in the white milk.

"Yeah, me too." Dad concurred.

With a little giggle as Dad pushed his plate of empty shells to the edge of the table, I said, "But you didn't love the oyster shells."

Dad scowled at me in response. Our entire yard in Cecil Cove was littered with oyster shells. For at least the first two hundred years during the development of our part of Maryland, the thick hard calcium-rich oyster shells were considered perfect for road surfaces and landfill, somewhat to the detriment of the Chesapeake oysters as they need the old shells for the young oysters to grow on. When the original farming family sold off the acreage that ultimately became our waterfront community, the first builders that came through dumped thousands of tons of oyster shells as fill to level the plots of land. Below that level, some of the shells had been part of colonial roads as evidenced when we would occasionally dig up clumps of oysters still bound together by some type of mortar with a faded yellow-ochre color. The shells turned up everywhere when anyone tried to do yard work. Even in areas of the lawn Dad had mowed hundreds of times, the lawn mower would suddenly catch a shell and either grind painfully or kick a piece out the side. Mom constantly bemoaned the difficulties they caused working in her various flower beds, even after Dad dumped a load of topsoil on the beds.

Although the shells drove my parents to distraction, I remembered how I had played with the oyster shells as a kid. I would get a Frisbee and pile them up as if I were making a plate of raw oysters. I would then offer them to Brian or Julie or any adult, as if I had my own restaurant.

The waitress put our entrees down. Dad had ordered a crab-stuffed fish that turned out to be enormous. "I would have been a whole lot of pissed off if I lived there when they passed that rockfish moratorium a couple years ago," Dad noted as he squeezed lemon on his fish. "Even when I was there, I watched one buddy after another give up on being a waterman. You just couldn't make a living anymore. And then, because of some damn rich folks who wanted to be sure they could catch a rockfish when they took the boat they barely knew how to drive out on the weekends, the paid off politicians put a total stop to fishing one of the best fish in the bay. Damn environmentalists, and also the spoiled rich sport fishermen."

I wasn't sure I knew what he was talking about, and I also wasn't sure whether I was that interested in a tirade on the fate of the Chesapeake watermen, but on the other hand, Dad was not normally so passionate and I didn't want to deter him. Ana must be rubbing off on him. I decided to bite.

"I didn't even know they had stopped rockfish fishing. I guess the ban happened when I was up at school."

"Yea, I guess you were. The moratorium started in 1985. You and your mother weren't ever much for eating fish either."

That was definitely true. Mom would cook, clean and eat as many oysters or crabs as Dad would bring home, but she categorically refused to clean fish. She had told Dad that if his buddies gave him fish, he needed to clean them before he got home.

"I liked the fish sticks Mom would make." I protested.

"Blasphemy. Those were frozen mincemeat of some cheap white fish of who knows what sort. Rockfish is too sweet and delicate to waste on mushing up into sticks and frying. You should try more fish now that you're more grown up, you might like it more."

My culinary tastes had expanded exponentially during my time in New York. Culturally, Western New York was an odd blend of rural, conservative farm folk, some ageing hippies who hid from mainstream culture in rural Western New York, and some fairly affluent liberal college staff and faculty who clustered around the college towns. The farm folk and hippies got along ok. I had been surprised to find one of the most famous vegetarian restaurants smack dab in the middle of the Finger Lakes region, but Moosewood and its cookbooks were legend. The seasonings and spices of these oddities had been completely foreign to me at first, raised as I was on Old Bay and Campbell's soup casserole recipes. Once I got used to the exotic tastes, I found myself trying them out and becoming pretty adventurous in the kitchen. One more way in which my choice of college had expanded my horizons.

JULIE NOVEMBER 1983

I was in the kitchen of a frat house on the horseshoe shaped fraternity row in College Park. One of those perfect brick buildings with the Greek letters right over the columned entry way. I was drinking some form of Jesus juice and talking to some sisters at a sorority where I was thinking of pledging.

Lo and behold Bobby Owen with his thick blond hair and china doll blue eyes comes in the kitchen looking for more to drink. I knew he was attending University of Maryland at College Park, but this was the first time I'd run into him. Since he appeared to have had a fair amount to drink, he took a few seconds to recognize me, but he came over, hugged me, spilling some vile-smelling draft beer on me in the process. We asked the usual "What is so-and-so doing" questions about the Cecil Cove folks, and then he unbelievably asked me if I knew where Siobhan had ended up for college.

I turned my look as frosty as possible and declared, "I don't speak to her, and I don't care what she's doing."

With less alcohol on board Bobby might not have spoken, but he did, "Haven't you gotten over blaming her yet?"

And with less alcohol on board I might have just walked away, but instead I flew back at him, "She destroyed my whole family. You think I should get over that?"

At this point, the sorority sisters and anyone else unfortunate enough to be in the kitchen were trying to melt into the walls to surreptitiously watch what appeared to be a good fight coming.

I expected Bobby to back down at that, but his retort left me breathless: "Destroyed YOUR whole family. Your parents killed her brother. They destroyed her whole family. Her brother is dead. Her dad left. Her mom spends most of her days taking Valium. It was your parents who destroyed your family and your life, not Siobhan. Your parents killed Brian and then hid. What did you think Siobhan was supposed to do when you all found the boat, quietly bury the fact that the killer of her brother was right there in front of us all? You think she could have sat on that for all her life? That's insane. Yes, Brian was stupid going out on the river in a canoe on the Fourth of July at night. Jim was stupid. I was stupid, and my parents damn sure made sure I knew how stupid they thought I'd been. But Brian has already paid for his stupidity with his life. You're looking for someone to blame for your life being a mess, be honest and admit that it's because your parents hid that boat in their garage instead of doing the right thing once they found out someone had been hurt." He walked out the back door of the frat into the night.

I ran after him, ready to give it right back to him. But right before I caught up with him, and I was opening my mouth to come up with some stinging response, for the first time I realized that he was right, 100% dead on right. Just because Siobhan had been my best friend didn't mean she could let her brother's killer off the hook. And had my parents called the police as soon as they found out that someone had been hurt, Dad might have gotten off with no jail time at all. After all, Brian, Bobby and Jim had been stupid. In the pitch dark, no one could see the canoe, no less a head right next to it. My parents lost their security clearances and their jobs because they lied and covered up. Instead of the zinging retort I had planned to make, I threw my arms around Bobby and started sobbing.

I started seeing a counselor not long after that night, and I finally started to accept who truly had responsibility for that night. The repercussions of that night hadn't ever seemed to end. I never had precisely known what my parents did for a living since they weren't allowed to talk about their work, but their original skill set did not translate well into the civilian world. Mom couldn't afford our Annapolis house without her and Dad's high-paying consulting work. Mom ended up renting a cheap townhouse north of

Baltimore from a cousin stuck with the house until her divorce finalized. Surprisingly, Mom didn't linger on the loss of her job. She enrolled straightaway in a night time computer programming two-year program and worked for a temp service to pay the bills.

Mom's new career plans meant that once again I was without parents to take care of me. At first Grandmom spent more nights than not in the basement of the townhouse because she would not abandon me to my mother's career ambitions. Even though I know she hated giving up her cottage and resented my mother for having to do so, she turned the cottage over to her nephew and moved in with us full time while I finished high school. Grandmom had a hard time suppressing her criticisms of her own daughter but she struggled to maintain enough of a relationship with my Mom that she didn't introduce any further discord in my life.

My parents' marriage tanked while Dad was in jail. He only ended up serving about a year and then somehow convinced his parole board to let him move back to California where his parents were. Grandmom was able to kick in enough money to allow me to go to College Park, but I had always dreamt of Columbia or NYU or Ann Arbor or some exclusive small liberal arts college for foreign languages and writing. So I had a huge chip on my shoulder. The counselor helped me let go of that and start to view my life going forward as my responsibility to make into what I wanted, not using other people's mistakes as an excuse for not getting what I wanted.

Bobby and I started dating not long after the episode at the frat house. I was surprised to find that we quickly ended up in a serious relationship because he was a senior and was headed to law school in the fall. But our relationship worked not just because we grew up together, but because we had the same goals for a family and for a life.

Bobby got into the law school at American University, his dad's alma mater, making continued dating possible without my leaving

College Park. He proposed marriage in his 2L year, presenting me with a small but exquisitely clear diamond ring. I was unintentionally pregnant almost instantaneously after the wedding. Without his parents, particularly his mother to help me understand what being married to an aspiring big firm litigation lawyer was like, I'm not sure we would have made it. Summer after second year is critical for law students to do clerkships and make the connections they need to land jobs in the big firms, which left me without Bobby during much of the pregnancy. Even though Bobby was likely to get an offer from the law firm where Bobby's father was a partner, Bobby was working constantly in order to prove that he deserved the spot and to put himself on a partnership track if he did get a spot.

I didn't want to give up on my degree because of the pregnancy either. I wasn't exactly sure what a degree in French literature was going to do for me, but I had spent too much time translating Corneille's *Le Cid* and *Polyeucte* not to have anything to show for all that work. My degree ended up taking five years but I still did finish. Bobby's mother did tons of babysitting for us as we both finished up. Then when Bobby did get the dream job in a litigation group of his dad's D.C. law firm, he was around even less, working the insane hours that are expected of new associates. It's a wonder we even managed to have two more kids.

I was thrilled to be a stay-at-home mom. Although I spent a lot of time doing arts and crafts as a kid and I was good with foreign languages, I never had any particular vocation or dream career I wanted to pursue. When guidance counselors or relatives would ask me what I would do when I grew up, I would always invent some art-related career, too ashamed to admit that I didn't see anything wrong with the Ward and June Cleaver life where Dad brings home the bacon and Mom raises the kids.

Bobby hadn't believed me at first when I said that I believed staying home to take care of kids was a great idea since most of the other girls my age were career-oriented. He finally started to understand when I explained that I had always sworn when I had kids, I would raise them. My children would not be raised by a grandparent or by the next door neighbor's parents, and that if I wasn't prepared to put in the time to raise them right then I shouldn't have them. For his part, Bobby was only too thrilled that I wanted to stay home as the hours he was expected to work meant that his partner through life would be handling most of the quotidian household affairs and childrearing. We were doubly lucky that Bobby's mother was always available to help too. And, Bobby's salary and bonuses gave us financial flexibility that none of our friends our age had.

CHAPTER SEVEN

The wakes from the boats on the river had diminished to low ripples by the time they reached the cove, but they were still making soft slap-whapping sounds against the neighbors' bulkheads. The sunrise this morning was one of the most unusual I had encountered since moving back and starting my quest for the perfect photo. We had had a cool evening producing a water temperature at dawn that was higher than the ambient air temperature. Mist was rising off the water in columns like an army of wraiths was being summoned from the depths of the cove. The sky was largely overcast, but a tiny hint of pink was seeping through, infusing the negative spaces around the trees.

I sat on the dock with a tripod, my new digital camera, two new lenses, some filters, and a handful of instruction books. I had decided that merely going out and seeing the sunrises wasn't good enough. I wanted to take some distinctive pictures of them, but I remembered distressingly little about the photography classes I took freshman year of college; I'd never even used a digital SLR. While I wholeheartedly embraced online shopping in general, I found myself offended by the fact that camera stores have largely become extinct. I would have loved to speak in person to someone knowledgeable about buying the right equipment and get some pointers. Instead I read reviews and tips online. The UPS man brought my boxes, and here I was sitting with a bunch of manuals trying to figure out how to take my perfect sunrise photos.

At least I had the tripod and remote shutter set up correctly to allow for some longer exposures although I wasn't sure that would help capture the mist. I drank some more coffee, leaned back in my chair and sighed. I remembered the last time I'd seen a tripod on a dock was the last trip we took as a family to the Outer Banks. I had found an overpriced photographer to take some professional photos of us on a boat dock on the sound side. On my orders, the boys and Bobby put on pastel polo shirts and khaki shorts. Caitlin and I had on flowing sleeveless dresses in matching pastel colors. We stood on the end of the dock with the sunset behind us, turning our heads this way and that at the direction of the photographer. I had an enlargement of the best one printed on canvas and professionally framed. I hung it on the family photo wall in the den, the centerpiece of which was our best wedding photo.

We had kept our wedding small. For his part, Bobby didn't want to be distracted from law school by plans for a big wedding. For my part, I certainly didn't want Dad to walk me down the aisle, meaning the huge traditional wedding was out. My Grandmom had already spent enough money making sure I could go to college, and I did not want to take any money from her for a wedding. I had guilted Mom into contributing a couple thousand bucks.

Bobby's parents had wanted a bigger affair but since we put the wedding together in a matter of a few weeks, they were limited in how much they could expand our plans. Bobby's father's firm gave a lot of meeting business to a hotel near their D.C. offices, allowing Bobby's father to get us a reception room on short notice. The Owens offered to pay for every guest that they added to the list, leaving us no basis for objecting to the size of their guest list. Mrs. Owen twisted some printer's arm to do up the wedding invitations as a rush job because she was appalled at the notion that I would buy some pre-printed party invitations and fill in the details. She and I drove up to some outlets in Pennsylvania and found a wedding gown that needed virtually no alteration.

From the wedding photos, you would have had no idea that the wedding had been thrown together in such a short period of time. Instead of doing pictures in the church, we drove to a few monuments in D.C. and I froze standing outside with the photographer snapping photos against iconic backdrops. I had used some of the cash we'd received as wedding gifts to print and frame a huge enlargement of the two of us with the Lincoln Memorial reflecting pool in the background that I was determined to display prominently on a feature wall in our home, even if at the time that home had been a student apartment.

SIOBHAN CHRISTMAS 1985

I came home from New York for Christmas to visit Mom. We bought a small ham, covered it with brown sugar and pineapple, and baked it until warm. Mom made her famous potatoes au gratin from the box and green bean casserole. Mom was never a gourmet cook. She had taken home economics in high school, and she had a handful of go-to recipes from the well-worn church cookbook with its red plastic spiral comb that was perpetually on a small slanted stand in the corner of the kitchen counter. Our meals during childhood were decent but without a lot of variation. We had spaghetti, macaroni and cheese, tacos made from the Old El Paso kits, hamburgers, fried chicken, and shake-and-bake pork chops. Holiday dinners were slightly more elaborate than weekday cuisine but she always made the same meals for every holiday. Nevertheless, having Mom's cooking for Christmas was comforting in a nostalgic way. I did bring some good Finger Lakes rieslings to elevate the meal.

As an effort to liven the place up, I took Mom's basket of Christmas cards that she had sitting by the fireplace and started to spread the cards across the mantel. Most of them were from her church friends. I was almost to the bottom of the basket when I found the wedding invitation, which was already out of its envelope. When I read the names of the happy couple, I let out my breath all at once.

"Mom, when did you get this?"

"This what?"

"The wedding invitation for Julie and Bobby. Did you know they were getting married before you got the invitation?" I looked back down at the invitation. "Holy heck, it's next week." I looked through the pieces of the invitation to see if the response card was still there. "You're not going, are you?"

"No, I told Bobby's mom it conflicts with one of the church Epiphany concerts."

"But otherwise you would go?" I asked aghast. "Mom, how could you even think about it? And how could Bobby of all people marry her?"

"Siobhan, you need to get over being mad at Julie. You may never be friends or like sisters again, but she was...."

I interrupted her. "She told me it was my fault that her parents went to jail. How can I forgive that?"

"Siobhan, she was a kid, she was scared to death that her parents would get sent away. If she didn't get mad at you she'd have to admit that her parents did something wrong." Mom held her hand up to stop me from interrupting her again. "Look, I can't say I've forgiven her parents because I haven't, but Julie was just as much a victim as we were. Bobby's mom and I went to high school together, and she was hoping to make some peace. I talked to her. She said that Julie's dad isn't coming, and he's the one that I really have an issue with. I still thought going to the wedding would be awkward, so I gave Bobby's mom a plausible excuse rather than make things worse."

"I just can't believe any of it. I can't believe Bobby would want anything to do with her. He and Brian were best friends."

"Siobhan, you are still looking at the accident from a kid's eyes. At some point you need to step back and re-think things like an adult. I don't want to ruin our nice holiday. I'm not going to the wedding so stop glaring at me like I did something wrong by receiving a wedding invitation that I didn't even ask for."

I breathed. I apologized to Mom. She was right about having no right to be mad at her. We watched our favorite old Christmas movies and finished off the wine.

When I went off to bed though, I found myself lying in bed unable to sleep, despite the wine. I couldn't believe Bobby would marry Julie. I was seething. I tried never to think of Julie, but whenever I did this medieval black bile crawled up from the pit of my stomach through my veins to my heart, seizing it with lancing pains, and then continuing on into my head blurring my vision with vitriol. I could never forget how, at the worst time of my life, she blamed me for ruining her life and getting her parents in trouble.

I spent the next couple days with Mom and then packed up for the drive back to New York. Only when I was on I-81 did Mom's scolding words come back to me. Mom usually had no motherly advice at all. The only time Mom spoke up was when I had pushed every last one of her buttons, and she couldn't take me anymore. Was I still looking at the accident through a kid's eyes? What did she mean by that? How did Mom think an adult would look at what happened any differently? Although obviously she did, and Brian had been her son. What was the perspective she had and would I hurt less if I could see things that way?

I didn't come to any brilliant revelations on the drive but somehow the poison that infected me at the mere thought of Julie seemed a little less viscous like it might one day be able to drip away.

CHAPTER EIGHT

I heard Guilty making an unholy high keening noise intermixed with pained yelps out in the yard. I ran out the front door to find out what was wrong.

Siobhan was climbing over the fence from her yard. I must have looked surprised as she started explaining, "Guilty got nailed by one of your cousin Bill's feral cats. I was cleaning up leaves and walnuts when one of the cats ran through my yard and headed into yours. Then I saw Guilty charge the cat. Ginger there," and Siobhan pointed up into the nearest tree where a ginger tabby was sitting on one of the branches with the hair on its back bristled up doing a perfect imitation of a Cheshire Cat smile, "gave Guilty one good swipe across the nose and ran up the tree. I didn't know if you were home so I was hopping over to make sure Guilty wasn't too badly hurt."

"Thanks," I said. We had both reached Guilty by this point. I started petting him to calm him down while Siobhan tried to inspect his nose. We agreed that the damage didn't look too bad, and I made a quick dash in the house to dampen a kitchen towel and grab the antibiotic ointment that any mother of three buys in bulk. I wiped the blood off his nose while Siobhan took her turn trying to hold him still. He had three distinct claw marks down his poor little snout, but they weren't deep. We smeared some antibiotic goop on the nose.

Siobhan observed, "He'll probably lick most of it off as soon as we let go of him, but I guess it's better than nothing."

"Yup. So you called that menace one of cousin Bill's cats?" I inquired.

"Oh yes," Siobhan answered. "Bill put food out for the ferals daily. Probably five or six of them came here pretty routinely in the last couple years. They avoid my yard when my labs are out, but otherwise they roam the whole neighborhood. None of them appear to be starving so I'm sure someone else picked up where Bill let off."

I thought for a second and then asked rhetorically, "I wonder if Grandmom knew Bill did that? She hated the cats around here because they would go after all the little birds she fed. She'd be having a conniption now knowing that her precious yard had been a feeding spot for the beasts that attacked her birdies all these years."

"Oh, that's right," Siobhan laughed. "She would have a fit if any of the neighborhood cats climbed onto her bird bath for a drink. She even yelled at King occasionally for not doing a good enough job of scaring them away."

We both laughed at that.

"I still miss her. I can't imagine how my life would have turned out if she hadn't been there to take care of me."

JULIE MAY 1989

Grandmom's senior community was one of those with everything from regular condos to assisted living apartments to nursing home facilities. I had a hard time thinking of someone as feisty as Grandmom being in a senior community. When I questioned her choice she observed that she'd had more than enough of living with Mom, who had thrown herself into her new career in computers with the same zeal as she had her prior defense consulting job. She also noted that she refused to displace Bill at this point, and she didn't believe she could handle the upkeep of the waterfront property by herself.

I still found the common areas of the senior community institutional and therefore depressing, and I tried to tell her that now that Bobby and I were out of college and law school and were getting a place of our own I would make sure we had a room for her. She laughed at me, "Child, you two are just starting your life. Marriage is hard enough, and marriage with small children is even harder. You don't need a third wheel around. Besides, I love it here. Everyone else is as old as me, and that means I have plenty of bridge partners. Some of us may forget what we bid or who led, but it might be more fun that way. I don't have to take care of a house. I get up, make myself some cereal and have my banana. I pay for their cleaning service. And I can do what I want. Just make sure you don't forget to visit me and bring my great-grandchildren"

I didn't. Grandmom was the one person on my side of the family who was both mentally competent and not narcissistic. Bobby and I made sure that she came to all of the Easters, Thanksgivings and Christmases even on the rare occasions when they were at Bobby's parents' house. I brought Caitlin to visit her regularly.

I did keep asking her if she wanted to move in with us. "Surely, this place must cost a fortune Grandmom. I don't want you to end up broke."

She replied, "That's not how this place works dear. I bought into it lock, stock and barrel. I'm guaranteed housing for the rest of my life. I may have to be a little nasty if they try to move me into the nursing home side when I still think I can be on my own, but I reckon I can take care of myself. My social security covers my little living expenses, so don't you worry about me and money."

"I'm being nosy, but how did you afford that without selling the cottage? I thought you pretty much had to turn over all your assets to get the sort of deal you're talking about."

"Your grandfather believed in life insurance, and he didn't believe in spending extra money. I invested the life insurance money in some good solid investments. I never considered myself rich, but I was happy to help make sure you got to a decent college. As for Bill, he can handle buying his frozen dinners and going to the same job day in day out by himself, but some crooked landlord would have taken advantage of him if he had to rent a place, making my old cottage the perfect place to plunk him. Thankfully, my older sister had the means and the sense to buy a life insurance policy to protect Bill after she was gone. She put me in charge of the funds from the policy. I use that money for the utilities and upkeep on the cottage. Once I'd helped with your college and set Bill up in the cottage, I had enough to set myself up here, and I have enough to live decently. Who could ask for more? Do keep visiting me. And keep bringing my great-grandchildren to visit me."

For being in her eighties, she was in pretty good health and remained quite active right up to the final weeks. I saw no evidence that her mind had slowed down. Pneumonia however is difficult to beat at that age, and what had started as a little cold wouldn't go away.

I had brought Bobby Jr with me on a visit not long before she got sick. At least, I consoled myself, she got to meet her great-grandson.

Grandmom had already made all of her own arrangements. She had told me this when I first got out of college. I would have been happy to take care of things for her, but she refused to be a burden to me and she didn't trust Mom to do it. She had already distributed most of her personal possessions, although she did leave me her jewelry box of mostly costume pieces. In terms of cash, her social security stopped at her death and she had had to invest the bulk of her savings into the senior community to buy in. By that point, neither I nor Mom needed money, and I was glad that Grandmom had spent the money in a way that made her life better. Mom grumbled a bit about "wasting" the money on some "predatory" senior community and leaving the cottage to a half-witted cousin.

The funeral home was absolutely packed. Grandmom had made dozens of friends in her new community. A lot of people from the Cecil Cove neighborhood came out too. Bobby's mom had spread the word, and Grandmom was remembered quite fondly.

I flushed when I saw Siobhan's mom come in the parlor, and I was glad that I was at the far side of the room in a group of people. I knew I would have to thank her for coming, but I needed a little bit of time to compose myself. Fortunately, no one expected you to explain or thought ill of you for emotional outbursts at a funeral home.

"Thank you for coming, Mrs. Barrett," I offered as she walked up to me.

"I'm so sorry about your grandmother, Julie. She was a great friend and a perfect neighbor. I really missed having her next door."

"Thank you," I replied. So far, so good, standard funeral talk. "I know she was very fond of you. I wasn't in favor of the senior community at first, and tried to convince her to move in with us, but the senior community turned out to be great for her. Most of the people here," and I pointed around the room, "are from the new place. She did great there and made lots of friends."

"Yes, she seemed happy when I would call her periodically. Mrs. Owen told me you had your second not too long ago. Are your children here?"

"No, they're too young. One of my neighbors has them. Bobby and I were thrilled to have a son as well as a daughter."

Mrs. Barrett hugged me and said, with her face behind my back, "I am so so sorry about Lotty, and I know you'll miss her a lot, but I am glad to see that your life is going well after all you went through."

I sniffled a little and thanked her again. Fortunately, enough other people were waiting to offer condolences that I didn't have to extend the conversation any further.

Only after we were cleaning up and piling the flowers into the car did I find the flower arrangement from Siobhan. During the events I hadn't had time to look at the cards to see who had sent what. The card hiding in the lilies was a standard sorry for your loss with the florist's contact information at the top. The card had "Siobhan" typed at the bottom. Nothing else. The card was probably typed up at the florist's after a phone order. I wondered if Mrs. Barrett had guilted her into it, but then probably not. Siobhan didn't do something just because her mom wanted her to. Of course, she hadn't addressed the flowers to me or to anyone in particular. I could be sure however that Siobhan would not have sent them to my mother. She could have sent them solely out of respect for my grandmother, without feeling the need to address them to anyone living. I wanted to believe the card was a positive evolution though.

I had been thinking about Siobhan since Grandmom died. Many of my best memories of Grandmom were as a kid at her cottage, and Siobhan was as much a part of that landscape as the water itself. With Bobby's and the counselor's help I knew that I had had no right to hurl my venom at Siobhan, and that was the last time I had seen her. The counselor told me that apologizing to Siobhan would help me move forward. I always used the excuse that Siobhan wanted nothing to do with me, and therefore apologizing wasn't possible.

SIOBHAN MAY 1989

Mom and Dad both offered to come up to New York for my Pharm.D. graduation but, as all of us agreed that graduations were stultifying affairs to be avoided whenever possible, I proposed instead to visit each of them after graduation but before starting to study for my licensure exams.

I was surprised to find Mom a little choked up when I arrived at the house. When I asked her what was wrong she related that she had just heard that Julie's Grandmom had passed away. My lips involuntarily tightened, and I could feel that bitter chemical that poured out at the very mention of Julie's name creeping up from my stomach. I looked at my mother's face though and saw the genuine grief there. I bit on the inside of my cheek and hugged Mom with my face over her shoulder to avoid giving any feelings away.

"Lotty was a good woman. I don't know how she ended up with such a worthless daughter, who wouldn't even take care of her own child 90% of the time, no less how she acted you know when. But Lotty was a great neighbor and one of my only real friends. She spared no kind words for her daughter either. She told it like it was. When she moved out she told me that she wouldn't uproot her life for her daughter but she couldn't let Julie get hurt any more than she already had been, so she had to move close enough to keep Julie safe."

I eased my grip on Mom and stepped back. Amazingly, the bile was sinking back down. "Mrs. Marconi was always around for us." I managed to splurt out something reasonably positive. Then I grabbed my bag and headed toward the house. "You ok if I go wash up a bit?" I wanted a few minutes to pull myself together.

Mom wiped her eyes with the back of her hand. "Yeah, I'm ok. Go ahead."

I was glad I had held myself together in front of Mom. She and Julie's Grandmom had been close for years. I had allowed my own anger to blacken everything associated with Julie for so long that I hadn't considered how much Mom probably missed having a good friend right next door, especially since Mom didn't exactly make friends easily. Mrs. Marconi's nephew Bill was a poor substitute for Mrs. Marconi. I decided I probably needed to spend some driving time on the way back to New York drawing a little smaller box around my anger.

Mom and I went to a local crab shack to celebrate my graduation. When we were kids Dad would drop our allotted two crab pots off the dock and catch whatever he could or go out crabbing in a boat with Grandpa. We would then eat the crabs Dad caught on our dock on the weekends. Putting the crab pots out without eating all of them quickly is wasteful though as the crabs will cannibalize each other. Now that Mom was by herself, she didn't put the crab pots out anymore. She reported that she went out occasionally when the church was organizing a crab social. At a restaurant or on the church grounds, you didn't get the fun of throwing the crab shells right in the water as you were done. For me as a kid tossing the crab shells right off the dock back into the cove water gave the sense of uncivilized behavior being sanctioned, probably the same primordial joy as some people have throwing their peanut shells on the floor of a bar. Besides, throwing the shells and the guts back in the water was good for the marine life. Within minutes of throwing a pile of guts and shells in the water, the water would be teeming with small fish snapping up the tasties. I assumed that the large parts of shells got used somehow, because whenever I inspected the water a few days after having dumped shells in, they would have all disappeared. I knew that new oysters needed old shells to form on, which is why whenever we found oyster shells in the flower beds, we gathered them in a bucket and dumped them in the water. I'm not sure if crab shells helped new crabs like oyster shells did for oyster spat but I didn't see any harm.

Picking crabs is a great opportunity for conversation between two fairly introverted folks. If you run out of things to say, you look down at the crab, start peeling the devil's fingers off and clean out the mustard. On this occasion, talking about my upcoming job prospects with Mom was fairly easy. I told her about the exams I would have to take to get my pharmacy license. I was excited because the Finger Lakes region had a fair number of openings for pharmacists. That part of the world had difficulty attracting professionals who wanted to live in a fairly rural environment. What urban centers existed were for the most part economically depressed. I would have to make some huge misstep or fail my exams not to get a job up there. I wasn't sure what Mom's feelings were about the fact that I had never talked about coming back to Maryland after graduation, but I figured the fact that the job prospects in Western New York were better for a new graduate than they were in Maryland would suffice as a reason that wouldn't hurt anyone's feelings.

After a handful of days at home, I could tell that a constant presence in the house was a strain for Mom as she found more and more excuses to end up in her room. I guess she was so accustomed to being by herself in the house that even her own daughter was a bit of an invasion, which helped wipe away any concern I had that she might be upset that I was staying in New York.

The last afternoon of my visit I took my latest novel down toward the dock to give her some time to herself. A female mallard that had been snacking near our shore swam off as I approached, leaving a V rippling in the water behind her. I sat down in the chair closest to the end to have the broadest view out toward the river. When I happened to glance down at the piling nearest me, I saw a blue crab clinging to it. I stood up to take a better look. He was facing downward, more concerned about what was likely to come at him from the water than me, even though I could have taken a long pair of tongs and snatched him right off. I wondered if he was about to peel and was looking for a place to hide to keep his own brethren from eating him. Then I remembered that crabs like to eat the barnacles off the pilings. A turkey vulture soared over, wings unmoving, catching the breeze while I was staring down at the crab, and I found that I had spent a fair amount of time remembering one of our best crab feasts on the dock rather than reading.

Dad, Grandpa and Brian had gone crabbing early that morning in one of the marina's boats. I was not initially happy to have been excluded from the trip, but when I found out they were setting the alarm for 3:00 a.m., I changed my mind. I hadn't even heard the alarm go off, and they were long gone before I even opened my eyes. The paradox with my Dad was that on the one hand he wasn't around all the time like Mom was. On the other hand, when he was around so much more happened that those times were much more memorable than when he wasn't. Mom was largely content to make sure we got to school, got fed, were reasonably clean and then go do her own thing. When Dad was home, Brian and I were usually hanging out watching him work in the garage on some engine project or going with him to the marina to help Grandpa. Dad didn't talk a lot, although he occasionally surprised us with bursts of loquaciousness, but watching whatever he was doing was generally more interesting than how we amused ourselves when we were hanging out with Mom.

The evening before the crab feed Dad had taken me, Brian and Julie over to the marina where he and Grandpa chopped up chicken necks to use for bait. Grandpa had a pile of hooks for the trot line stored in an old gallon can with "Maryland's Finest Oysters" emblazoned on it. Brian helped with the bait but Julie and I were a little grossed out. Grandpa was grumbling about how much the bait had cost. Dad teased him a bit saying, "Well, you could have gone out and shot a few of those wild turkeys that hang out in the woods near the community park. Then we'd have our own turkey necks."

We did occasionally see wild turkeys along the road, although nothing like what we saw in our school books about Thanksgiving. I never saw any magnificently spread plumage on the birds near the park. They were a boring gray with a red head and wattle. Somehow I found equating those birds with the main course of Thanksgiving dinner difficult.

Grandpa groused back, "Shite, do you know how many of those things, I'd have to shoot in order to get enough necks to be bait for this trip, and how many feathers I'd have to clean up."

Julie and I had wandered up and down the docks of the marina while we were waiting for them to finish with the bait. A derelict skipjack was moored at the end of one of the forks of the pier. I had never seen the sailboat out of that spot in all the times I'd been to the marina. Grandpa and Dad were friends with a number of oystermen. Grandpa noted that a lot more of them used to come to the marina, but the marina was becoming too expensive for most of them, and the super-rich folks with the big yachts didn't like having smelly fishing boats too close to their fancy ships. Some half-broken hand tongs leaned against the back of one of the marina sheds, and when Dad had explained what they and the skipjack were, we took the tongs up on the dock near the old skipjack and stuck the tongs down in the water pretending we were catching oysters. For the most part our catch consisted of some trash and a few rocks.

While the men were out on the boat crabbing, I kept asking Mom when they would be back with the crabs and was bursting with impatience by the time they came back in the middle of the afternoon with four dozen crabs for our family, Julie and her Grandmom. They had caught a little over a bushel but since they knew we couldn't eat that many, Grandpa had sold a few dozen to a local waterman who would sell them to a restaurant with the rest of his catch. Grandpa and Dad were crowing that selling the excess crabs had paid for the bait and the gas.

Dad had set up the propane tank and portable burner in the driveway and put the huge crab pot with steamer basket on top. He poured a few beers in the bottom of the pot, and then started to use a pair of long kitchen tongs to toss the crabs in, followed by a layer of Old Bay seasoning after every handful of crabs. Every now and then a crab would escape from the wooden bushel basket and try to make a run to Mom's bushes on the side of the driveway. Brian was literally sitting on King to keep the lab from trying to chase the escapees. Only one crab got to the cover of the bushes before Dad's tongs caught up with him. The crab had turned around to face out, its dark little eyes looking at us malevolently and its two front claws snapping continuously as Dad tried to get the tongs around it. Dad won eventually, and then all the crabs were in steaming away. As the crabs were cooking, Mom boiled the corn she and I had shucked earlier in the day.

Julie and I spread newspapers out on the wooden picnic table out on the dock, weighing sections down with the crab knockers and bowls for the vinegar and seasoning. Julie's Grandmom brought over some of her killer homemade potato salad as a side. When the crabs were done, Dad brought them down to the dock in the wooden bushel basket.

We sat around the picnic table picking the crabs. Dad would help me break open the main shell with the crab knife, and either he or Mom would make sure I got all the devils fingers out. Once the main shell was open, I would pick out every last morsel from every last crevice in the cartilage. When I was a little younger, the claws had been my favorite, but now that I had the hang of the body, I wanted the whole crab. Dad would still grouse that I was making a mess by beating the crab with the wooden crab mallet far more than necessary to pull out the meat. The best part about eating the crabs down on the dock was that we could throw the shells and guts right into the water. The corn cobs went in too. Fish would come for the delicacies we dropped right away.

Periodically Mom would call my attention back to eating rather than watching the fish. Brian tried to gross me and Julie out by talking about putting the hooks with chicken necks on the trot line when they were out catching the crabs. He also kept reminding us that he had gotten to go on the boat trip but we hadn't. Of course, Julie and I were still wide awake since we had slept to a decent hour, but Brian was paying the price for getting to go on the trip and was already yawning by around 5:00.

A pair of turkey vultures soared silently as we ate, circling the cove. Once they got up to cruising altitude, they floated on the air currents unlike the sea gulls that needed to flap much more often to stay aloft. "I hope they're not going to come attack us for the crabs," I worried.

"They know better than to come around people. Besides they'd much rather have a big fat dead raccoon off the side of the road than a little bit of crab." Grandpa reassured me.

"Ooooh grosss, road kill eaters." I cried

"That's their job in life honey," Grandpa said laconically.

The present day turkey vulture was similarly uninterested in me once he'd made a loop over the dock and went off to settle in a tree. I managed to read a little bit. The next day I left for New York to start studying for my licensure exams. Once I got my pharmacy license, finding a job in a community hospital pharmacy outside of Binghamton was not that hard. Binghamton had a rundown downtown, with a lot of abandoned factory buildings. Hospitals were thrilled to get trained professionals willing to live in the area.

The work wasn't hard for me. Pharmacy requires great attention to detail, and I was tailor-made for that. The biggest difficulty in that economically challenged area was keeping my opiates from being stolen.

CHAPTER NINE

JULIE NOVEMBER 2014

I celebrated Thanksgiving at Caitlin's. Having her take over the center of the family role was a little weird for me. Ever since Bobby and I were well-established in our house, we had hosted the big holidays except for a handful where we had gone down to Florida after the Owens became snowbirds. Now we were in the same house that had seen all of those holiday meals, but I wasn't the orchestrator of the events.

Bobby's parents came up from Florida. I had invited them to stay at the cottage with me, but they chose to stay in their own house where Bobby's sister was still living. Bobby's sister had some new boyfriend, and she was in Cancun with him for the holiday. I couldn't tell how Bobby's parents were reacting to having their remaining child uninterested in spending Thanksgiving with them.

Even though the Owens didn't stay with me they did pick me up from the cottage and drove me out to Caitlin's for the meal. Bobby's mom decided that I deserved the chance to drink as much wine as I wanted at the holidays without having to worry about driving home. Drink wine I did.

An obvious subject of conversation at the dinner table for the whole family was my adjusting to life in the cottage. While the family had supported my decision to renovate and move into the cottage, they were all also somewhat concerned about how I would cope, even though they were variable in their willingness to admit any degree of worry. The men, however, accepted my simple response of: "I love the cottage. It's exactly how I hoped it would come out, and it's awesome not to have to clean up a place as big as this one. "

Bobby's dad, Caitlin's husband, and my two boys moved out to the den to watch football after helping to carry everything out to the kitchen after the meal.

Bobby's mom, Caitlin and I cleaned up and drank more wine. Caitlin apparently had not been satisfied with my response at the dinner table and inquired, "But isn't it weird for you to not be in your home?"

"Cait," I answered, "Don't you remember how early I started bringing you all out to your grandparents so that you all would grow up in and on the water? I put you and your brothers in summer camp on the Chesapeake as early as you were ready for it. The best times of my childhood were on Cecil Cove. By bringing you out to your grandparents' and getting you in camp, I was trying to give you the best parts of my childhood. This house isn't the only home I've known and been happy in. My Grandmom's cottage was too."

JULIE JUNE 1994

Bobby's mother invited me to bring the kids out to their house during the week while Bobby was working. With the kids being so young, I usually found having people visit us easier than going to visit, avoiding the headaches of making sure I had all the right toys and items in the diaper bags. Bobby's mom however pointed out that the weather was perfect for swimming in the creek. Didn't I want our kids to have the same experiences Bobby and I had had growing up near the water? As usual, any argument that related to being better for the kids won me over. I felt like I had to stuff the entire minivan full to go an hour east though.

I had never spent any amount of time in the Owens' house growing up. Although I hung out with the boys when we were all outside, Siobhan and I didn't get invited inside the boys' houses. For that matter, during the summers we all spent more time outdoors than anywhere else. Bobby's sister is exactly 10 months older than he is, which made her more than four years older than me. She had not wanted anything to do with either me or Siobhan back as teenagers so I hadn't seen their house through her either.

Mrs. Owen helped me unpack the minivan and get the kids settled. She already had the kids' favorite brand of macaroni and cheese and some hot dogs ready. She had also picked up some fancy salads for us. After lunch we carted all the kids' stuff down to their dock including the playpen for David. We raised the big umbrella to keep David in the shade, and he was largely content to hang out with his toys. Bobby Jr had no patience for the life vest. Since we weren't letting him in the water without it, Bobby's mom mostly followed him back and forth as he marched up and down the dock waving a bright green foam floatie.

Caitlin, however, was in heaven in the water. She had taken swimming lessons last summer, and she was a natural swimming in the creek. Wearing my bathing suit and some water shoes, as I had become much more squeamish than I used to be about standing on the silty bottom, I stood about waist deep in the water ready if Caitlin needed any help. As the tide was full, Caitlin's head was above water only until she walked out about half the length of the dock. Once she got that distance from the shore, she swam back and forth on a parallel line to the shore between the Owens' dock and the neighbors on the right about forty feet away. I let her go back and forth like that until I saw that she was getting a little sloppy from fatigue, and then I reined her in.

After that, I brought the kids out to the Owens' regularly until the sea nettles started to appear that summer. I hardly had much choice as Caitlin begged at the dinner table almost every night to go to Grandma's to swim the next day. I also realized that Mrs. Owen had been right that I didn't want to deny my kids the chance to experience the waterfront life. I knew therefore that driving out to the Owens' would be part of many future summer days.

Since Grandmom's old cottage was less than two miles away from the Owens' house, I periodically entertained the notion of a drive-by, but I always came up with an excuse not to do so. The kids were the easiest excuse. Someone was always tired, or had fallen asleep in the car seat, or wasn't feeling well. If I was honest though, I just wasn't comfortable going by there. I had never been entirely at ease around cousin Bill myself, but I was even more worried about how the kids, particularly Caitlin, would react to his irregularly slow speech. I was afraid she would ask some embarrassing question about why he was like that, or even worse, ask him why he was like that.

Also, Mrs. Barrett was still next door to Grandmom's old place. She had been kind enough at Grandmom's funeral, but I still wasn't sure I was ready to randomly run into her, or even worse Siobhan, if I had the bad luck to drive by when she was visiting from New York.

Caitlin was going to spend a week at summer camp in mid-August of that year. Camp Tidewater, where I had gone, had closed and been turned into an expensive waterfront community, but similar camps were still available all over the Chesapeake. I picked a place on a cove off the Susquehanna because the water that far north was reputed to always be too fresh to support sea nettles. I knew the early summer time at the Owens' house would be good prep for her, getting her used to going out into the water before she got to camp. The camp had all the activities that I had loved: canoeing, kayaking, sailing, swimming, horseback riding, arts and crafts.

Bobby was able to clear enough time on the Saturday Caitlin was due at camp to drive the whole family there. I was doubly glad Bobby was able to come because the traffic on I-95 north of Baltimore, an area with which I'm not familiar, turned out to be absolutely horrendous. The boys were restless with boredom in the back by the time we got there, whereas Caitlin was restless with excitement. I leapt out of the minivan with relief at the end of the long ride.

Bobby took the boys to a playground area to keep them occupied as I got Caitlin checked in. All the campers next had to have a lice check in the camp's medical trailer before signing up for activities. While she was in line for that, Bobby and I walked the boys down to the water where the different types of watercraft were. Despite my efforts, both boys managed to get shoes and socks soaking wet by getting too close to the waves as they came up to the shore. When Caitlin was done with the medical trailer, she picked her activities, which I had to sign off on for costs. Fortunately, everything she wanted was available. However, since we were so late getting there because of the traffic, only lower bunks were left in her cabin by the time we got there. I know she was disappointed, but her cabin counselor assured her that she would be outside so much she shouldn't care which bunk she was in. I hid a tear or two as we started to leave Caitlin. Caitlin, however, was already caught up with the kids in her cabin. She hugged me and Bobby perfunctorily, then went back to the tetherball being violently centrifuged by her fellow campers.

The traffic had eased considerably by the ride back home. The boys were worn out and both fell asleep barefoot. Bobby and I were able to converse like adults, and I had his undivided attention for over an hour. Naturally we reminisced about our own Camp Tidewater experiences, although due to age and gender difference, we had never run into each other at camp.

The boys ultimately joined Caitlin at the camp up off the Susquehanna as they got old enough. I was pretty sure that I'd instilled a love of the water in each of them as canoeing, kayaking and sailing were always their first picks for activities. Not surprisingly, each excelled at different activities: Caitlin like me at arts and crafts; Bobby Jr at diving and competitive swimming; David at archery. As they bragged about their successes on the car rides home, I couldn't help but remember how Siobhan and I would show off our strengths.

SIOBHAN 1975

Julie's sand candle was a perfect purple heart. I had intended mine to be a star shape. One arm of my star had collapsed overnight, and the other four were all different lengths, widths and shades of green. Worse still a mosquito had become trapped in the wax at the edge of one of the arms. This was the first year that my parents had decided I was old enough to stay over at Camp Tidewater instead of just showing up for the day sessions. Last night, my first night ever, as darkness crept in, we all made sand candles on the shore, carving out spots past the high tide lines. The counselors gave us soap-sized bars of clear wax and boxes of old broken crayons to melt over the campfire in old coffee cans. I wanted a green star, but obviously I hadn't mixed in enough green crayons and hadn't mixed them evenly. This morning after breakfast, we all headed back to dig our candles out. I pouted all the way back to our cabins to put them away as Julie spun hers around in her hands over and over again.

The first activity of the day was archery, where our triumphs and frustrations were reversed. Julie had strung her bow backwards, making the shape of a parenthesis mark instead of the correct sinuous recurve shape. She twanged the inside of her arm the first time she tried to draw the bow. I helped her re-string her bow and then went back to my own target. I crowed as my fourth shot was in the yellow, and then on the seventh shot hit the bullseye. With her bow properly strung, Julie finally got a couple in the black at the end of the session.

After archery we ran to the pool house to change for swim lessons. I was still somewhat annoyed that Mom would only buy me one-piece bathing suits, while Julie sported a red, white and blue flag-patterned bikini. We were both great swimmers for our age although hardly surprising since we'd been swimming in the cove all our lives. Mom, Dad and Julie's grandmom had all insisted that we learn early on. Even Brian had been involved, holding his hand under my stomach as I held onto a kickboard and learned how to do frog-kicks. The camp counselors started me and Julie on the backstroke and sidestroke since we were notably ahead of the others.

All of the kids of all ages ate lunch together at picnic tables in a huge barn-like building on stilts. By the time we all filed in and sat down, each table had pitchers of "bug juice" and cold cuts with plain white bread from which we made sandwiches. Wisely the boys were kept on one side of the aisle and the girls on another to prevent too much horseplay.

Horseback riding was first after lunch, and there, Julie and I were both novices although we had grand plans for being master jumpers. The fact that we spent most of the time walking around in a circle trying to keep our heels down and our fingers properly wrapped around the reins with the right tension was a bit of a letdown.

Then we were back to the shore for canoeing and sailing lessons, which was a relief after the heat and the biting flies of the horse paddocks. We all stood in about thigh-deep water with paddles, learning our I, J and back strokes. I'd been out in our canoe dozens of times, but Dad or Brian always did the bulk of the paddling. With them, all I did was sit in the middle seat, and get yelled at when I leaned over one side or the other, which threatened to flip us all in the water. Brian had christened our canoe *The Colt,* and every time he got a new Baltimore Colts sticker we added it to the decorations on the hull. Some of the stickers that were too close to the waterline were starting to come off though.

Dinner was served in the same hall as lunch, but usually consisted of big platters of spaghetti or so-called campfire stew. Staying over at camp was much better than having to go home every day because we got to go to campfire every night after dinner. No way would Mom have let us make s'mores every single night. We belted out camp songs until the mosquitos started their voracious biting, and then the counselors would push us back to our cabins where we would tell ghost stories in our bunks until we fell asleep.

A few weeks of summer remained after camp was over. Mrs. Marconi's rule was that Julie and I were only allowed to swim in the cove if an adult was out on a nearby dock, which was true most days. Brian was sometimes with us and sometimes with Jim and Bobby on the other side of the cove at Jim's family's dock.

Julie and I were the only two girls our age on the cove although a few other girls lived closer to the community beach area. Julie and I would probably have been close friends no matter how many other girls were around. Most of the families in our community were traditional ones where dad went to work, mom stayed at home and raised two to three kids. Neither Julie nor I could call our family traditional. Julie was practically being raised by her grandmother particularly during the summer. Even during the school year, her grandmother ended up driving her to her expensive private school a lot of the time. Her grandmother was also the one who made sure she did her homework and helped her if she needed it. My family was unusual in that Dad was down at the oil rigs and tankers in the Gulf of Mexico so often that we were effectively being raised by a single mother at times, which was virtually unheard of in our little neighborhood.

Brian must have noticed the difference between our family and others in the neighborhood to a certain extent, but not nearly as much as I did. He probably missed working with Dad on all the little engine projects that Dad did when he was in town, but our neighborhood had enough boys his age that he was never without playmates when Dad wasn't around. For me, if neither Julie nor Brian were around, I mostly read on the dock or in my room.

During the school year, when all the other kids got called into traditional dinner around the table for the family, Julie's grandmother, Julie, Mom, Brian and I would set up our flowered black aluminum tray tables in the family room of our house, eat some macaroni and cheese with hot dogs, and watch *Happy Days*.

CHAPTER TEN

I carried a few new junipers down to the dock to replace some evergreens that hadn't taken near the shoreline hoping to get them to take root before the first frost. Then I went back up to the garage to grab my gloves and tools. When I returned to the water side, I saw that a dozen or more mallards had floated right up near my shore to feed. To avoid scaring them off, I quickly hid behind the horrible gumball tree that I had unsuccessfully begged the county for permission to take down; the tree partially obstructed my view and made a total mess of my yard when the spiky balls fell, but neither of those concerns overrode the tree's positive environmental impact according to the county.

I had loved watching the ducks ever since I was a kid, when I used to take any stale bread that Mom had and toss it in the water. Water fowl take advantage of low tide where food on the bottom is easier to reach. The exceptionally low tide that came with this new moon had pulled the water well out from my shore, exposing the acorns that roll down into the shallows from the oak trees above. I watched the whole fleet of mallards bobbing their heads in and out of the water as well as clustering around the pilings of my dock to pull off some adhered food source. When they floated a little farther out and started to flap their wings in some sort of grooming exercise, I came out from behind the tree and got back to my new plants.

Halfway through my planting, a flash of black fur appeared in my peripheral vision, and all the ducks took off at once. I looked over to see that Guilty had been made a beeline down to the end of Julie's dock as soon as someone on the inside had opened the door and released him solo. He barked futilely at the departing ducks and ran back and forth along the dock hoping they'd return. Fortunately my two were inside as they would have only created more noise. I went back to my new evergreens that I was hoping would hold my hill in place without getting too tall and blocking the view.

"You know you're just making a salad for the deer, don't you?" Julie's voice came from over the fence. I started and nearly fell onto the dock as I hadn't heard her come outside to retrieve Guilty, who had been too distracted by the ducks to take care of his business.

"Yard work not your thing, huh?" I tossed back at her.

"I love having a beautiful yard, but it should get beautiful the way God intended, by paying someone to do it for you." I laughed. She continued, "I got that one from Dad."

"Do you ever see him?" The words were out of my mouth before I could stop them, but I immediately wondered if I should have asked as Julie had never brought up her father since she moved back.

JULIE 1996

If not for my own kids, I'm not sure I would ever have considered getting back in touch with my father. Although counseling had helped me with my anger, I still had no desire to try to recreate a relationship that had barely existed in the first place. After all, Mom was barely tolerable even in small doses. Why have two intolerable parents in the mix?

My kids though were curious about my father, in part because they had such terrific relationships with Bobby's parents, their grandmother first and then their grandfather as well once he retired from litigation. Bobby's parents came to their recitals and sports events. They babysat and, when I couldn't be in three places at once getting each kid to his or her respective event, they were willing chauffeurs. We shared holidays with them. Our home was the nexus of a large family, and I basked in the warm blanket of a family as family was meant to be, as I'd always wanted to have, a family that embraced and supported but didn't smother.

Because I had still lived with Mom after the accident, we'd been forced to come to terms with each other. However, she was a driven career-focused person. She had taken a lot of computer programming classes even before I went off to college, and had climbed to the top of a computer software firm with the same dedication that I assume she had given to the defense consulting she used to do. I always invited her to holidays and birthday parties but more often than not the kids just got a card or a present in the mail from her. At least the kids knew her. As far as I could tell, they assumed that she loved them, but that if they didn't see her that she was working a lot, not that different in fact from Bobby as he made partner.

The kids therefore did not understand why they'd never even met their maternal grandfather. I had never told them about the accident or the subsequent jail time. I assumed I would at some point once they were old enough, but I still viewed that as being years in the future. They didn't ask about him every day, but at large family occasions or when I forced everyone to the photographers for another set of family photos, I got the queries.

Then in March 1996, I got a thick cream envelope in the mail addressed to Mr. and Mrs. Robert Owen & Family with a return address in California. Holy shit, I swore to myself when I opened it, he was getting married again this June. And he had the abject gall to invite me and Bobby, and the kids no less, to the wedding, when the kids hadn't even met him. I was at turns furious, bewildered, and anxious. I had no idea what to do.

Bobby was preparing for a big trial in a couple weeks and was getting home after 9 o'clock every night. I told him about the wedding invitation, and like the rock he always was for me he said, "You know I'll support you 100% whatever you choose to do, but he's your dad so it's important for you to decide. Write the date down for me, and I'll make sure to clear the calendar at work in case you decide you want to go." All supportive words, caring, but they didn't help me decide what I wanted to do in the slightest.

I was so torn I even contemplated calling the counselor I used to see, but Bobby found his own way to help me. He told his mom about the wedding invitation, and when she brought the boys home from Bobby Jr's beginning basketball practice one day, she fixed us iced teas and patted the chair next to her at the breakfast table. "You don't have to talk to me about this if you don't want to, but Bobby thought you seemed really upset about the wedding invitation. I'm all ears if you need them."

I stared at my tea for a few minutes, but I'm not taciturn by nature and once I start to speak, words just spew out of me. Part of me supposed I still hated my Dad and that I had probably hated him even before the accident for being such a nonexistent parent. The side of me that had spent years in counseling wanted to believe that I had forgiven him a long time ago as part of my own healing process. But, just because I'd forgiven him didn't mean I needed him in my life when I had such a wonderful life without him. The mom in me reminded myself that not having a chance to get to know their grandfather was unfair to the kids. But what if he was a jerk to them? What if his wife was horrible? How could I bring the kids blind into that? Bobby would be ok no matter how Dad acted. If Bobby could stand up in front of a judge and opposing counsel time and again, my ex-con father couldn't intimidate him, no matter what Dad brought.

After having allowed my volcano to pour lava in every possible direction, Bobby's mom cut through all the angst with a suggestion that hadn't even crossed my consciousness. "Dear," she said, "if he were a completely unfeeling oaf with no love for you whatsoever, he wouldn't have invited you to the wedding. He's trying to reach out. He must be pretty socially inept or scared to death to think that a wedding invitation was the best way to reconnect with you. I agree with you that the kids might find walking cold into a wedding difficult. Why don't you call your dad and see if you can go out for a few days by yourself before the wedding? You can meet his bride-to-be. You might even meet whatever family your dad has left out in California. We can watch the kids for you. If your visit goes well, you can all go to the wedding. If it's a disaster, you come home. You know that you tried, and you move on."

Her plan made so much sense that my stomach stopped doing its Mary Lou Retton imitation. I was still nervous when I picked up the phone later that night, waiting until the kids were in their rooms so they couldn't overhear me and also giving Dad plenty of time to get home from work three time zones away. When a woman answered the phone, I clenched my fingernails into my palms so hard they left impressions. I asked to speak to Charles Johnson, please.

"Who's calling please?" she politely replied.

"His daughter Julie."

The pause was long enough that I knew she was surprised, but when she spoke she responded quite neutrally, "Of course, please hold on."

Dad came on the line. "Julie, it's great to hear from you."

I stumbled and stammered a lot but managed to get out, "Well, er, um, I got the wedding invitation, and well I um wanted to. Well, first off, congratulations. My kids you know have asked about you and I was thinking it was only fair that they had a chance to meet you, but I was um well really worried that it might be awkward too. My mother-in-law, who's just terrific, well she er suggested that I might want well that it might be less weird if I came out to visit you before the wedding. You know, meet your new bride and all. Then if all went well then I'd be able to answer the kids' questions and we could see about coming out as a family for the wedding. Well, um" I trailed off not sure how to wrap up.

Dad responded simply, "I'd be happy to have you visit."

We sketched out some dates that might work, subject to my in-laws being available to watch the kids. He sounded a little nervous when he said, "You know, Claire and I are just in an apartment right now. We wanted to wait until after the wedding to buy a house, so well, we have a pull-out couch in the living room, but you might be more comfortable in a hotel. There's a few decent ones nearby. I don't want you to feel unwelcome, I just thought…." It was his turn to trail off.

"A hotel would be fine, Dad." I was inwardly relieved. A hotel would mean I'd have a place to which I could retreat if things were awkward or intense or downright awful.

I journeyed out a couple weeks later. I'd never flown anywhere without Bobby. We usually drove to the Outer Banks with the kids for a family vacation. If Bobby got through with a trial and got a brief break, he had occasionally surprised me with last minute trips to different places in the Caribbean. But I'd never had any reason to travel anywhere without Bobby, and I had never been on a cross-country flight before. Here I was though, getting off a plane at LAX.

Dad was at the gate. His hair was virtually all gray and his face had more lines than I remembered. "Julie," he greeted me with a genuine warm smile. "Claire's at work. I figured you and I could spend a little time together alone first and then you could meet her this evening. I hope that's ok."

It was. In fact it was preferable.

"Have you ever been to southern California?" he asked.

"No, Bobby's firm has an office in L.A., but when he's come out here, it's been all business and I've had the kids."

"Well, we can drive you around some, do a little sightseeing while you're here too." Dad drove us along the coast a bit since I had never seen the Pacific before. He asked about the kids, and I was able to relax because I could talk endlessly to anyone about my kids; the listener was the one at the disadvantage once I got going.

Like Mom, Dad had made a second career in the computer industry. I got the impression that he was more hands on in the hardware side of things than Mom; however, some of his more technical descriptions of what he did went way over my head. I found out that Dad had been introduced to Claire by some colleagues of his and that she was a fairly recent widow. Apparently her kids were unhappy about her re-marrying, and they were unlikely come to the wedding. I found it ironic that I was considering attending the wedding of my ex-con father, but Claire's kids might refuse to come to their mother's wedding when, as far as I learned during my visit, her only crime was failing to mourn endlessly for their father.

I had only planned for a two-night trip as I was worried that anything longer would be a strain on all of us, not to mention on my best babysitters. After we'd run through the easy topics of kids and work, I can't say we didn't have a few awkward silences during my visit, but Dad was so obviously trying that I felt sorry for him.

Even as a kid I remembered Dad as a boastful man. I didn't see any of that tendency anymore. In fact, he was almost embarrassingly self-effacing at times.

Claire was pleasant enough although somewhat shy, understandable when meeting your fiancé's long-estranged daughter. She was about Dad's age, but stereotypical of a Southern California woman, I suspected she'd had plastic surgery as she didn't have a single line on her face. Her neck and hands gave her age away though.

Both Bobby and his mom called me the first evening to see how things were going. Bobby was obviously exhausted. Even though it was almost 10 p.m. in California, he'd only just gotten home from the office prepping for trial. I told him that things were going fine, but I didn't want to keep him up listening to my play-by-play. Bobby's mom made sure I knew everything was good with the kids, and then she listened to me prattle about the events of the day.

As Dad was dropping me off at the airport at the end of the visit, I saw him slide an envelope in the front pocket of my suitcase. He obviously hadn't wanted me to see so I pretended I didn't. I hugged him and headed for check-in and my gate. Since I checked the suitcase, I didn't pull out his envelope until I was home and unpacking. I didn't know you could buy a Hallmark card for apologies. Dad, however, had found one. The front of the card had a rose and read, "I'm sorry." The inside was unprinted. Dad had written, "I know I was wrong back then, and I know how much it hurt you. I'm sorry I don't have the nerve to say this to your face. Dad. P.S. No need to reply." Dad would never win any awards for eloquence or sharing his feelings, but he was a far humbler man than when I had been a kid. And, a Hallmark card was more of an apology than I was ever going to get from Mom. As I stared at the card, I was reminded of a book I read in college about the Victorians. They gave different meanings to different flowers. So, instead of sending notes or telling people what they felt, they sent particular flowers. I wondered idly if roses corresponded to apologies in any of their books.

We brought all three kids out to California along with Bobby's mom for the wedding. I was still a little nervous about whether the kids would ask awkward questions about where Dad had been all these years, but I was sure that with Bobby and his mom there, I could get through it. We only planned to take Caitlin to the wedding itself as the boys were too rambunctious and too young to appreciate the ceremony anyway. Two nights before the wedding, we all had dinner with Dad and Claire at a family style Italian chain restaurant in the suburbs near their apartment. The kids were shy at first, but after a few initial awkward moments of trying to make conversation with a total stranger, they started playing hangman on their paper placemats with the crayons the restaurant had the foresight to have on the table. The day before the wedding we took the kids to SeaWorld and had dinner at an authentic Mexican place in San Diego. The kids largely filled up on tortilla chips because they were intimidated by the menu, with ethnic cuisines being a relative rarity at our home.

The wedding was a small quiet affair fairly typical of later life marriages. Dad was an only child, and his parents had passed away years ago. We met a few of Dad's cousins but I didn't get the impression that Dad was particularly close to them. Dad and Claire were heading off to Maui for a short honeymoon the following day. We headed home the next day. The boys told Caitlin all about how Grandma had taken them to Disneyland, while she had been stuck going to the wedding with us. The squabbling on the plane made me wish we'd taken the redeye so they'd have slept through it.

My relationship with Dad never became what I had with Bobby's parents, but he did start sending the kids birthday and Christmas cards. I talk to him on the phone occasionally. Dad flies out to the East Coast every couple years for a short visit. We may not be close, but at least the kids know their grandfather, and there's no drama.

CHAPTER ELEVEN

Guilty made yet another raid on Siobhan's yard as I went into the garage to look for Christmas decorations. The poor mutt had grown up with my energetic boys roughhousing with him. Now that he had just me as a poor substitute, if Siobhan's dogs were out, he would immediately soar over the fence and fulfill his unrequited need to socialize.

Siobhan didn't seem to mind the invasions as Guilty did no more damage to her flower beds than her own two did. I had to ask to make sure though.

"I know you love dogs, but if Guilty is a problem for you when your dogs are out, let me know. I can force him on a leash if he needs a pit stop when yours are outside. It's obvious you love your gardening." Even as I said this, Siobhan was trimming up mums in her yard circled by the three happy canines.

"No, it's fine. My Mom would probably view it as some sort of divine retribution for all the times I let King run amok, or hopped over someone's fence myself, for that matter." Siobhan smiled.

"You remind me of your mom when I see you working in the yard," I observed over the fence. "Same auburn hair, same freckles, same gardening gloves. At least you don't wear those godawful housedresses."

"Oh lord no. I think she and your grandmother bought them in bulk together. When I cleaned out Mom's clothes, the house dresses went straight to the trash bin."

"I think Grandmom gave them up when she moved into the senior community. At least I didn't find any when I cleaned up her stuff. Managing all of your mother's arrangements while you were living in New York must have been hard on you." I hoped Siobhan didn't mind my continuing the subject of her mom, since her mom had been gone for at least ten years.

SIOBHAN MARCH 2003

I came back to Cecil Cove with the osprey. According to folk wisdom the osprey come back to the Chesapeake from their annual migration to South America on St. Patrick's Day, but both they and I were a few days early for that holiday this year. The osprey picked a bad year to come back early. The ice had covered the cove late but hard and had stayed well past the time when the waterways were usually clear. My mother's and all the neighbors' deicers were still bubbling away under the docks preventing ice from locking onto the pilings and thrusting them out of position. Pieces of ice were only now starting to break off the solid pack; they would float toward a dock, only to be bounced back out into the cove by the bubbling deicer, then trying again at another dock, being rejected yet again by the rippling circles made by $\frac{3}{4}$ horsepower engines that had been submerged for over six weeks. Our own mini-Antarctic, complete with calving icebergs.

The intense cold seemed to contribute to exceptionally low tides. In summer even at low tide, most people had a good five or six feet of water at the ends of their docks. Now, I could walk halfway out on Mom's dock before the water and ice even started. As I watched one of the osprey fly overhead with a new stick for its nest, I idly wondered whether the salt in our brackish water made the cove ice contract on freezing rather than expanding the way fresh water did. One of my old chemistry books undoubtedly held the answer, but I'd probably never get around to checking.

I had come back because Mom was ill. Lung cancer. Unresectable. Metastatic. I assume she knew long before she finally went to the doctor coughing up blood. Dad was the one who called me, guessing quite correctly that Mom would bite off the end of her tongue before she would "bother" me with her little problem. I knew Mom and Dad had never officially divorced, but I had never realized that he continued to cover her health insurance all those years. He received an explanation of benefits from his insurance for an expansive and expensive list of diagnostic services from various doctors' offices in Maryland. As he knew that Mom only went to doctors for emergencies, he called to tell her someone had possibly stolen her insurance information. When she told him the charges were valid, she had no choice but to tell him the diagnosis.

Dad was been worried enough by the insurance paperwork to ask some of his old friends in the area to do some snooping. He found out that Mom was missing lots of choir practice and was not looking well when she attended church, which alarmed Dad enough to call the pastor. The pastor had noticed the unusual absences, the fatigue and the weight loss, but he had incorrectly worried that Mom's occasional benzodiazepine habit had gotten completely out of control. The pastor reported that Mom had brushed him off when he'd tried to make polite inquiries about what was wrong. When Dad told the pastor the real diagnosis, the pastor showed up at Mom's house and was shocked by the state of disrepair of the house. The pastor called Dad back, telling Dad that he was quite worried, and that he had immediately asked some of the choir folks to help her out. Somewhere in that conversation, the two of them realized that Mom probably hadn't even told me yet, which is how Dad finally ended up calling me. The pastor also called me after he was sure that Dad had broken the news, saying that he was pleased to see that Dad still cared enough to check on Mom. He also inquired as to whether he could do anything else before I had arranged a visit, which was his not so oblique way of reinforcing that he felt Mom needed someone with her.

When I told Mom I would come back to help her, she had tried to brush me off saying she just got tired easily but she was otherwise ok most of the time. Armed with all of Dad's background detective work, I was not fooled by Mom's attempts to downplay the situation. I did however have to dissemble a little with her. At first I told her that I would just come visit for a week because I was overdue to visit her anyway. I told both my work and my landlady, however, that from what I was hearing from my Dad, that my Mom might be sick enough that I would need to move in with her for a little while depending on what sort of treatment she might need. By the end of the second day back home, I knew that she needed me way more than anyone or anything in the Finger Lakes needed me. Mom had never aspired to the cover of *Good Housekeeping* with her housecleaning, and she was prone to clutter, but Mom had never allowed the house to be dirty; the house though was grungy when I arrived. As I began to observe for myself, some days she barely had the energy to do the dishes or take the garbage out. The church choir had started to fill the fridge with casseroles by the time I got there, and I had to push down my involuntarily remembered distaste of the almost burdensome charitable offerings that came when Brian died.

After finally convincing Mom to let me go to one of her oncology appointments and doing some of my own homework on her prognosis, I quit my job outside of Binghamton, canceled my lease on the house I was renting and moved in with her. The great thing about being a pharmacist is that you can get a job anywhere in the country with some fairly minor paperwork to become licensed in the new state, so I knew that whenever I was ready to get a new job, I'd have no problem. For now, I had saved plenty of money working. I had no rent once I moved in with Mom because Mom inherited our house free and clear from her parents.

As I had visited over the years, I knew that Mom had grown accustomed to living by herself and that after a few days with me on a normal visit, she was ready to have her peace and quiet back. I didn't even tell her that I'd quit my job and canceled my lease until after the arrangements were a fait accompli so that she couldn't try to stop me from moving back with her. Within a few weeks of my moving back, while she might still have been longing for her privacy, I could tell that she was grateful to have the help with the house.

Mom initially refused any treatment saying she would not claw desperately at the false salvation of not particularly effective but overtly aggressive treatments to line some doctors' pockets. She reasoned that modern medicine wasn't going to cure her and therefore was going to do nothing. After some coaxing by me, she did consent to palliative radiation and a little chemo solely to reduce her discomfort.

Neither of us were big talkers. Mostly we read, and I would often read in my room to give her the illusion of privacy downstairs. All of my old fantasy books were still stacked in my room, and I re-discovered old loves between their pages. During the evenings when she was too tired to read anymore, we would watch television together. Given Mom's lifelong love of choir, I shouldn't have been surprised that she loved *American Idol*; I pretended I was watching the episodes for her sake, too ashamed to admit that I also quickly fell in love with the show. I tried to get her to play chess with me early on. She shook her head and said, "It's time you knew the truth. I despise board games. You drove me to distraction with your constant pleading to play." I had had no idea.

When the weather warmed up, I set her up in a lawn chair outside and had her tell me what to do with her flower beds. Every now and then she would have a good day and would be able to do some herself. Getting down on the ground wasn't possible, but if I put all the pots, tools and plants on a table she would fuss over the plantings there.

As I looked around the house and started to see how little had changed, other than a new layer of dust and nicotine, I couldn't help but reflect on how hard staying in this house after Brian's death and my departure for college must have been for Mom. Despite the fact that I knew I had visited and developed a stable relationship with her over the years, I still suffered from guilt. Yes, I had lost Brian. But Mom lost everything. She lost her son. Then she lost her husband. And she effectively lost me when I pulled completely inside myself during high school and then ran away to college as soon as I could.

Mom couldn't drink much with the chemo. But one night when I lit a fire because her cachexic body just couldn't be warm enough, we had a little wine, and I finally asked her how she put up with me as a teenager when I was such nasty bitter pill. I cried. Mom didn't, she never did. She just said, "From what I hear all teenaged girls are nightmares. At least you had a real reason to be hurt and upset." I never succeeded in engaging Mom in any real discussion of that time in our lives.

In mid-May, Mom and I were watching the Blue Angels off the dock practicing for the Naval Academy graduation, combatting our instincts to look toward the source of the sound rather than in the opposite direction where the supersonic planes had already reached. In the midst of our viewing, to my surprise Dad ambled down the walkway and onto the dock. I knew he and Mom had been talking on the phone periodically since he found out about the cancer. Mom's illness seem to have brought on some sort of rapprochement between the two of them. Dad was still living with Ana. I had no idea how she felt about his supporting his ex-wife, but on the other hand, Ana could hardly view my dying mother as a threat to her relationship. However, neither my parents' relationship nor Dad's relationship with Ana was any of my business.

As a child I had never considered my parents' relationship much; they would have told me it was none of my business if I'd thought to ask anyway. As an adult looking back at their marriage, I wondered how they'd ever gotten together in the first place, although the reason may not have been any more complicated than the fact that less than nine months had elapsed between their wedding date and Brian's birth date. Dad is a little taciturn, but his hobbies guaranteed the presence of a constant string of people with whom he worked on his handyman projects. Mom on the other hand seemed happiest with her solitary pursuits of reading and gardening. Neither of my parents struck me as particularly devout, but all of Mom's meager social forays were centered on her volunteer work at the church. I suspected she liked the sense of a community that unquestioningly accepted people, particularly volunteers, not to mention that she genuinely loved choir.

She and Dad first saw each other at some of the fundraising all-you-can-eat pancake breakfasts and fried chicken and oyster dinners that the church hosted in the fellowship hall, often in combination with some Boy Scout troop. Mom was volunteering. Dad was not a churchgoer, but right out of high school he had a voracious appetite and not much money, and all-you-can-eat suited him just fine. Dad eventually asked her to the movies with him. Most dates they went to a park and went swimming or did something else free to allow Dad to save his money.

Dad grew up learning how to tinker with almost any inboard or outboard engine because Dad's father worked at one of the local marinas. Dad's mother had gone deaf following some uncontrolled infection when Dad was a small child, and she committed suicide when Dad started high school. Grandpa and Dad never talked about her; they just put their heads down and worked. Dad wanted more than doing service work at a marina all his life though. He put himself through College Park by working any odd job he could find. He came out with an engineering degree and a four-month contract to work on an oil tanker that took oil from the rigs down in the Gulf.

Mom found out she was pregnant with Brian while he was away. When he finished his first contract, he came back and married Mom. Working for the oil companies was his dream job. I would bet Mom was only too happy with a part-time husband, as even before Brian's death she relished her periods of solitude.

Mom never left her mother's cottage; Mom's dad had died at 40 of a massive heart attack so her mother would have been alone if Mom had moved out. When Dad was home from his job, he stayed there as well. Mom continued to do her church work, and they paid her for some secretarial chores which gave her a little extra pocket money. Dad sent home money. Mom's mother died, and my parents took over the cottage completely, but not much changed for their marriage, except eventually me. And then when Brian died, they seemed to stop talking altogether. If they fought, they kept their conflict from me. From my perspective they just stopped being together.

During Dad's brief visits once Mom got sick, they didn't seem to talk much either, but they did seem to take some comfort sitting in silence with each other. During those moments, I tried to make myself invisible.

I became a self-proclaimed goddess of soups over the summer. Mom had mucositis from the radiation, rendering the swallowing of solid food painful. I made vegetable soups, having learned that you could puree almost anything with an immersion blender after a long enough boil, and when I was feeling ambitious, I would push the puree through a chinois to make it even smoother. The secret to my best meat soups was nothing more than soaking bones in water all day long and then adding seasonings and vegetables. I bought rotisserie chickens just to have the carcass for soup. Trying not to eat foods Mom could no longer digest in front of her, I indulged in spiced shrimp when Mom was napping and then used the shells to make stock for more soups. Since Mom had always made oyster stew when I was a kid, and since I had always wanted to try the she-oyster stew in James Michener's *Chesapeake*, I tried my hand at making that for her. I loved the stew with its rich mix of milk and butter infused with the salty oyster taste, but Mom's fragile system couldn't tolerate the richness; hence she-oyster stew did not become a permanent part of the soup rotation.

I also re-discovered the neighborhood as Mom napped. As a child Brian, Julie and I had covered every square inch. No fence or dog was an impediment to our tromping through the whole community. We would head to the community center to play kickball in the fields when we weren't out on the water. Once we were allowed to bike beyond our gravel lane, we would ride everywhere on our bikes, leaving them parked in the grass wherever we happened to be going.

As an adult, the focus of my perambulations was decidedly different. I was enamored of the fiercely familial osprey that determinedly built their nests at the top of any available lamppost or piling. In the mid-1970s, the osprey population had fallen to an all-time low due to the depredations of DDT so they weren't a major feature of my childhood. The osprey had now rebounded with the help of environmental regulations, to the point that nesting spots were in such short supply that local Boy Scout troops took on service projects to build these birds of prey nesting platforms on small uninhabited islands in the Chesapeake. One day as I walked by the lacrosse field, the mother osprey in her nest started a more urgent cheeping than her usual inquisitive single note. For a bird of prey, the osprey's normal cheep is distinctly and surprisingly delicate. The urgency in this particular call was so different from the norm, I looked up and saw not an osprey but a bald eagle streaking away from me. Immediately after the eagle came the daddy osprey, hell-bent on making the bald eagle feel unwelcome and ensuring the safety of momma and the babies. I guess the osprey hadn't gotten the message about the bald eagle being the national bird. The eagle certainly got the osprey's message though and cleared out.

When I wasn't watching the birds, I studied the houses as I walked. Virtually all of the houses in our community were built during the 1940s and 1950s. In some cases, they were pre-fab houses from the Sears catalog, brought on a trailer and dropped onto a slab. In other cases, the original cottages were decommissioned military housing; when the owners of these specimens started renovations they were astonished to find not a single nail in the place, just tongue-and-groove holding the whole place together. Over the course of 50 plus years though, most families had added on or renovated or lifted the roof, making each house unique; I had to stare hard to find the original footprint of the cottage.

At some point I was determined to get out on a canoe or a motor boat to look at all the houses from the water as people often put much more effort into the waterfront side of the home. In part I was curious, but my ulterior motive was to get some renovation ideas as Mom's cottage hadn't been updated since my parents took over after Mom's mother passed away, leaving our kitchen and bathrooms long overdue for some updating. I felt strange twinges of guilt when I entertained renovation ideas for the cottage as making future plans went one step further than accepting the inevitable denouement of Mom's condition.

When Hurricane Isabel hit in September, Mom and I were relatively lucky in the property damage department, especially compared to many along the river. With the massive storm surge of Isabel, extensive flooding occurred on both sides of the Chesapeake and its tributaries. On our river, the houses had a small slope if any to the river surface, and most homes directly on the river incurred some degree of flood damage. Further back on our more protected cove the houses were more elevated than the houses on the river. The water got up over the top of the pilings of our dock, but didn't reach the actual foundation of the house. Our dock and those of all of our neighbors were completely submerged. Only where people had taller poles or showerheads mounted on their docks could we tell that the docks were even out there.

Kayaks, canoes, and even motor boats broke loose from moorings and floated randomly for days. Going out on the water was irresponsibly dangerous for a couple days after the storm itself passed because the high water obscured bottom-reaming obstacles. Lots of boats that had sustained little actual damage in the storm itself were subsequently damaged as they were smashed into pilings or into each other as the water levels fell. At local restaurants and all over downtown Annapolis, people marked the high water marks and ordered plaques to permanently mark Isabel's zenith.

Mom didn't fare as well in the storm as our house did. We lost power for about 60 hours. Being on a gravel road at the end of the community, we could count on being one of the last to have power restored. Most of our neighbors had long ago installed full house back-up generators but Mom had never seen the point. When I was a kid Dad had always run a portable generator in the garage that kept the refrigerator and the well equipment working. We were still on a well, and when we had no power, we had no water. Prior to the storm, I had filled up the bathtubs with water we could use to flush the toilets and filled big kitchen pots for drinking water in case I had any problems with the generator. I had filled up a few five-gallon cans of gasoline prior to the storm and had cleared the area around the portable generator Dad had left in the garage. I didn't have Dad's knack with things mechanical or his years of practice though and when the power did go out, getting the generator going, running extension cords and connecting the well equipment took me a maddeningly frustrating hour.

While Mom may not previously have seen the point of a full house generator, in her immunocompromised state, she did. The portable generator was not powerful enough to run the air conditioner. Without air conditioning, the humidity crept in almost visibly under the doors and around the windows, making her breathing even more labored, notwithstanding the little portable oxygen tank that she was carting around by that point. She was so uncomfortable by the second night that I packed small bags for us and insisted on checking into a local hotel that had power until ours was back. I didn't see that she sustained any permanent damage from the whole experience but we both realized how fragile her physical equilibrium had become.

After the storm, she let me call a contractor to install a full house standby generator. She declared she would never go through days without power again.

She was right about not going through an epic power loss again, but unfortunately not for the right reasons. Dad came up for Thanksgiving, and the three of us went to a local waterfront restaurant that had assured me that they would have butternut squash soup on the menu for Mom. In our rather quiet way we enjoyed the holiday. By Christmas, Mom was in no mood or condition to go out to a restaurant.

She passed away in January 2004 at home with a hospice nurse present. Not that I've had a lot of experience with people's final days, but she seemed reasonably comfortable; she spent more and more time asleep, and then she was gone.

When the pastor had asked me about any favorite songs of my mother's for the service, I drew a total blank. I decided to let the pastor and the choir handle the service; in that regard, they knew her tastes better than I did.

I come to the garden alone
While the dew is still on the roses

My memory may have failed me in preparing the service, but I was instantly flooded with flashes of Mom working in her rose garden singing.

And the joy we share as we tarry there
None other has ever known

The cold was too intense to have the entire service at the community beach, but Dad and I did take a small box of her ashes out there. A few of the choir members followed as well. A great blue heron was standing in the dead rushes at the far end of the beach. When we approached the water, he took off in a long arcing elegant circle. We sprinkled the ashes in the water where Mom could be with Brian.

I'd stay in the garden with Him
Though the night around me be falling,
But He bids me go; through the voice of woe
His voice to me is calling.

When most of the people had headed back for the warmth of their cars, I wrapped myself a little tighter in my coat, stared out at the horizon and listened to the little sucking sounds the water made as it slid in and out of the rushes by the shoreline.

I had arranged for one of the local waterfront bars to put out an appetizer buffet open to anyone who wanted to come. The church had offered up the fellowship hall for free, but I required at least a few beers if not something stronger if I was going to cope with Mom's funeral meal, so I politely declined the church's offer.

Not that I'm a connoisseur of funerals, but I'm always amazed at who shows up and how people hear about these events. I found myself speaking to a woman who had been in Girl Scouts with Mom and hadn't seen her since eighth grade. Perhaps impelled by a couple whiskey sours that I drank too quickly on arrival, I found myself wondering if she expected me to fill her in on everything Mom had done from age 13 on, or if we were going to talk about Mom's sewing merit badges.

Among the visitors were Bobby's mom and dad. Of course they had known Mom, and of course they were of a generation where going to funerals of even mere acquaintances was the right thing to do. Bobby's mom hugged me and offered the usual condolences. Then she added, "You may not have had a chance to notice them yet, but Julie sent some flowers and a card." She looked like she wanted to say more, but I was saved by another guest coming up.

I did find the flowers and card from Julie. I sent the same thank you card I sent to everyone else simply signed Siobhan. I suppose 25 years after the accident, we should be able to exchange basic social graces.

My unease at making plans for the future while Mom was alive had blocked me from asking myself why abandoning my life in the Finger Lakes had been so easy and whether I was willing to do so permanently. A few days after the funeral, I stared at a murmuration of starlings as it melted into the sunset with a glass of red wine in hand and decided I owed it to myself to weigh the options for my future. No one special waited for me in the Finger Lakes. My job there had been satisfying but hardly unique as pharmacy work went. Only having ticked through those initial considerations, I found myself transfixed by the view out of the sunporch windows, and I realized that the choice between Cecil Cove and the Finger Lakes was not a choice at all. Cecil Cove had always been my home. The Finger Lakes had been a refuge where I could heal and grow up. But just as the waters of the Susquehanna were destined for the Chesapeake, I belonged in Cecil Cove.

In practical terms, I rented a U-Haul and made a final trip to New York to retrieve a few boxes from a friend's basement. Then, I turned in earnest to the work of making the cottage my own.

Dad had never canceled the modest life insurance that he got through his work for Mom with me as beneficiary, giving me a nice chunk of cash to do some of the renovations the house desperately needed. Mom and Dad had thankfully expanded the cottage when her mom died, in the era before the environmental agencies went ape about any sort of expansion for waterfront homes. I was therefore spared the nightmare of trying to get permits for exterior work that would disturb the Chesapeake Bay watershed.

On the interior, the kitchen however needed a complete makeover. As I had become a much more adventurous cook than Mom ever was, I would have wanted fancier upgrades than anything Mom would have installed even had her kitchen been in good shape. During the several weeks of renovations, I microwaved aliquots of my frozen soups in the living room while I waited to have a functioning kitchen again. I ended up putting the same ceramic tile through the whole first floor except the downstairs master as part of the renovations. Other than the fact that carpeting was the trend of their era, I could never understand why my parents put carpet all over the first floor so close to the water where all of us were constantly dragging in sand and silt, dripping all over everything. I made my old bedroom upstairs into a library and work area with a futon in the unlikely event that I ever needed the extra sleeping capacity after I took over the master bedroom.

Brian's bedroom was painfully untouched. When I was in high school, Mom and Dad kept the door locked, and none of us ever went in there. I had been home long enough to realize that Mom hadn't done much more after I left, but when I finally mustered up the guts to go in there, I was still somewhat dumbfounded.

His felt pennants from Kings Dominion, Hershey Park, Animal Kingdom, and his beloved Baltimore Colts were still tacked into the paneling, rather dusty, and faded by the sun from the window in places. A big Confederate flag covered one wall. Thankfully, all of his clothes were gone. Mom probably donated them at the church as leaving good clothes unused when others were in need would not have sat well with her. The comic books were still on the shelf of his closet where he'd stashed them when he decided he was too old for them but couldn't bear to throw them out. I couldn't help the tears from falling when I saw the college brochures from the Naval Academy, College Park, Penn State, and Johns Hopkins still in one of the desk drawers. Underneath the brochures and some intentionally scattered loose leaf paper in the same drawer were a couple issues of *Playboy* as well. Obviously Brian had had dreams about his future as well as other more carnal pursuits, and here they still were dusty and faded in a drawer in a room that had been shut down for more than two decades.

I donated all his furniture to the church. I packed up the pennants and some other souvenirs in a box I put in the attic until I was sure what I wanted to do about it. I sold the comic books, all save one that I kept as a reminder, to a store that specialized in such collectibles. The storeowner at first thought I was nuts for wanting to get rid of them at all, and then probably offered me a fair amount less than what they were worth to a collector, but I still couldn't believe they paid me over a thousand dollars for one of the old *Spiderman* issues.

To make sure I was done with the closet, I swept my arm across the top shelf one last time and bumped an old Mason jar at the very back. The bottom of the jar was covered with a layer of grimy black chunks. As I carried it over to my trash pile, I saw that the jar's lid had been punctured several times with an icepick and in a luciferase flash I realized they were the dessicated corpses of lightning bugs.

SIOBHAN JUNE 1972

"But it's still light out. How can I go to bed when it's still light out?" Brian protested. I nodded in vigorous agreement next to him. Brian held our jar of fireflies that we had spent the last hour or more running around the yard catching. At first I was squeamish about holding a bug in my hands, but I didn't want Brian to call me a chicken, so I started catching them anyway only to find that touching them wasn't so bad after all.

Over the roar of the midsummer cicadas, I could barely hear Dad's sotto voce "Oh, for Pete's sake...." And I knew the evening was doomed for me and Brian. In a rare burst of socialization, Dad had invited over some couples who kept their boats at the marina where Dad's father still worked. The men were all drinking beer, and the women had fussed in the kitchen over the blender coming up with some concoction they called a Peach Fuzz. I knew they wanted us to go to bed so they could sit outside and talk and drink in peace.

Mom got up and shooed us into the house. "Brian, you can read your comic books for a half hour. Not a minute more, and I'll know if I see your light on in the window. Siobhan, go into the bathroom and clean your teeth." Another summertime battle lost, I harrumphed into bed after washing up.

A little while later, I heard a knock on my door and Brian came in. "C'mon, you gotta see this."

I followed him into his room. We crawled into his closet under the hanging clothes, and Brian pulled the door shut. The fireflies were magical in the dark. Brian had the jar in the darkest corner of the closet. Individual flies would light up and then go dark, but a few were always lit up. I watched entranced until Brian realized the trance was the onset of sleep. We'd both be in trouble if Mom and Dad found me asleep on the floor of the closet, and Brian wasn't big enough yet to carry me.

We didn't get to do much more lightning bug chasing for the next week or so. Hurricane Agnes stormed up the Chesapeake Bay wreaking devastation as she went, and then causing more damage as all the rain water she dumped into the Susquehanna had nowhere to go except flow down to the Chesapeake, drastically altering salinity levels in the bay. While the storm was passing over us, I wouldn't go upstairs where I could hear the rain beating on the roof. Dad was in and out of the house checking on the generator. The house was hot and sticky but we couldn't open the windows with the storm still raging. The winds were so violent that windows and door jambs that had never leaked before had trickles of water coming down on the inside of them.

When the next high tide came in during the daylight, the water was no more than 10 feet from our back door. I was excited and wanted to go out swimming. I thought finding the dock in the flood would be fun. I had no idea at the time how dangerous that was. Dad wouldn't let either me or Brian go out of the house.

On the far side of the cove, a huge tree had taken down a power pole and the flood waters reached within a foot of the downed lines at high tide. Jim and his mom came over to our house that afternoon because their house was frighteningly close to the downed lines that were still live. I had slept through the tree falling, but Jim told us about the huge crack and the sparks that continued every time a new branch got tossed against the live wires. Jim's dad worked for one of the power companies so he had been working non-stop for more than 24 hours, only allowed to come home long enough to make sure his family got out safely and that the house was ok, but otherwise having to sleep in his truck or the dispatch center.

Dad ventured out to check on his father, to get more gas for the generator, and to get whatever supplies he could find for us and for any of our neighbors. He came back with all the local newspapers, and Mom and Jim's mom clucked worriedly over them, puffing heavily on their cigarettes.

As Brian and Jim were trapped in the house with me, we got an epic game of Monopoly going. I went bankrupt after an hour or so. I had spent every last dollar I had buying properties but had to mortgage them when I kept landing on Brian's and Jim's houses. The two of them duked it out for another two hours until Brian finally ended up with all the money and most of the property.

Sometime during the night a power company crew finally arrived to restore electricity to the cove. The big gum tree that had fallen took hours to cut up and get off the lines. Then the lines had to be fixed. We had peanut butter and jelly sandwiches for the second night in a row for dinner while the repairs proceeded.

SIOBHAN 2004

When cleaning out Brian's room got to be too much, I would walk out onto the dock for some of the cold fresh air and to watch whatever wildlife was in action that day. The ice was not quite as intense this year as last, but still a tongue of ice was projecting from the creek into the cove. One of my biggest wildlife watching payoffs came the day I saw an initially unidentified creature crawl up out of the water onto that mini-iceberg and shake itself off. I stared, squinting my eyes trying to identify the creature, and wishing I had brought the binoculars that I always leave at the door. "Holy shit, it's a raccoon." No sooner were the words out of my mouth than the raccoon scampered across the tongue of ice and slid into the water on the far side. I watched it swim to the other side of the cove and come out on the little beachlet left by the low tide at one of the neighbors. The raccoon disappeared into the dead cattails. I had had no idea raccoons were swimmers.

The raccoons in general were a nuisance. Our whole community had to use bungee cords on our outdoor trash cans to keep the raccoons from scattering the trash all over the yard. Of course, we worried about rabies as well, although that concern was likely irrelevant in the instance of a swimming raccoon.

Once I had finished with Brian's room, I had to clean out Mom's room in order to create my new master bedroom, which I also needed to tackle in small doses. Mom was not much of a clothes horse and most of what she had was worn to the woof. However, since she didn't have many clothes, as I pulled them out of the closet I found myself picturing her wearing practically all of them either as she was gardening or going to church. Her horrid old cotton housedresses were the first to land in the rubbish pile. Some of her church dresses were in good enough shape to donate. I kept a few of her bulky sweatshirts for myself. The rest went in the rag box.

Mom had left books piled on any available surface. I moved the ones I definitely wanted into my library. She had a huge pile of Nora Roberts, Danielle Steele and Harlequin romances, a genre that I remember being one of her favorites but one that held no appeal to me. I packed those right up for donation. Surprisingly she had quite a number of stream-of-consciousness books: *Catch 22*, *Gravity's Rainbow*, Kerouac's *On the Road*, and several Henry Millers. I couldn't remember her ever reading anything of that ilk, but I reminded myself that I had been gone for over a decade. Even Miller's phenomenal sex scenes weren't sufficient inducement for me to choose him over a good fantasy novel. I started to move these right to the reject donation boxes, but the cover fell open on one and I saw that Dad had inscribed his name and English 203 on the inside cover. I made a separate box for him in case he wanted to take some of them.

Mom also had some shoeboxes full of my letters and cards home from New York. I was somewhat surprised by this as she had never struck me as sentimental enough to keep such things. I packed them up for the attic like I had with Brian's memorabilia since I couldn't decide what to do with any of it. I'd probably find them a decade letter and still wouldn't know what to do.

At the back of the top dresser drawer were a couple old Valium prescription bottles. Outside of the house or her familiar church activities, Mom had been an anxious person. She didn't like crowds in shopping centers or new places in general, and she had only been too thrilled when my driver's license relieved her of responsibility for getting me to various public fora. I considered asking Dad whether Mom had subscribed to Mommy's little helpers back in the 60s and 70s, or if she started needing help only after Brian's death. Then I decided I didn't need to know at this point.

After about eight months following Mom's death, I got a part-time job with a health care organization that ran a large network of assisted living, rehab and nursing home facilities throughout the county, more to keep busy and keep my professional skills sharp than an urgent need for money. I did all the same dispensing and drug accountability that any pharmacist does anywhere. For a small additional fee, the facilities offered services such as filling a 7 x 3 gridded pillbox with a week's worth of medicine for residents who had difficulty figuring out which medicine to take when or opening the pill containers. Occasionally, I would have to track down a special compounded formulation of a medicine for a patient who had difficulty swallowing. The company liked rotating me through their different facilities as the problems of drug mishandling, particularly opiates, were as present in affluent Anne Arundel County as they were in economically challenged Western New York. Having a separate pharmacist periodically rotate through the various facilities offered a fresh set of eyes to make sure no bad staff habits that would facilitate patient drug diversion developed.

I did not have an extravagant lifestyle. The house was paid off. I had some of my own savings from the years in New York, plus I still had a smidgeon left from Mom's life insurance after I got the house remodeled. Part-time work was enough for me to cover the property taxes, the homeowner's association fees, the utilities, food for one and still save a bit. I could have spent a fortune on books, but I forced myself to go to the county library. When I exhausted their repertoire, I made myself buy the used copies I found on Amazon instead of the new copies. One of these days, my ancient Honda Civic would finally give up the ghost, but I also had Mom's Toyota Corolla, equally ancient. I traded days driving them and would only buy something new when both of them were declared moribund.

I took a lot of weekend and holiday shifts as I got overtime pay or a shift differential and could make more money without working more hours. The management was happy to have someone who would take shifts when other pharmacists requested off. I was left with plenty of time for reading and gardening. I splurged on a new kayak to allow paddling around the cove and creek. I'd venture into the river early in the morning when no boat traffic was out yet. Since my days off were often in the middle of the week, I didn't have to deal with all the crowds on the weekends either on the river or at the garden store.

Mom had been passionate about her yard. While I had been in New York, I hadn't done much more than plant some annuals, but back home I took up gardening with as much zeal as Mom had ever had. When I worked I often found myself remembering her. I could picture her out with her white cotton gloves and shears. I was surprised to find how much of her gardening skills she obviously engrained in me as a kid. All of her beds were in good shape except for some minor neglect after the illness got to her.

After a couple years, I got two chocolate Labrador retriever puppies from a local breeder and christened them Godiva and Hershey. I hadn't had a pet since King died when I was in college, and until I got the pups, I hadn't realized how much I had missed the sight of an animal bred to hunt water fowl flinging itself joyfully off the end of the dock into the tidal waters. Since I was the one now dealing with wet dog when I indulged in this passion, I could better appreciate Dad's grouchiness when I had released King as a kid. Dogs, however, are terrific channels for socializing without having to exert much effort. I wasn't as shy as Mom was, and I wasn't anxious in public places like she had been, but I was certainly no flaming extrovert either. With two pups, I could hook up the leashes, head down the road, and invariably come across a handful of neighbors doing the exact same thing. Instant socialization.

I did have to control my temper when the pups destroyed some of my lovingly planted annuals in their zesty exuberance for life, but the affection the pups transmitted was worth it. I got them each a huge soft dog bed. I loved them but I wasn't sharing my bed with them; I trained them early with rewards of Greenies for staying in their dog beds when I went to bed. Even with ceramic tile all over the first floor, the dog fur required almost daily vacuuming. I didn't know how Mom and Dad could have stood having a dog with wall-to-wall carpet.

I found that with the renovated cottage, the job and the dogs, I was quite content, even happy.

CHAPTER TWELVE

Nathan from my company's corporate offices hand delivered for my review the investigator's brochure for some new drug being tested in a clinical trial at our facilities. Apparently the timing and the procedures for making up and administering the IV solution were tricky. After a junior pharmacist had botched the process once, the management wanted a senior pharmacist to review and make up some local procedures to use for training our staff. I agreed to review the materials over the weekend as an extra shift, but only if I didn't have to go to headquarters in Glen Burnie to pick them up. The pharmaceutical company would not allow their documents to be e-mailed, sticking Nathan with the job of personally delivering them.

The dogs rushed outside with me as I walked Nathan to his car. Guilty had been curled up peacefully in Julie's yard until my two came out. In seconds, Guilty had hopped the fence in what was becoming his routine fashion.

Nathan evaded the slobbering onslaught of three dogs, got in his car, rolled down his window and offered profuse thanks for the extra work I was taking on from the safety of his car. Julie came

155

out to retrieve Guilty while all this was going on. After Nathan had driven off, Julie gave me a sly grin and said, "Hope Guilty didn't scare off someone special...."

"Nope, sorry to disappoint you." I rolled my eyes at her as I scratched Godiva's head. "Just one of the managers from work."

"It's not disappointing me. It's just I figured there must be someone special." Julie looked a little abashed. "I know that's nosy, but that's me."

"Again, just a colleague. There hasn't been anyone special in a long time." I replied.

SIOBHAN 2002

Jacob and I agreed that we were effectively calling it off for good when he decided to move back to New York City. We had had more of a friends with benefits relationship over the last seven or eight years, rather than a traditional boyfriend and girlfriend or live-in set up, never making any promises about the future. His second stepfather had been a financial guru up until September 11th, and his mother was not coping with her loss well, not that I blame her. I knew what losing Brian had done to me and my family, and Brian's death had been a stupid accident. I could only begin to imagine what coping with the loss of a family member to a terrorist attack must take. Jacob was not close to his mother. In fact, his disapproval of her lifestyle was a large part of what led him to leave New York City and end up in the Finger Lakes. Despite any disapproval though, he felt the need to help her through the loss.

Jacob worked as a registered nurse at the same hospital as me. Along with a number of other hospital staff, we would hang out at one of the local bars or restaurants when our shifts were over. As such, I can't even say exactly when I met him. I do remember that one early spring evening when we all were beginning to hope that the cold might have finally let go for good, Jacob threw out into our group of eight or ten co-workers, "Anyone want to do the Gorge Walk at Watkins Glen tomorrow? The weather's supposed to be glorious, and the gorge should be roaring with melt off."

I was the only one in the group who immediately responded with enthusiasm, "I love the Gorge Walk. I haven't done that since I was waitressing on Seneca." Watkins Glen State Park is only a mile or two south of the bottom tip of Seneca Lake. The most famous and best trail at the park follows Glen Creek up through the gorge that it carved out of the native rock over millennia. Sometimes before the dinner shift, the other wait staff and I had hiked the trail, leaving enough time to clean off at the mini-hotel across the street from the restaurant that was owned by the same couple.

Jacob and I both tried to convince a few other of our hospital colleagues to join us the next day. Failing at that, the two of us stood at one of the bar tables for the rest of the evening comparing our favorite Finger Lakes nature spots. Although I believed I had done some exploring of my adopted region, I realized that I'd only scratched the surface once Jacob got going about all of his hiking adventures. Jacob professed his unqualified love for the Finger Lakes region, and he appeared from that first conversation to be a bit of an amateur ecologist and geologist.

The next morning Jacob picked me up at the house I was renting and drove us to Watkins Glen. During my college summers, when I had waitressed on Seneca Lake, Watkins Glen had quickly became one of my favorite places. I had never gotten tired of the Gorge Walk. The twists of the canyon were sinuous and curvaceous, glistening with the waters of Glen Creek, almost sensual at first glance. Sensual in the same way that a Rodin structure is sensual, but on touching the white marble or the hard shale of the gorge wall the illusion is broken by the cold hardness of the rock.

That first day with Jacob, Watkins Glen was even more spectacular than I remembered. With the spring runoff pouring over the rocks in torrential cataracts, the volume of water was twice as great as the summer days of my college memories. Despite our good walking shoes, we both slipped a couple times on the uneven rocky path, which was slick with spray. Jacob stopped every few minutes to point out some feature of the rocks themselves or interesting flora clinging to life in the cracks of the phyllo dough-like layers of rock.

At the top of the gorge, just past the decaying railroad bridge that frighteningly was still in service, we caught the shuttle bus back to the main parking lot at the base. Jacob surprised me by pulling an insulated backpack out of the trunk of his car, revealing a lunch that he had packed. "How 'bout we eat at Lodi Point?" he asked.

"Where?" I responded cluelessly.

"What, you worked on Seneca Lake, and you don't know Lodi Point," he teased. He drove us about twenty minutes up the east side of Seneca Lake, then turned down a sketchy road marked only with a brown park sign. The road led down to the water, and Jacob parked in the almost empty lot of the state park.

As we headed toward a picnic table with the backpack, I joked, "Well, I worked on the west side of the lake, so clearly I wouldn't have known about this place."

Jacob just shook his head, smiling, and unpacked the lunch. After we had eaten, we walked along the shore, which consisted of thousands of small flat grayish black rocks. I picked up a handful and said, "When my friends and I would go swimming in the summer during college, these damn rocks cutting into my feet would drive me bananas. Where I grew up swimming as a kid, the bottom might be a little squishy, but at least it didn't hurt."

Jacob took my hand with the rocks in it and pointed out, "These are nothing more than broken off pieces of the same shale that makes up the walls of Watkins Glen."

He was, of course, correct, and I was a little abashed that in all the times when I was cursing the stony hard bottom of the Finger Lakes and wishing for the almost slimy alluvial cove bottom where I grew up, I had never seen the connection with the walls of the Watkins Glen gorge that I loved. I was still processing the geological revelation when Jacob tugged me closer with the hand he was still holding and kissed me. I dropped the rocks.

Back in the car, Jacob said, "I'd like to go on more of these hikes with you."

Over the next several years, we explored dozens of hikes in the parks all around the Finger Lakes. We usually ended our outings at a local winery close to whatever park we'd explored that day. The Cayuga Whites, made from grapes developed by Cornell scientists particularly for this region of the country, grew to be my favorite. We would taste at the winery and then buy a couple bottles of whatever had appealed to us most that day. Then we would head back to one of our places and make some meal that would be complemented by the wine. My cooking skills expanded dramatically as we found local ingredients at the farmers' markets and paired them with local wines.

We enjoyed each other's company and enjoyed the physical relationship that we developed, but although I felt affection and friendship, I never felt that infatuated love about which I would hear coworkers talk. Jacob gave me no reason to believe that his feelings for me were any different or stronger than mine were. And never once during our years together did Jacob and I ever discuss moving in together. We would have our outing, have our dinner, stay over, and in the morning go back to our separate lives.

We never even specifically discussed whether we were exclusive or not. I did not date anyone else, but I honestly couldn't say whether Jacob did or not. As I watched colleagues at the hospital get married, or received wedding invitations from friends, or heard from Mom that so-and-so from three blocks over was pregnant, I would wonder why I had absolutely no such urges. Maybe because I hadn't had the greatest examples in my childhood. Or maybe Jacob just wasn't the one to inspire such feelings in me, but then no one else came along either.

When Jacob moved back to New York City, we parted with no rancor, but no particular sense of loss either.

In 2006 Jacob came to visit me at Cecil Cove in the late summer. He was planning to move back to the Finger Lakes area, and he had tried to look me up there. Some friends of ours told him that I'd moved back to Maryland when Mom got sick. Jacob related that he and his mom had cohabitated peacefully when he first moved back to help her. Once she got over the legitimate shock of losing his stepfather though, she had rather quickly moved on to another potential stepfather. Jacob's prior stepfather was already husband number three, so his mom was only conforming to pattern. Jacob wasn't keen on the new potential stepfather, and the greater New York City lifestyle still wasn't for him.

I invited him down for a weekend, telling him I had a guest bedroom. I had no idea whether he had any hopes of restoring the prior relationship but I didn't want him making any assumptions.

I hadn't talked much about my home life when we had been together in New York. He knew that my parents were split up and that my only sibling had died in an accident. I had never talked about the house or the community in which I grew up, although I knew I occasionally compared some aspect of the Finger Lakes to the Chesapeake.

When he arrived though, I could tell he was surprised by the vista from the house. "Wowww, look at that view. I drove through Baltimore on the way down, and it's not that far away? Do a lot of people work there and live here?" he asked.

"Both Baltimore and D.C. are commutable. Lots of people around here work in one or the other city. The political types work in Annapolis which is only 10 or 15 minutes away. These homes were almost all originally summer cottages for wealthy or almost wealthy Washingtonians. In the early 20th century, the waterfront closer to Annapolis on the north side of the river and Chesapeake Beach about a half hour south of here at the end of a railroad line were quite the playgrounds of the well-heeled. This peninsula was farmland until somewhat later on, but eventually farmers sold off the waterfront areas to developers to make summer cottages for those with post-WWII disposable income. In most of the houses, you can still see the outlines of the original summer cottage if you look hard enough. I'll show you when we go kayaking."

"So this was like a mini-Hamptons, huh?"

"I don't know New York as well as you, but my neighborhood was probably more the Rockaways. Once the Chesapeake Bay Bridge opened in the fifties and more families had cars, people started going to Ocean City and Rehoboth. People also eventually realized that you could commute to D.C. from here, so they moved in permanently rather than making this a vacation destination. Baltimore was pretty rundown until they started working on the Inner Harbor in the seventies, and I-97 didn't open until after I was in college, so commuting north came as a later phenomenon."

"Hard to imagine coming from NYC. This place would easily be a couple million up there."

"No such luck here, although compared to the Finger Lakes, this is a pretty expensive area. When the place next door sold last year, I looked up its sale price online because the acreage and the waterfront are comparable to mine. I have no idea what condition the inside of that house was, but since it was a vacation cottage for two or three decades, I'd bet my place has been more lovingly tended over the years. Anyway, whoever bought the place next door paid about 40 times what my grandparents paid when they bought this place after World War II. The return on investment is awesome, but I'm not going anywhere, so the sale price is just a point of curiosity."

We got up early the next morning to go kayaking, hoping to get down the river to the next creek south of mine before the boat traffic chopped up the river too much. The creek below mine is a terrific place to watch wildlife because it borders a large county park on one side. By happenstance, all of the creatures iconic to my world on the cove obligingly put themselves on display for me to show off to Jacob. After about a half hour of paddling in virtually flat water down the river, we turned into the creek. We heard the cries of the osprey before we could see it. We had to paddle away from the shore to see over the cattails that were five or six feet tall at the edge of the water. The osprey, who hadn't yet started his South American migration for the year, was sitting on the branch of a dead tree about twenty feet inland. As we paddled further around the cattails and into a little covelet, we startled a red fox that was sniffing curiously along the tiny strip of silt, exposed by the falling tide, between the rushes and the water. The fox disappeared in a break in the rushes, his coat the exact color of the lower stalks of the rushes.

We continued paddling down the shoreline of the creek, one little nipple of water after another. In one crevice, we were berated by a great blue heron that had been standing in a few inches of water, probably looking for breakfast. With a series of guttural cries, he took off, tucked his long legs back behind him and flapped until he reached treetop level where he landed on a dead limb. He continued to vocally protest our presence until we paddled out of his fishing grounds.

As promised I also showed Jacob how many of the houses on the water had been built up. Only a few unimproved cottages remained along the shorelines. Most at least had had a second story added on. The state was increasingly reluctant to grant permits to expand the footprints of the houses, but most people had done the additions a couple decades ago when regulations had been much looser if they existed at all.

As we headed back, the river traffic was heavier with the early morning fishermen finishing up and the earliest pleasure boaters getting started. We hugged along the shoreline of the river and paddled back without too much difficulty even though the water was choppier. As we pulled up to my dock, both of us hot and sticky, Jacob asked, "How 'bout we take a dip?"

I backpaddled my kayak a little bit and pointed in the water with my oar. "Take a look at that and tell me if you still want to swim."

Jacob maneuvered his kayak close to where my oar was pointed. A large almost translucent white sea nettle was pulsing just below the surface of the water. Its tentacles were about a foot long, and its body was four or five inches around. Jacob stared down at it as its body flattened out like a puff of air had started to hyperextend an umbrella and then closed in until it resembled a mushroom cap.

Jacob said with a look of distaste, "On second thought, a shower sounds good. Do all the jellyfish mean you can't ever swim here?"

I answered, "Oh, you can swim here earlier in the season. The nettles like salty hot water. As the weather gets warm, they move up to this part of the bay from the south where the Chesapeake meets the ocean. Some years they don't make it this far north, but this late in the summer we usually see a few.

"And in years where we get a lot of rain, the water isn't salty enough for the nettles. But lots of rain means more runoff from the farms around the area. Here on the Western Shore we've got more housing developments than farms these days, but still enough for some runoff issues. And the Eastern Shore is still mostly farmland. All of the big communities around here with private beaches monitor the water for *E. coli* and other bacterial contamination after a big rain storm. Some close their beaches preemptively for the first 24 to 48 hours.

"I spent my whole childhood plunging into the water without a second thought for pollution, long before the communities thought to monitor. I was never sick once, and the Bay has been cleaned up a lot since then, so I find it hard to get alarmed by the pollution warnings. Still, I don't want to tempt fate, so if we get a huge thunderstorm with a ton of rain in the summer, I try to hold myself back from swimming for the first day."

As I was going on about the hazards of swimming in my cove, we pulled the kayaks up onto the shore and stowed the paddles. Then we cleaned up and went out for lunch at a local waterfront restaurant.

Later that afternoon, we were sipping some red wine in the sunroom looking out at the water when the sky turned dark gray.

We had heard vague rumbles of thunder off in the distance for the last half hour, but nothing close. Then, nature's best light show started out on the water. The unique aspect of this particular storm was that we could see the rain marching across the water toward us. First, the rain started out on the river with the whole area between the clouds and the river surface a dull dark gray, but from our distance, individual rain drops weren't visible. As the storm advanced onto the creek and then the cove, we could see the rain hitting the surface creating concentric circles that merged into each other. For at least five minutes, rain fell on the water no more than thirty feet from the house, but not on the house itself. Then the storm moved overhead and pounded on the roof.

"Your view is incredible." Jacob returned to our earlier conversation as we watched the storm on the water. "You grew up in this house, right?" He didn't wait for an answer. "I mean I love the Finger Lakes, and NYC can't compare to being out there, but whatever made you look elsewhere?"

"My brother died in an accident out on the river. He and his buddies were out in a canoe watching the Fourth of July fireworks when they shouldn't have been. The canoe flipped in the choppy water. The kayaks we have today are lower slung and a fair amount more stable than our old canoe was, and you felt the difference in the choppiness of the water when we paddled back after the motor boats had time to stir things up." I paused to see if Jacob was following and then continued. "It was already dark out when the canoe flipped but lots of boats were still moving around heading home after the fireworks. A boat ran into the canoe which then hit my brother, who was swimming right next to it, in the head. The head injury wouldn't necessarily have killed him if he'd been helped right away, but he couldn't swim with it, so he drowned. His buddies assumed he was swimming right behind them, so it was only when they got to shore that they realized he wasn't there and must have been trying to tow the canoe behind him." I left out the part about the identity of the boaters. Jacob had never heard any of this from me. I imagine he was so stunned by the story that he didn't even think to ask.

"And you're ok with staying here now?" he asked.

"So far. It's been almost thirty years. I ran away to college and stayed up in New York thinking I would never get over it. You can't stay mad forever though, and when I came back for Mom and started helping her I realized how much I love this area.

"I was in New York for twenty plus years, and I never even thought about buying a house. I just rented apartments or floors of those historic old houses that are all over the area. I guess it says something that I could live there all that time and never once think about putting down roots, but when I got back here I was relieved that I'd finally healed enough that I could plant myself."

Jacob nodded. I suppose I was saying something about our relationship as well when I talked about being unable to put down roots in New York. But then, Jacob was in his own way escaping from his past when he moved out to Western New York. He couldn't handle his mom's revolving door relationships and wanted to live away from the hustle and bustle. Now that he had helped his mom move on, I wondered if he would be looking for a more settled life. I knew it wasn't with me though.

Then he inquired, "Even if you can get over staying here, how did you get back out there and kayak on the river?"

"I never really thought about it. I mean, people lose loved ones in car accidents all the time, but they still get back in their cars and go to the store and work every day. Being on the water in this community is part of daily life in the warmer weather. No matter how experienced you are, you can get in trouble whether you're swimming or in a canoe or in a monster power boat. I grew up swimming and canoeing and being ridden around in other people's boats. That wasn't what freaked me out about Brian's death. It was that I couldn't picture the place without him. I hated the ill-disguised pity from all the neighbors. Between our roaming the whole neighborhood as kids, my Mom being in the church choir, and Dad's father having worked at the local marina most of his life, I couldn't go anywhere without feeling like someone was feeling sorry for me. The cove had been my haven and then it became a trap. I wasn't afraid of the water, just anchored down, unable to escape from what had happened."

CHAPTER THIRTEEN

The wind picked up and started whipping the last straggler leaves off the trees just when I thought no more leaves could possibly fall. The surface of the water close to the shore disappeared under yet another blizzard of dry, crinkly orange and yellow leaves. The wind had also flipped over a few of my dock chairs that I had left out too late in the season. I went down to the dock to bring them in. From the dock, I shielded my eyes from the bright early winter sun and looked back at the shore to admire the mums I'd planted earlier in the fall and trimmed up earlier in the day. The wind gave a good gust at that instant, and I heard a crack. Looking around for the source of the noise, I saw that the wind had broken a major branch of a small dogwood on the other side of the property line in Julie's yard.

As I was inspecting the dogwood, I noticed that the water had cut a deep groove into the soil in between the dogwood and her riprap line. I had never seen cousin Bill do more in the way of yard work than pushing a small lawnmower back and forth, so Julie was going to need some major erosion control work. I remembered when Dad had done both our and Mrs. Marconi's riprap back when we were kids. Over the years, Dad, Mom or I had kept up with ours, adding some new dirt in between the filter cloth and the rocks, re-piling the rocks or sticking a few new ones in here and there. Although none of us would have hesitated to go over to help Julie's grandmother with yard upkeep, we all had allowed the riprap in her yard to slide once Bill moved in.

Erosion is a significant problem all over the Chesapeake because the inexorable nature of an estuarine system is to move earth back and forth. The tides cut away at the land in some places and pile up the silt in others. My favorite and only dog beach in Anne Arundel County had been closed for a couple years due to erosion, although the county continued to make non-specific promises of its re-opening. We were comparatively lucky on Cecil Cove with its gentle slope to the water, in contrast to the Severn River, where the banks were actual cliffs being undermined by the tides to the point that the houses above would eventually fall into the water.

As I hauled the chairs up to the garage for the winter, I was relieved to see Julie and Guilty coming out so that I wouldn't forget to mention the erosion.

"Hey, Jules. You know you need some serious erosion control work at your shoreline, don't you?" I was leaning against the fence separating our yards as she carried a bag of garbage out to her garage.

"Siobhan, you know I don't speak landscaping. What do you mean?"

"The water has undercut a chunk of your shoreline. You're going to lose some trees soon. Eventually, the supports for your dock where it joins your yard will go, and you'll have to do a long jump to get out onto it." Julie gave me a fatigued stare. I continued, figuring she could use some pointers, "These days you need a permit to do most erosion work. Contractors are out there who will get the permits and do the work for you. Hiring someone to fix it should be right up your alley." I grinned as I teased her.

"Oh crap. There's no end to fixing this house up, but you're right, as long as I can pay someone to do the work, I'm good." Julie held her hand up to shield her eyes from the direct sunlight. "I hope to hell you were wearing sunblock out there when you were doing all that yardwork."

"Nah, it's December. With the sun at that winter angle, I won't get burned, and besides what's a little skin cancer."

Julie burst into tears. "What did I say? What's wrong?" I asked anxiously.

"Bobby…."

"I heard it was his liver, Jules."

"No, no, it was skin cancer that spread to his liver."

"Oh, shit, Jules, I'm so sorry. I had no idea. Open mouth, insert both feet."

JULIE 2012

We had left the balcony doors open all night in order hear the ocean and smell the tangy Aruban air. I was languorously spooned against Bobby's back. By the position of the sun, I'm sure it was at least 8 o'clock in the morning. At home, Bobby never ever slept this late, even on weekends without any trials in the immediate horizon. I was in a delicious half-doze state where the noises of early morning beachgoers and the resort staff setting up the lounge chairs awakened me from mini-dreams about undone household tasks just enough so I could remember that I was in paradise and slide back into blessed unconsciousness until the cycle of dreaming and wakening repeated.

I don't think I had ever seen Bobby as stressed, tired and, frankly, grumpy as he was leading up to this trial that just finished. He left the house before dawn, returned well after dark, ate a fraction of the dinner plate I'd made for him, and then headed off to bed immediately complaining his whole gut was killing him. One night I made the mistake of asking him if he might be getting an ulcer. He snarled, "That's the last thing I have time to worry about right now," and went off to bed.

Three days after the trial was over, the alarm went off at 5:30 a.m. Bobby snapped up, but unlike most mornings where he would quickly move into the bathroom and shut the door to avoid waking me, he turned on all the lights in the bedroom. "What's going on?" I protested, pulling covers up over my head.

"Get up and get packed," he directed, grabbing the blankets and yanking downward. "The flight to Aruba's at 11:30, so we've got to be at Dulles by 9:30, so we leave here by 8:30. That gives you three hours to wake up and get packed."

I stared sleepily at him, trying to figure out if he was joking or not. He was smiling from ear to ear, and he flopped down on the bed next to me. "I know I've been a total grizzly bear these last six weeks, so I wanted to surprise you. We have four nights in paradise coming, and I know I need it." He kissed me and then pulled me out of bed.

Bobby had planned surprise trips following major trials before, but this time was the first time that I got only three hours' notice of one. "What if I have a major commitment this week that you didn't know about?" I tried to tease him.

"I looked at your calendar in the kitchen AND I told Mom what I was planning a few weeks ago, so she could set up the dog sitter and all that other stuff I know you'll worry about." He grinned. His mother had been more curious than usual about what was going on this week.

Six hours later, we were on our flight. We both had champagne on the plane down, and we kept going with the rum drinks as soon as we got to the resort. We spent most of the next day on the beach nursing our hangovers. The second full day, we rented a Jet Ski and cavorted around the coastline. Bobby teased me about how I used to flirt with Jim when we were kids to get rides on his Jet Ski. We had dinner at one of Aruba's terrific South American style steakhouses.

By the third morning, as we were lying in bed dozing, I felt like all the stress and tension with which Bobby's work had filled our lives for the last few weeks had finally slipped away. At home Bobby slept in a T-shirt and boxers, so I was enjoying rubbing his naked back and shoulders when my left hand felt a bump right at the back of his armpit. I pulled back to see what I was touching. A large brown and black mole almost half the size of the end of my thumb was there.

"Bobby, have you seen this mole? I don't remember this being here last summer when we were at the beach. Or if it was there, it just blended in with all your freckles."

"I don't know. I really can't see back there," he mumbled sleepily.

"Yeah, I know. It's sort of tucked almost in the back of your armpit. It's super ugly, and its edges are all uneven, like the kinds of moles everyone says you need to watch out for. You should get it checked out."

"I guess. I think I should go to some sort of gastro guy first if this refluxing pain in my gut thing I have doesn't go away now that the trial's over and I can relax."

He did make an appointment with a gastroenterologist not long after we got back from the trip. The stomach pains hadn't gone away. Instead, they were getting worse. Of course, the closest appointment with the specialist was three weeks out, and during that time he ate a lot of antacids and not much else. He had lost at least ten pounds by the time the appointment rolled around in the middle of the summer. We were both worried by that point, but after a battery of tests including a CT scan, endoscopy, colonoscopy, MRI and other tests of which I'd never even heard, we were both blind-sided by the diagnosis.

Bobby had skin cancer that had spread to his liver. That horrible mole on his back was cancerous. The pain in his gut was from the cancer that had moved into his liver. The whole family was completely stunned. All of us knew that skin cancer could kill you, but none of us had any idea that it frequently spread to the liver. I had childishly assumed that you only needed a dermatologist to hack off the mole. After all, this thing was smaller than the tip of my thumb. When I had heard of people dying from skin cancer, somehow I pictured people waiting until these moles were the size of baseballs or until dozens of them had popped up all over their bodies and then, well, it was their own fault if it was too late to get rid of the cancer.

None of us could believe the doctors when they advised us under intense questioning from my litigator husband that Bobby would be lucky to live through the next year. Bobby's mother was the ultimate activist. She moved up from Florida and into our spare bedroom "until things were better." She called anyone she knew for advice or information. She went on the internet for hours at a time. She went to the library. She went to the appointments with the oncologist with us, and she barraged the doctors with questions. She found clinical trials of new drugs and new liver surgeries, and she contacted the people who ran them.

When none of the treatments worked, she demanded of the doctors, "I've read that this new antibody is a miracle cure for melanoma. How come it hasn't worked?"

Even the simplest language made no sense to me. Something about antibodies targeting particular substances or particular genetic mutations, and Bobby had the bad fortune not to have the particular variants that the drug worked on. Instead, he had some sort of surgery where to the best of my ability to understand they pumped chemotherapy directly to his liver.

Bobby could barely sit at the dinner table by Thanksgiving. For the first time since I had started dating Bobby we didn't celebrate Christmas. The kids came home and had their private moments with him. He was home with hospice care in between occasional three or four day stints at the hospital to fix various complications. We had enough pain medicine in our house to supply a small street cartel.

Once again, my own ignorance of all things medical set me up for more surprises. One night between Christmas and New Years', the night nurse came and queried me about when Bobby's last bowel movement had been. I had to admit that I didn't know. "Doesn't the day nurse record stuff like that?" I asked somewhat puzzled.

She showed me Bobby's distended stomach, stating that she was worried that he had ileus. I stared blankly at her. She explained to me that pain medicines often cause constipation and bowel blockage, i.e., ileus. She said that if the blockage was bad enough, surgery might be required. I responded, "Well, we go to the doctor again in two days, so I'll ask what we should do."

The nurse tried to correct me without making me feel like a complete idiot. "Dear, if his bowels are completely blocked, waiting two days could be life-threatening. I think he needs to go to the emergency room. Now."

The bowel blockage was the end game. His bowels were blocked by more tumor, and the only option left to try to correct the blockage was surgery. All I can console myself with is that at least Bobby had no idea what was going on at that point. They kept him sedated with some milky white fluid that dripped steadily through his IV. Although the surgery corrected the blockage, it weakened him, leaving him in the ICU.

Bobby's mom was a tiger in the ICU waiting room. She would assault every nurse, doctor, technician, or social worker who came to talk to us or who just had the bad luck to walk through the ICU waiting room. "When is this condition getting fixed? When can we get back to treating his cancer?"

Most of the ICU staff evaded questions about continuing cancer treatment, but one young doctor looked at Bobby's mom with surprise and told her that he wasn't the oncologist but in his opinion Bobby was way too weak to even consider chemotherapy any time soon.

Bobby's mom then demanded, "Well, who screwed up the surgery? What went wrong?"

The young doctor winced at the onslaught and mumbled out some response that Bobby's mom clearly found wholly unsatisfactory. One of the senior ICU nurses fortunately overheard the end of the exchange and rescued the doctor. She sat down right across from me and gently urged Bobby's mom into the chair next to me. She looked unflinchingly at us and calmly stated, "No one did anything wrong. No one screwed up the surgery. Unfortunately, with cancer, we have bad outcomes all the time even when everyone does everything absolutely right. We don't have the tools to beat some of these cancers. There's no one to blame. No one's at fault. I'm really afraid we're not going to win this one, and I am very sorry."

I doubt that anything anyone said would have changed Bobby's mom. Someone was responsible for her son's impending death and she wanted to know whom. She stormed off in a huff mumbling under her breath about finding a supervisor and the gall of nurses claiming her son could not be cured.

For me though, the nurse's words were an earthquake shifting a fault line. Everything bad that had happened in my life up until now could be blamed on someone. I could blame Brian for trying to save the canoe. I could blame my parents for hiding the accident. I could blame Siobhan for telling on my parents. I spent years in counseling trying to get over the anger and the blame when my world got dumped upside down in high school. But back then, somebody's choices could have made a difference in what happened to my life.

Bobby's skin cancer was, in the words of the medical staff, extremely aggressive. I'm not sure whether the staff were just trying to console me or whether their words were true, but they stated that even if Bobby had been getting regular skin checks and had caught the mole earlier, they weren't sure he could have beaten this particular cancer. All they would offer is that he might have lasted longer.

So, in Bobby's case, I was left with no one to blame. He was going to die of his cancer within the next few days most likely, and it was nobody's fault. I was going to have to find a way to cope with losing Bobby, and I couldn't even use anger at someone to help me through it. Some people rage at God, but since I wasn't religious, I wasn't going to start believing in Him now just to have the satisfaction of being able to blame Him for what happened.

CHAPTER FOURTEEN

Caitlin was hosting Christmas at her place because she wanted her kids to wake up to presents left by Santa and be able to stay at home playing with them. I, however, claimed the privilege of having the Christmas Eve lasagna feast at the cottage as my first family celebration in my new place. Unfortunately, David was still in Chicago in some sort of training; the Navy did not grant him leave. Caitlin and Bobby Jr were both coming though. Dad was staying out in California. Mom, true to herself even in her seventies, was traveling somewhere for work and sent presents for the kids and grandkids. The Owens were spending Christmas Eve with Marie and then coming to Caitlin's for Christmas Day.

I had invited Siobhan to come over for the Christmas Eve dinner a couple weeks ago, inwardly hoping that we could move our recovering relationship past the fence post conversations. When I had asked her what she had done for Thanksgiving, she had replied that she volunteered to work a shift for one of the other pharmacists who had requested off. I told her that she couldn't spend all of her holidays like that, and that I expected her to come for Christmas Eve lasagna. I ignored all protests about

179

intruding on family time and told her she could bring some Chianti.

We ate dinner somewhat early in order for Caitlin to get the kids back home and in bed in time for Santa to arrive. Each kid and grandkid had been allowed to open one present on Christmas Eve, and we had finished cleaning up all the wrapping paper. As Caitlin would be driving, she was abstaining, but all the other adults were sprawled around the living room with glasses of red wine. The grandkids were playing in the den with the new toys.

With no warning whatsoever, the front door swung open and in walked Mom. "Surprise and Merry Christmas Everyone! I'm sorry I didn't call, but the company where I was consulting gave all their employees Christmas Eve and Boxing Day off at the last minute, so I had nowhere to work until Monday. I'm ultra ultra platinum member with the airlines so I bullied my way into a standby slot. I hope there's a couch somewhere. God, this place is still a backwater. The gas station off the main road isn't even open 24 hours, and the road is still gravel."

As she was saying all this, she moved into the living room and started kissing people on the cheeks and hugging everyone. When she got to Siobhan, who was sitting next to me on the hearthstone, Mom remarked, "Oh, you have extra company. Hi, I'm Donna." Clearly Mom didn't recognize Siobhan after all these years.

The color had completely drained out of Siobhan's face, and before Siobhan had to say anything I jumped up and inserted, "Mom, you remember Siobhan." I figured I'd try nonchalance. It didn't work.

Siobhan leaped up, mumbled, "I'll go," and tried to get around Mom and out the door.

If Siobhan got pale, Mom flushed to her hairline with color. Before I could intervene, Mom got out, "What the hell is she doing here?"

I'm not sure what Mom would have done if left unchecked, but I grabbed her arm, hard, with one hand and put the other hand up to her mouth not quite touching. I hissed, "Don't you dare!" and hustled her into the hall powder room. The room was barely big enough for both of us. I was whispering angrily, "Don't you dare make a scene in my house on Christmas Eve. I invited Siobhan, and you will not treat any guest of mine like you just did."

Mom was livid. "You know what she did to our fam…"

I cut her off before she could finish. "That used to be my line Mom, but 10,000 dollars of therapy later, I finally figured out that the only people to blame for the mess our family got in was ourselves. Maybe you should see if you can use some of those frequent flier miles for some gift cards to a counselor."

I shouldn't have made that last remark, but as usual my mouth was open before my brain engaged.

Mom was only further infuriated and tried to push past me. Fortunately, she couldn't.

"Mom, I invited Siobhan here. I am trying to put the past behind me. If I had known you were coming, I wouldn't have invited her. I doubt she enjoys seeing you anymore than you want to see her. But you will not start a brawl on Christmas Eve. You will also not bring this up in front of your grandkids and great-grandkids. All I have ever told the kids is that there was an accident a long time ago and things got pretty messed up for everyone involved. I have no intention of going into the details right now."

I heard the bongs of the security system twice while I was making this speech, knowing they corresponded to Siobhan opening and closing the front door. With my meanest glare I admonished Mom to stay in the bathroom until she could pull herself together and go greet her great-grandkids without causing a scene.

Miraculously, she did. Perhaps because Caitlin's kids had come up to the living room even Mom realized that she couldn't let loose in front of a 6- and 4-year old. Caitlin was obviously curious, but her husband was gathering up the toys and preparing to get them back to Chevy Chase. She invited everyone to be at their place at 8 a.m. for presents from Santa. After the usual hustle of getting two small kids moving, they were off.

Mom had been talking to Bobby Jr while Caitlin's crew was packing up. She had never been good with small children, even her own, so I wasn't surprised that she had done little more than hug her great-grandkids and then moved on to someone adult-sized.

Once Caitlin and crew were out the door, only Bobby Jr, Mom and I were left. "Bobby Jr is already set up in the guest bedroom, Mom, but the den has a pull out. I'll get you some sheets."

I pulled some linens from the upstairs hall closet and walked Mom to the den. I told her, "I'm going over to Siobhan's to apologize. When I get back, you and I can talk if you like. Or not. You will NOT under any circumstances discuss this with my son because if you do you can try to find a hotel on Christmas Eve. Ask him how law school's going."

I grabbed a bottle of Chambord, some Christmas cookies and walked next door where I was relieved to see that lights were still on. I wasn't sure what reception I was going to get, but I was determined to try. Just as I was about to ring the main doorbell, I had a strategic thought. I went to the sliders on the water side of the house where she could see me when I knocked. I yelled, "Please let me in. I have booze and dessert."

Her dogs were my allies. They heard me, ran right up to the sliders and started barking. I knew they wouldn't shut up as long as I stood there, and I wasn't going to leave. Siobhan came out of the bedroom area after about a minute and let me in. As soon as the slider was opened an inch I started talking, "I am so so sorry, Siobhan." I had gained the sunporch by this point. "I had no idea she was going to show up. She never shows up for anything. She sends cards and money and thinks that counts as being a grandmother. I would never have put you in that situation. She has never accepted responsibility for anything about the accident. I believe she truly convinced herself that since Dad was driving the boat she was nothing but an innocent bystander."

I had walked to the kitchen by this point. I randomly opened cabinets and found two glasses. I poured and handed one to Siobhan who just stood numbly with her hands at her sides. In the light of the kitchen, I could see that she had wiped away some tears before she opened the door.

She looked like she wanted to say something, but she was obviously only holding back tears by keeping her lips pressed tightly together. I pressed the glass of Chambord into her hand.

"I should have said this years ago, Siobhan, but I had no right to blame you for what happened to my family back then. Mom and Dad were big fat selfish cowards. They were so worried about what would happen to their damn security clearances that they acted inexcusably. I spent a lot of time with a therapist figuring out that Mom and Dad were to blame, not you and not Brian. So, it may be 30 years late, but I owe you a huge apology for how I acted back then. When Bobby died, I couldn't see how I could ever be happy again, but since I've been back here at the cottage, I've started to feel alive again. And, I have really enjoyed getting to know you again. I don't want Mom to screw that up."

I took a big gulp of Chambord, barely able to choke down the sweetness, still not sure whether Siobhan was going to throw me out the second she got control enough to speak.

Siobhan poured down a bit of Chambord too, also wincing at the sweet taste. "I guess we were bound to have to talk about that damn accident at some point. Part of me was hoping we could just start to be friends again and leave the genie in its bottle forever."

"Mom fixed that one, that's for damn sure." A weak attempt at humor, but it worked. We both smiled.

I hugged her tightly saying, "I really am sorry. I want my Siamese sister back."

She hugged me back, almost at the expense of the Chambord. "I owe you an apology too. I shouldn't have blamed you for wanting to protect your parents. We were still kids. No kid wants to worry about mom and dad getting locked up. God, I didn't have a clue what would happen to your whole family when the truth all came out. I didn't know beans about security clearances. I was used to thinking about your Grandmom as your parent."

I poured more Chambord and pulled out cookies allowing us both to stop talking and get ourselves under control.

"So, we're ok," I asked.

"I think we're more ok than we've been in a long time."

We ate some more cookies and drank Chambord. After a few quiet minutes of digesting, both thoughts and dessert, I said, "I hate to say this, but I do have to go back to Momzilla. I want you to understand that I know what she did back then was wrong, but she is the only Mom I've got. If nothing else, for the sake of my kids, I can't cut her out of my life. I will, however, tell her she can't make any more surprise visits and will give you plenty of warning if she's going to be around here. But, I've left Bobby Jr alone with her, and I have to go save him."

Siobhan smiled at the Momzilla appellation. "Yes, go, I understand. We're fine really. Thank you for coming over right away. And good luck with Santa presents tomorrow morning"

I walked back home happy that I'd saved one aspect of the evening, but I wasn't sure the rest of the evening would go as well.

Mom and Bobby Jr were chatting amicably, but I could tell she was seething by the way she was drumming her fingers against the side of the couch out of Bobby Jr's sight. I played dumb and joined in the conversation about law school, throwing in some anecdotes from when Bobby had been slogging his way through law school while I was pregnant with Caitlin. We called David on the speaker phone feature of my cell to wish him a Merry Christmas Eve, but he had only a couple minutes to tell us that Navy life was going fine. Bobby Jr went upstairs to call his girlfriend on the West Coast.

Now alone with Mom, I decided to try to take control of the conversation first, saying, "I'm glad you want to spend Christmas with all of us. I'd like to enjoy the holiday with you. I think if we want to do that, we should pretend you just got here. Can we please please please do that?"

She stared stonily for long enough that I was sure my pleading was not going to work. Then she forced her obstinacy down with a hard swallow and a weak smile, "Should I go outside and charge through the front door yelling 'Surprise' again?"

I sighed with relief and laughed at her joke.

Knowing that we had to get up way too early tomorrow to be at Caitlin's for Santa presents, we headed off to bed.

Mom drove her rental car to Caitlin's the next morning since she was going to stay at an airport hotel and head back the next day to wherever her job was. Hence I was in the car alone with Bobby Jr for a good solid hour driving to Caitlin's. He was too much his father's son not to want to dig out the truth with that much opportunity.

Lying in bed this morning before I got up, I deliberated on how much of the story of the accident I wanted to tell the kids. I quickly came to the conclusion that after Mom's reaction last night I wasn't going to be able to hold much back.

"OK, here it is. I know that I told you kids that there had been an accident a long time ago, and it messed our family up. That was the reason I gave you for your grandparents being divorced and for your grandfather being out in California and for not being part of your lives."

Bobby Jr looked over at me, but since he was driving I joked, "Eyes on the road please, or I'm pleading the fifth."

He chuckled and turned back to the road.

"In 1979, my parents were out in their boat on the Fourth of July watching the fireworks, and they hit an overturned canoe in the water in the dark as they were headed back home. They thought it had broken loose from someone's dock or had been abandoned when it flipped over. Unfortunately, Siobhan's brother Brian was swimming next to the canoe trying to tow it back to shore. When their boat hit the canoe, the force apparently pushed the canoe and the canoe hit him in the head. He drowned because he couldn't swim back to shore after he got hit. I swear to you they didn't know he was there." I paused for air.

"But why would Grandmom yell at Siobhan like that?" Of course, Bobby Jr had leaped right on the crucial point.

"Well, that's where your grandparents did something wrong. When they learned that Brian had been killed that night, that they hadn't simply hit an abandoned boat, they didn't come forward and tell the police about the accident. If they had, things would have gone a lot better for everyone, me included. Being out in a canoe on the river in the dark on Fourth of July is not safe. The water gets chopped up by all the power boats coming out to watch the fireworks, and it's not hard for a canoe to get flipped. Everyone at the time understood how foolish it had been for Brian to be out there like that. So, if my parents had gone right to the police once they learned Brian had been killed and explained that they didn't realize that there was a person anywhere near the boat, my Dad may not have even gone to jail, and Mom probably wouldn't have lost her security clearance." I paused again. I had never told anyone the full story except my counselor.

"Still not getting how that makes Grandmom angry at Siobhan, Mom." He'll make a good lawyer. He won't let up, I thought to myself.

"Siobhan and I were best friends back then, almost sisters. We were always together the whole summer long, at camp or at her house or at my Grandmom's, my current cottage. Siobhan was totally depressed after Brian died and hid in her room as much as she could. Then this one day after Brian died, her parents made her come over to my parents' house with me because they were trying to force her to do something other than just cry in her room. We spent the afternoon hanging out around the dock with some rafts, and we went into the garage to put them away before Siobhan's mom came to pick her up. Dad had hidden our boat in the garage after the accident, and Siobhan saw the damage to its front end. Their canoe had had a bunch of stickers on it, and part of the stickers had come off onto my parents' boat, making it undeniable how our boat got damaged."

"Siobhan had to tell her parents what she saw, and they of course told the police. Siobhan couldn't hide that she knew who had been responsible for her brother's death. It killed our friendship for decades though. I blamed her for telling on my parents and messing up our lives. She blamed me for caring more about protecting my parents than her brother."

"Holy cow, Mom, how come you never told us any of this before? What happened to Grandmom and Grandfather?"

"Hiding was wrong. At that time, both your grandparents had high level security clearances and were defense contractors. They made boatloads of money. They lost their security clearances as soon as DOD found out what had happened, particularly that they covered up the accident. They lost their jobs. I'm pretty sure that Dad would have lost his no matter what once the prosecutor brought charges. But Mom wasn't driving the boat. If they had gone straight to the police, she might have been ok. All the fuss killed their marriage. Mom had to rent a cramped little townhouse from a cousin who was getting divorced because she and Dad couldn't afford their house anymore. Mom got probation, maybe because I was still a minor and the court didn't want to take both my parents away. Dad went to prison and then moved back to California after he was released. Our lives were pretty screwed up for quite some time." I paused for a sip of coffee.

"Wow, no wonder Grandmom hates Siobhan." Bobby Jr chimed in.

"Whoa, whoa, whoa, Bobby. Don't make the same mistake I made. I wasted a lot of years being angry at Siobhan and lost my best friend for over thirty years because I blamed her instead of my parents. Siobhan couldn't have done anything other than what she did. I was crazy to think that Siobhan could figure out that her best friend's parents killed her brother and then keep her mouth shut. Your grandparents are the ones who did the wrong thing. They should never have hidden the truth from the police. They were responsible for what happened to themselves and to me. Not Siobhan. By the way, your father was the one who taught me to see that I had been blaming the wrong person. He was the one who opened my eyes. Of course, I needed a couple years with a therapist to really get over it."

Bobby Jr took a few seconds to chew on my words. "Yeah, I guess there wasn't anything else for Siobhan to do. You still haven't answered me about why you never told us any of this."

"Obviously your grandmother has never accepted responsibility for her part in covering things up, but she is still my Mom and she is your grandmother, and I wanted you all to have some sort of relationship with her. She made her own choices about how much time she spent with you, but at least I gave you kids and her the chance to have a relationship. Dad and I had no relationship until he got in touch just before he re-married. Dad, however, always realized that he was responsible. When the police showed up at our house he told them everything right away, while Mom sat on her white couch in the living room and pressed her lips together. I snuck out of my room on my stomach and watched from the balcony over the great room as they talked to the police. Dad was a pretty arrogant man before the accident. He was an only child of wealthy California parents, had gone to expensive private schools out west, and got a high-paying important defense job. When he was around when I was a kid, I always remember him comparing how well he and Mom were doing to other people. He completely fell apart when the police came. I doubt anything had ever gone wrong before in his life and then when something bad finally did happen he did the wrong thing. I think he felt so guilty about that that he didn't get in touch with me until he got himself together again. Not a great answer, but I always figured I would tell you at some point when you were all old enough, but I never saw an easy approach. 'Hey kids, did I ever tell you your grandfather was convicted for manslaughter.'"

"Right... I get it."

We were almost at Caitlin's. "If you don't mind, I'd like to tell your siblings myself, my own way."

I got a grunt.

"Well, at least, please don't post it on Facebook. And, no, I'm not going to talk about it in front of your Grandmom nor in front of Caitlin's kids. OK?"

"Yup, got it."

Caitlin's kids were apoplectic by the time we got there. They'd woken up at 6:30 to see if Santa had been there, and they were not happy about waiting until we arrived at 7:53 to open presents. Caitlin was barely able to pour us cups of coffee before they started tearing into the pile.

When the Santa presents for the kids were done, Caitlin and her husband called for silence. "We have a Santa present for parents and grandparents." They were smiling so broadly I knew what they were going to say.

"We won't be able to open this one for several more months," Kevin grinned, patting Caitlin's stomach. "We're having another one."

Congratulations were spread all around, and then Caitlin took the breakfast strata out of the oven.

I did eventually tell Caitlin and David what I had told Bobby Jr about the accident. I knew that if I didn't Bobby Jr eventually would, and I wanted to tell them my way. I was able to talk to

Caitlin in the kitchen after we'd cleaned up and her kids were still in toy rapture. I called David two days later. I hated having to tell David over the phone, but I didn't know when he'd be in town for me to tell him in person. Even so, I still didn't tell any of them that their father had been in the canoe with Brian that night, and even my budding attorney son didn't ask whether anyone else had been with Brian in the canoe at any point. I'm not sure why I held back. Bobby hadn't done anything stupider than Brian in going out at all, but I somehow didn't want to tell the kids something that made Bobby look foolish when he was no longer here to defend himself.

SIOBHAN CHRISTMAS DAY 2014

I had planned to sleep in but some damn duck hunter started blasting off his shotgun at around eight in the morning. Originally, I had also planned to spend the day lolling about the house with the dogs and a new fantasy book. Spending holidays alone had never bothered me. I occasionally worked on holidays, and I had learned to treat them just like any other day whether I worked or not.

Today, though, I knew if I stayed at home, I would obsess over the events of the prior evening. Once I had made sure that all the cars next door were gone, I took the dogs down to the park for a good long walk. Then I showered up and made some coffee. While I was drinking the coffee, I called Dad to wish him and Ana a Merry Christmas.

I used the iPad to pull up the schedule for the local movie theaters, which do a booming business on Christmas Day from all the people who don't celebrate that particular holiday, and found the earliest show in which I was interested.

Of course I couldn't stop myself from mulling over the encounter with Julie's mom the night before even on the relatively short drive over to the mall and even with the radio turned up to blare inane holiday music. But on the way there, I suddenly burst out laughing. Once I had deduced that Julie would be moving back to the cottage, I had obsessed over what having Julie next door would be like. I had worried endlessly about how she and I would get along for all the months that her cottage was being renovated. After she moved in, I had felt hopeful about how our relationship seemed to slowly be building back up. But as I drove over to the mall, I realized that for all my obsessing for all those months, I had never once even considered the possibility that I would run into Julie's mom or dad with Julie living right next door. I couldn't believe how I had missed that elephant in the room.

192 SHANNON O'BARR SAUSVILLE

I watched a movie at the mall and then indulged in a loaded
burger at one of the chain restaurants near the theater. I then
decided to further indulge in a second movie.

On the way home, I was once again replaying in my head the
events of the prior night. Julie had done all the right things
yesterday. And I decided I truly was happy to have her back in my
life and was happy that she was next door.

I was not at all ready to forgive her parents yet.

From my conversation with Julie back in the fall where I
blurted out a question about her dad, I got the impression that he
was truly sorry about everything that had happened back in 1979. If
I encountered him in the course of his visiting Julie on one of his
rare trips to the East Coast, I think I could handle being around
him for the five minutes that politeness would require. That didn't
mean I'd forgiven him, as when I thought about him I did feel a
twinge of that black poison that I'd felt for all those years. But I
guess thirty years later I didn't need to make a scene if someone
who'd done time in prison and professed genuine regret for what
he'd done happened to cross my path.

Julie's mother was another story though. Part of me was having
difficulty separating my feelings for Julie from my feelings for her
mother. Up until last night's encounter, I'd managed to make her
mother non-existent. Funny that in all the times I'd seen Julie over
the fence the past few months, I never registered that Julie did look
almost frighteningly like her mother did back when we were kids.
Seeing Julie and her mother together last night brought home their
physical resemblance, and I wondered if I could look at Julie now
without seeing her mom.

I tried to sort through how I could start being friends with Julie
if Julie's mom could pull one of her surprise visits at any time,
although I had to admit that wasn't all that likely to occur. But then
I remembered how Julie had rushed over to my house to make sure
I was ok and to apologize for Momzilla, as she called her.

And then, I started to see the path to separating the two in my head. First, Julie actually apologized and cared. Her mom did not. But further Julie herself was every bit as hurt by and embarrassed about her mother's behavior as I was. Like Julie had said, she was essentially stuck with her mom, for her kids' and grandkids' sake if nothing else. When we were kids Julie had tried to pretend that she wasn't hurt by all her parents' absences and their apparent willingness to divest themselves of their daughter at any chance. Julie had needed my friendship back then, in part, because the two people who were supposed to love her the most failed miserably at doing so. If I couldn't find some way to separate my feelings about Julie from my feelings about her mom, I'd be indirectly letting Julie's mom hurt Julie yet again, by depriving her of a friend. Julie deserved better than that.

That tiny corner of my heart where I had banished all the fury and loathing and bile related to Brian's death, I still reserved for Julie's mom. The woman not only wasn't sorry but she still didn't see that she had done anything that would require her to be sorry. So many people would have gone through a lot less pain if she and her husband had run right to the police and let them know what happened.

CHAPTER FIFTEEN

Through the winter months, I continued my quest to capture the best sunrises with my steadily improving photography skills. Thin layers of ice formed overnight at the water's edge but the bulk of the water was still liquid. On exceptionally cold mornings when the tide was full right around daybreak, the water, warmer than the surrounding air, had a layer of mist rising as if the arms of the water spirits were reaching up above the water level toward the sunrise. I learned quickly that the filters didn't do anything to help the photo but a good long exposure with a film camera on the tripod made a much better picture.

I wished that going out on the water were possible in order to get different angles, but I was not willing to risk hypothermia. The water temperature was in the thirties. Despite the cold, I did see early morning boaters, presumably fishermen looking for some type of catch or another, and I hoped they had wet suits on in case of a fall overboard. At that water temperature, they'd have less than ten minutes in the water before the cold paralysis of freezing muscles would make pulling themselves back in the boat impossible.

The photography was a good hobby, but as I set up my equipment on these morning adventures I found that I was increasingly wondering what I was going to do with myself. Bobby and I had only begun to discuss what would happen once the kids were done with college and Bobby was able to cut back on work. At first after Bobby died, I was numb, and my days passed without my being able to account for how I spent my time. Then, I'd developed my grand house shuffling plan, and I had no problem filling my days with packing things up for each of the kids and approving design plans for the cottage. I was making Caitlin store things for her brothers in the basement of the house until they were settled enough to want them. Bobby's mom had helped me go through Bobby's things, donating most of his clothes and dividing up the memorabilia. Now though, I was comfortably settled into the renovated cottage, the packing and storing was done, the holidays were over, and I was realizing that all of the kid-related activities with which I used to fill my days were gone.

Many of the life choices I pondered were not dissimilar from those faced by any empty nester who was previously a stay-at-home mom. The obvious difference with my situation is that most of my compatriot stay-at-home moms believed they would use the empty nest time to re-connect with their husbands and take the trips that they couldn't take with kids at home. Bobby and I had never managed more than short Caribbean getaways without the kids over the years, and I had longed to embark on some grand European vacations once Bobby cut back on work, particularly to France where I hoped to resurrect some of my language skills. Now, never having gone to Europe at all, I was intimidated by the idea of going by myself.

I knew some of the divorced women originally from my old neighborhood traveled together once their kids were grown. I could probably get along well enough with someone to go on a Caribbean weekend with them. Siobhan and I were too early in restoring our friendship for me to consider asking her to be a travel companion yet. Besides, I didn't get the impression that she was a traveler except for going to visit her dad.

Although I could foresee occasionally helping out with the grandkids, I wasn't sure I wanted childrearing to be my whole life either. I had loved taking care of my kids when they were babies, but I found myself much more tired after a day with Caitlin's little ones than I remember being with my own. When I reflected back on how much time Mrs. Owen had devoted to helping me with my kids, I wondered where she had found the energy and asked myself if that was the role that I saw for myself in the future.

As long as I lived somewhat modestly, I probably didn't need to work. I owned the cottage free and clear. I had used life insurance proceeds to renovate the cottage, and I had Bobby's retirement savings to cover my daily living expenses. Besides if I went back to work, I'm not sure what I was qualified to do. All I had done for the past decades was raise kids. My degree was in French literature, and *je n'ai pas parlé francais depuis longtemps.*

I had started looking in the community college catalog and the community center brochures for photography classes. At the least I could meet some people and keep busy by taking a few cheap classes. Maybe I could even get a part-time job working on some sort of arts class, more to meet people than to make money. I had no illusions that my photography was good enough to make a living on, but I could probably teach some basic skills at a community center level.

With these thoughts swirling in my head while I set up the tripod on the dock on a late February morning, my gaze fixed on a red object twisting out near the creek entrance. I looked through the telephoto lens to try to identify it. The object was a Mylar balloon, a Happy Valentine's Day balloon in fact. The red satin cord on the balloon had become frozen into the ice on the water, but the balloon itself was not. The balloon still had enough helium inside that it was trying to float upward, but only about two feet of the satin ribbon was free of the ice; the trapped balloon was therefore just bobbing up and down.

I snapped quite a few photos of the balloon with the zoom lens at full extension. I wondered who lost their Valentine. I entertained the idea of submitting the photo to some amateur photography contest in one of the local magazines as a good local shot. I could picture several different captions: Romance on Ice, Love Floats, Love Wants to Be Free.

The Valentine balloon reminded me once again of the call from Mrs. Owen on Valentine's Day that had spurred some of my thoughts about the future. She was religious about calling me at least once a week and on every holiday and on any day that was any sort of special occasion for our family. Most of the time she just filled me in on all the news and confirmed that I was "doing ok."

On the Valentine's call though, she had leaped on my comment about how this winter I had done my own snow shoveling for the first time in my life.

"You know, dear, we don't get snow here in Florida. We'd love to have you visit us."

"Of course, I want to come visit you now that I'm pretty much settled in," I had replied quite sincerely.

"Terrific. You know we have a spare bedroom down here. You could avoid snow shoveling altogether if you came down for the winter but I hope you'll come in the warmer weather too." Mrs. Owen responded enthusiastically.

I sucked in my breath when I realized the scope of the "visit" she was suggesting. "Oh, I think you'd get sick of me if you had me for the whole winter. I'll look at the kids' schedules and come up with some dates when I can get away for a visit though."

I loved the Owens, and they had been in countless ways better parents to me than my own parents. When Bobby had first died, all I could focus on was the cataclysmic loss, the irresistible vacuum threatening to drag me into the void like a passenger on a catastrophically depressurizing airplane. What took me longer to realize was that my loss was greater than just Bobby; all of my other relationships with people that had known me and Bobby as a couple would change.

Taking Bobby out of the picture but otherwise trying to keep old relationships the same as they had been wasn't possible, but I'm not sure the Owens had realized that yet. As the kids' grandparents, the Owens would always be part of my life with or without Bobby. Their mental picture though was a wedding photo of the two of us, and although Bobby was no longer here, I was still in my wedding dress in their heads. I had no real desire to date as of yet and hadn't met anyone that I considered interesting, but I couldn't imagine ever telling Bobby's parents that I was dating; in their minds I would always be Bobby's wife. I, however, wasn't sure I wanted to be "Bobby's wife" for the rest of my life. I was starting to realize that I needed to be "Julie," and that I had to figure out who Julie was.

If I weren't careful though, my life could get sucked into the Owens' without my ever having a chance to determine if I wanted something else. Emotional considerations aside, I jokingly thought to myself, I didn't golf and had never seen the appeal of the snowbird and now full-time Florida life that the Owens had adopted wholeheartedly.

Bobby's parents decided to become snowbirds when Caitlin went off to college in 2004, buying a large condo in West Palm Beach. The Owens' decision to become snowbirds partly related to their grandkids having reached their independent teenaged years, and partly because they wanted less housework and warmer weather.

After they bought the condo, we flew with the kids for Thanksgivings in Florida more years than not. Flying Caitlin there from college was just as easy as bringing her home for the holidays.

The first year we went down there, I found having palm and citrus trees as the backdrop for a winter meal a little incongruous. Their condo's kitchen was a little small for a full production dinner, but we got by because Bobby's mom ordered pre-fabbed Thanksgiving dinners from the local gourmet grocery store. All we had to do was put the turkey in the oven and warm up the sides. Part of me protested the lack of tradition in doing dinner that way, but the Owens had declared they wanted an easier life style and pre-fab fit right in with that choice.

Ostensibly, the Owens could have stayed at their own house with Marie whenever they came back north, but I had correctly foreseen that when they were in Maryland, they would spend a lot more time at our Chevy Chase house. Of course, I didn't mind. Over the years, they had become an integral part of daily life whether they came through to babysit or pick up kids or help out in any of a thousand different ways.

Bobby's sister Marie, who had never married or had children, had moved back in with her parents about a year before they bought the Florida condo because she took a job at an Annapolis interior designer firm for yachts. She had previously lived in New York doing interior design for wealthy Manhattanites who needed their apartments off Central Park re-decorated. She wasn't terribly open about why that hadn't worked out, but when she moved back home she claimed the yacht work was a better deal. Originally, Marie declared she'd be moving into the parental house on the cove only temporarily until she found something else.

The first summer without the Owens in town after they converted to full-time Floridians, I realized how much I missed not just their presence at our house but also visiting their house on the water. I had grown accustomed to taking the kids and their friends to swim off the dock in the middle of the week with no notice whatsoever. Bobby Jr and David were as piscine as their sister, and once they had learned to swim competently all Bobby's mom and I had to do was sit on the dock and make sure the roughhousing didn't get out of hand. Some part of me acknowledged that even if the Owens hadn't moved to Florida, the kids were increasingly less interested in being dragged to their grandparents'. But I still missed the summer swim days.

I never had the same open invitation from Marie to show up and hang out on the dock. I wondered how much updating Marie had done and would continue to do to the Owens' house. The house was considered a generous size for a family of four back in the 1970s when we were growing up, and it certainly had plenty of room for just the Owens. Standards, at least in this area, had changed though. Now everyone wanted at least 3,500 square feet for two people. Coming from Manhattan Marie might not demand a sprawling suburbanite-sized house, but as a fashion and design maven the Owens' 1990s update of their 1960s era house could not possibly be up to her standards.

Even though the kids got over the Owens going to Florida and not going to their waterfront home all summer long, I had still found myself hoping that Marie would decide that Annapolis wasn't tony enough for her and take off for New York or L.A. I had had fantasies that I could then convince Bobby to buy his parents out and move into that house once the kids were in college. Dreaming that we could even retire to their house once Bobby was ready to slow down and he didn't need to be closer to D.C was about as far as I had ever gotten to retirement planning while Bobby was alive, but I had never had the courage to mention the idea to him. I'm sure Bobby had known the details of who was continuing to hold title to the house and who was paying the bills, but as the in-law, such details were definitely none of my business. Now that Bobby was gone, I assumed the Owens would ultimately leave the Maryland house to Marie since she was still living there ten years after the supposedly temporary re-adjustment.

In all those years of enjoying the Owens' house on the water, I had been completely oblivious about Grandma's plans for her cottage. I had assumed that cousin Bill had owned the cottage outright. But if the Owens' house hadn't been the way for me to get back to the water, Cecil Cove had its own way of showing me that the ribbon on my balloon was only so long, and the love that tethered me to the water would find its own way to draw me back. And now that I was back, I would create my own new life here.

CHAPTER SIXTEEN

SIOBHAN JANUARY 2015

A Canadian goose armada was invading the community beach. Godiva, Hershey and I had just reached the edge of the playing fields adjacent to the beach when I saw a perfect V of geese floating in toward the shore and then marching up on the sand the community imported and placed past the high tide mark every few years. The geese were a real nuisance for the community. One of the neighbors at the park informed me once that each goose we saw was responsible for about a pound of poop in the fields. I had no idea where that measurement had come from or who had taken the time to study goose fecal matter. I did know, however, that I had to tread carefully and also wash off the dogs' feet before I let them back in the house.

I let the dogs off the leashes. The geese saw them before they saw the geese. Suddenly the armada was an air force, in not quite so perfect a V formation in their haste to escape the canines.

A golden retriever joined my two from the far side of the field. I waved at my neighbor Linda, whom I often saw here and who was my most reliable dog sitter, and walked in her direction.

"I haven't seen you around our little facility lately," Linda noted. She was referring to the small rehab center where she worked toward the south of the county; it also happened to be owned by the health care organization for which I worked. The company occasionally sent me there as a rotating pharmacist to fill in for vacationing staff. The company was also partnering with some drug companies doing dementia research, and they sent me to all their facilities to do internal audits of the pharmacy records.

"Don't worry, I'm scheduled to be there next month to audit," I said.

"Thanks for the heads up. I might feel the flu coming on." She held a hand up to her brow in mock distress. In Linda's role as nurse manager, she often got stuck sitting with me during the audits if I came across any issues with compliance in the nursing staff.

"However, I am flying down to Florida to spend a few days with my Dad before the audit. Would you be available to watch Godiva and Hershey?" I asked.

"Sure, Goldy always loves the company. Mind if I bring them to my place?" Linda responded.

We worked out the details and chatted for a few more minutes while the dogs played together. Neither of the humans was up for an extended outing, with the wind blowing straight off the water at us with a damp heaviness that suggested the weatherman's predictions about possible snowfall might be correct. With some reluctance on their parts, the dogs allowed me to clip their leashes back on and we walked home.

Out of the breeze off the water, the temperature was a little more bearable. The funny thing about living right on the water is that I have different weather on the water side of the house than on the road side of the house. In winter, that cold breeze picks up microscopic particles of water producing a damp cold that sinks right through any clothes, while on the road side of the house, the breeze is often blocked by the house itself and seems to get caught in the trees. The road side therefore feels about 10 degrees warmer. The same is true in the summer but with the opposite effect on the humans, with the air stagnant with humidity on the road side of the house. I am grateful during those times for the gravel as it traps much less heat than the asphalt driveways some of the neighbors have. The water side of the house during those summer heat waves still benefits from whatever breeze is available, moving the air enough to break up the humidity a little. The added bonus is that during all the stifling months of summer, the water is usually swimmable, and I can console myself with dreams of plunging off the pier.

A cold breeze slipped right through my clothes, and I snapped back from my summer musings to the winter reality. We did get snow later that evening, about four inches. In Western New York, especially close to the lakes, no one would blink at four inches of snow. In the greater Washington D.C.-Baltimore metropolitan area though, four inches was as calamitous as the volcano exploding over Pompeii.

Regardless of the snowsteria the next day, I got back and forth to work easily enough in my little Civic with front wheel drive. Fortunately, I was at one of the closer facilities on this particular day. To my great frustration though, the grocery store was completely wiped out when I stopped on my way home. No milk, no eggs, no bread, only a few rolls of the cheapest toilet paper. I bought the last two five-pound sacks of dog food. With two seventy-pound labs, that food would last about two days, and I needed enough to cover the time Linda would be watching my dogs. What had people been thinking? Oh no, snow might come, let me go buy 300 pounds of dog food in case we're trapped until March.

I wasn't unhappy to escape the winter weather a few days later to head to the Gulf Coast. I had been visiting Dad more regularly since his heart attack. On the plane rides down for these visits I always found myself slipping through more than a one hour time zone difference all the way back to the call from Ana in 2009.

I hadn't recognize the phone number, but I answered because I knew the area code was the Pensacola area. Ana was on the other end. Dad had had a mild heart attack, and she was calling from the hospital.

"You don't have to rush down here or anything, dear. We were in a restaurant when it happened, and there was a nurse right at the next table who knew exactly what to do until the ambulance got there. The doctors say it was a pretty mild attack, and they say he should be fine as long as he does what they tell him to do. He'll be weak for several weeks to months though."

I took down some details on which hospital and where and told her I'd be heading down to Florida as soon as I could make the arrangements. I called my supervisor and requested that he find someone to cover my shifts for the next few days. Linda, as always, agreed to watch the dogs. When she inquired if she could bring them over to her house, I countered, "Are you sure your house is up to three dogs running amok?"

She replied, "I used to have a husband, a son, and a dog running through the house amok, so I don't think three dogs can be any worse."

I ended up flying in to Tallahassee and renting a car to drive west toward Dad's part of the panhandle. The flight connections were so bad to the small airport closest to Dad that I made better time driving from Tallahassee.

Dad was still in the hospital, although scheduled to be released with some home health care and rehab in the next day or so. And from Dad's point of view, his discharge couldn't be soon enough. "You think you can sneak me some Beechnut in, Siobhan?"

"They still make that stuff? You can't be serious, can you?"

"Of course I am. I know someone will smell it if I try to light up a cigarette, but I figure I can chew a little without anyone noticing."

"No way José. You'll be home soon enough."

Dad was a little pale and drawn, but considering some of the people I had seen wheeled by pharmacy windows in the nursing homes who were recovering from major heart attacks, he didn't look too bad.

I had dinner with Ana that night at a local seafood restaurant. I had seen Ana occasionally through the years but I had never spent any time with her outside of Dad's presence, and I felt a little awkward. Ana, however, was not the sort to notice, and the words poured out of her mouth incessantly, not even pausing for me to nod or say yes to some rhetorical question she posed before moving on to something else.

"Of course, once we got to the hospital, the doctors and nurses wouldn't even tell me what was going on because I'm not related to your dad. All in the name of patient privacy. I can't say that this HIPAA thing's done anything helpful for me, but we're all supposed to feel better that our secrets are safe from everyone, even the person who's going to have to care for them when they get home. Your dad and I both had our reasons for never getting married. I had dependent kids, child support and alimony from my first husband that would have been messed up if we did. And of course now we're at the age where we know that you should have some sort of health care power of attorney, and even our friends would tell us to make sure to take care of it, but we never got around to it, so I had a hell of a time convincing the hospital that I was the decision maker when he couldn't tell them himself. Fortunately, your dad wasn't out of it for that long, and as soon as he knew what he was talking about, he told them to tell me everything.

"You know your dad was thrilled when I told him you were coming. Of course, he had told me to tell you you didn't have to rush down here or anything, and you really didn't have to rush down like you weren't going to see him again, but when I said you were coming anyway, I could tell he was happy. I don't want to push you or anything, but getting up to Maryland to visit is getting a little hard for him. I know he likes going up there, and seeing that old marina where he and his dad worked, and he still goes on and on about how special it is to live on the Chesapeake. He says that he spent years on oil rigs and tankers in the Gulf, so he's spent plenty of time on the water, but he said nothing was like that cove.

"I've always lived down here and they don't call this part of the world the Redneck Riviera for nothing. We have some of the best beaches in the world right here. I don't get the big deal about the Chesapeake with no real beaches at all and the water is so brown, but I guess you must love it too since you moved back there."

I was exhausted just listening to Ana. I tried to keep my focus, but outside the big picture window of the restaurant the pelicans were fishing in the water, their pointed beaks plummeting into the water like sewing machine needles dipping into fabric, and I found myself blinking in and out of the conversation periodically.

I had come down on a Wednesday. They let Dad out on Friday because the hospital wanted him out before the weekend. I stayed in Florida through the weekend, working with the home health care aide to get all Dad's medicines parceled out into 3x7 grid boxes just like I did at work. Dad and I played rummy when he was awake. He did nod off a couple times, but I had a book with me.

I headed back home and returned to my routine, but after the heart attack I made visits to Florida a more regular part of my schedule instead of relying on Dad's visits to Maryland to spend time with him.

The change in cabin pressure called me back to the present flight. I got off the plane and picked up the rental car to drive over to Dad's place.

Six years after his heart attack, Dad was never going to have the same level of vigor that he had previously, but he was still able to do pretty well for himself. Ana was some undisclosed number of years younger than him and in good health. Plus she seemed to do a good job of keeping him on the straight and narrow.

He snuck in too many cigarettes when he went over to the local marina where he puttered around helping out at the counter and doing some light handyman tasks. I went over there with him one afternoon. He had explained that he had cleared his schedule for my visit, but he had agreed at the last minute to take one afternoon shift for a guy whose kid got sick.

"One thing you can say about Florida is that the boat business doesn't dry up come November. It keeps going year round." Dad observed after about 45 minutes of non-stop customers. I was sitting on a hard wooden stool next to the counter trying to keep out of the way.

"Do you miss doing the oil rigs or being on the tankers? Or is this enough for you?" I inquired.

"Right after the heart attack, this level of activity would have been as much as I could handle. I was just starting to get well enough to think about going back to my regular job, and then BP had that accident and dumped a few million gallons of oil in the Gulf. I filled out all my permanent retirement papers not long after that. Let me tell you, you didn't want to be part of big oil around here right after that mess. I accidentally walked into a grocery store one day wearing one of my old baseball caps from the company. It wasn't even BP but the cashier let me have it for all the birds we big oil folks killed with our carelessness." Dad grinned at the memory. "I didn't throw out all my logo stuff, but it's all buried in the back of the closet. Nah, at this point, I'm just as happy hanging out here. Come full circle. Grew up in a marina, now I'm ending up at one. Hey, you never did tell me what happened to Lotty's place once Bill died. Who'd they sell it to?'

I flushed. Although I called Dad pretty regularly, I hadn't told him about Julie's moving back in. At first, I hadn't wanted to talk about it, because I wasn't sure what my reaction would be. Then after things seemed to be ok with me and Julie, I had forgotten that I hadn't told him.

"Julie renovated the place and moved in herself Dad." I paused to look at his reaction.

He kept a blank look on his tanned face, raised one still black-as-coal eyebrow at me, and chewed on his tobacco. I knew he was waiting for me to say more.

"Do you remember I told you that Bobby had died of cancer, right?" I asked.

He just nodded and kept staring.

"Well, so Julie was pretty much an empty nester in a huge house. Turns out Mrs. Marconi left the house to Julie after Bill died. Bill never owned it, he only had the right to live there as long as he lived. Julie decided to renovate the cottage, move in there, and let her oldest daughter have their big house in Chevy Chase."

Dad finally joined the conversation. "I never held anything against Lotty. She was like my own mom that I didn't have, and I'd've done anything for her. But, Julie's mom and dad are pieces of shit, always were and probably still are. And even if they're not, I'm not giving 'em any chance to show me. My engineering degree was every bit as hard to get as theirs, but they were always lookin' down their damn noses at me 'cuz I wasn't afraid to get my hands dirty. And then, to act like such frickin' cowards after the accident." I heard a slight choke behind Dad's words and I thought he was going to stop. He changed gear slightly, but went on.

"When you and Julie were such good friends, I hoped Julie would turn out like Lotty. But that day she laid into you, I was in the garage and heard every nasty word she said. It's a damn good thing Lotty rushed her in the house. I told your mother that night that it looked like Julie did get her share of her parents' genes with no clue how to put blame where it really belonged, she wasn't like Lotty at all, and you were just as well rid of her. Worst fight your mother and I ever had. Your mother trying to say what a shock

Julie had had and how she probably didn't know what she was saying."

I turned my face down and tried to hide my shock at Dad's words, because if I showed any reaction on my face, whatever had turned on my Dad's talkativeness would shut down immediately.

"And then she married Mr. Kiss-the parents-ass Bobby Owen. He was always too slick for me. He was always, Yes, Mr. Barrett, no, Mr. Barrett, right-you-are Mr. Barrett. I always wondered what he was doing when no parents were around. Lawyer was a good job for him. Not that I wish cancer on anyone, 'specially not after what your mom went through. I told your mom I thought Julie and Bobby deserved each other. Your mom thought I meant that in a positive way. She and I weren't talking much by then though."

Dad went silent. I knew he was waiting for me to talk about Julie being next door. He would never ask, that just wasn't Dad. He would keep mum until you figured out what he wanted to hear.

"Julie went to counseling sometime in college. By her account, it was Bobby who first told her what a damn fool she was being, and she needed to start seeing that her own parents were responsible for screwing up her life, not everyone else." I was phrasing my words carefully. I didn't want to overly defend anyone, because the slightest extra praise and Dad would tune me out.

"Probably the smartest thing I've ever heard that Bobby said." Dad muttered.

"She indicated that without the counselors and Bobby she would never have gotten herself together. She apologized for blaming me back then." I caught a slight rise of Dad's eyebrow and rushed on. "I was angry for long enough, and I'm sick of my world of family and friends shrinking, not growing. Julie seemed sincere when she apologized and she's going to be right next door to me whether I like it or not, so I'm gonna see if I can have my Siamese sister back." I had never quite admitted even to myself that I wanted that much from having Julie next door. Dad didn't say anything, a faint smile playing at his lips when I resurrected our old nickname, and just nodded his head after a few seconds.

"Her mom, however, is still total shite," I smiled, deliberately using Grandpa's Irish pronunciation. Dad gave a low little chuckle too. Once Dad had finished up his favor to his friend with the sick kid at the marina, we headed back to his and Ana's place. Ana did most of the talking all through dinner that night and any other time she was with us during my visit. I had been coming down approximately every six months since the heart attack. Dad kept saying how he wanted to visit me and see the cove, but I could tell Ana worried about that. I nodded and left travel debates up to the two of them.

CHAPTER SEVENTEEN

My barge appeared on the horizon one morning when I was out to photograph a particularly spectacular set of pinks and oranges in the sunrise. I was initially annoyed because the floating rust trap looked rather ugly in the picture. When the barge turned onto the creek appearing to head toward the cove, and I could see the mountains of rock on the surface of the barge, I realized that my erosion control crew was on its way. Siobhan had pointed the erosion out to me at the end of last year, and I had hired a contractor. The contractor had told me in mid-March that the permits had come through after "only" three months. I had assumed he was joking about the only part, but he assured me that three months to get permits from the county, state and no less than the Army Corps of Engineers was absolutely record-breaking. The deep freeze that had locked all of his barges in place had created a backlog of work for him, and he could not get to my shoreline for several weeks after the permits came through.

I wasn't exactly sure what the machine on the barge was, but its operator sat in a cage and moved a long bent arm with a big basket at the end. As the barge turned into the narrow channel to enter the cove, the operator carefully dunked the basket in the water first on one side of the barge, then on the other to make sure not to run aground. I noticed that the barge operator had wisely chosen to come in on a high tide. The barge anchored itself off my dock, the versatile basket at the end of the arm lifting up the poles at each corner of the barge in turn, twisting slightly and dropping them down to serve as anchors. For the next day and a half, the contractor's crew put down a bunch of new black filter cloth and tried to shore up what had been left of my riprap. They then unloaded, one basket of the rusted yellow machine at a time, another 100,000 pounds of rocks to bolster up the shore line. The men wore thigh high boots and overalls that looked like they were made out of plastic as they stood in the water and re-positioned rocks as they came out of the big basket. The water temperature was only in the low fifties at this time of year, and their legs had to be turning numb after a few hours of work.

When they were done, the shoreline looked much better. They assured me I'd be good for another 20 or 30 years. The barge slowly backed itself out, using the basket again to test the depth on the sides to make sure the large vessel stayed in the channel.

As the tide washed against my new shoreline, the water made an echoing sound sliding amongst the new rocks, with mini-caves between the rocks needing to be filled in and then drained as the tide went out.

The boys hadn't been able to come home for Easter. Law school spring breaks and military leave hadn't corresponded to the Easter holiday this year. I hosted an open house for the neighbors on the cove at the end of April to satisfy my need for a big gathering. I remembered what a tight community Grandmom had had when I was a kid. The water brought everyone together. Doing the open house as the weather began to turn pleasant would give me the chance to meet new folks or re-acquaint myself with some of the folks I had known years ago. Then when everyone started going out on their docks and swimming in the water, I would have already had a chance to meet them.

I took a page from Mrs. Owen's book and ordered numerous platters from the local gourmet store rather than trying to prepare food myself. When the day of the party arrived, I was genuinely amazed how many of the people I knew myself or recognized as a friend of Grandmom. Of the twenty plus houses on our gravel road, only three or four had changed families since I was a kid. In many cases, the parents had turned the houses over to the kids as they got older. Or like Siobhan or me, people had inherited the houses when older relatives passed away. In a few cases, the older generation was still hanging on, although some of them looked to me like they would have difficulty keeping up with a waterfront house much longer.

I had originally believed that when I moved to Grandmom's cottage, I would have less work to do because the house was smaller. I had underestimated how much work a waterfront home was though. Things like erosion control were not a part of keeping up a Chevy Case suburban home, and even if they had been, Bobby would have taken care of that sort of detail. Also, being at the end of all the roads in the community, the backup generator was essential. I nullified that concern by paying for a maintenance contract with guaranteed emergency service. But the day the weather got warm enough to turn on the water going down to the dock, and I realized that I was going to have to crawl into the two foot high space under the house with all the imagined spiders to reach the winter shutoff valve, I had a moment where I was almost ready to throw in the towel.

I now better understood why the Owens had wanted to go to a condo and why Grandmom had been so happy at the senior community, even though I absolutely loved being back on the water so much that I was not willing to consider either of those options. I had missed the easy access to the Chesapeake ever since the Owens had migrated to Florida.

The morning of my open house, I had tried to prepare myself for the questions about Bobby as most of the families knew the Owens; in fact, some of them had probably come to the funeral home, although those days were a blur to me. Although people did ask how I was doing or offer condolences if just learning about Bobby's death, I was surprised after the event that I hadn't had any full-blown tearful outbursts. Yes, I felt a dull pang in my chest, my eyes oozed a little moisture, and my stomach tightened up, but the knife-like sharpness of the loss had subsided somewhat. When Bobby had first died, lots of people had platitudinously told me that I would feel better with time, but I hadn't seen how that was possible. Now I was starting to believe.

Guilty was over in Siobhan's yard with her two dogs, allowing guests to wander through the house and down to the dock without being molested by dog tongue.

I was on the dock with a glass of my special party punch talking to my next door neighbors, the Thompsons, from the side opposite Siobhan. The Thompsons had been big time competitive sailors. They kept a small motor boat at their dock next door just to go to the marina where they kept a couple different sailboats; the water depth in the cove was not sufficient for their fixed keel sailboats. The Thompsons still sailed on a leisurely basis, but they were now past the age where they could safely compete. Their two sons, who were several years younger than me, had inherited the sailing bug even worse than their parents. The two boys traveled the globe entering into various races. I wasn't sure from where the money for all of this came. Sailing is an expensive hobby, and the whole family did enough boating that none of them could possibly have held down a full-time job. Sailing was all that the Thompsons could talk about though, and after a few moments of chit-chat I had exhausted my knowledge base; I had learned to tack a little Sunfish back and forth in summer camp but that was the extent of my sailing skills. I was inwardly relieved when a sandy-bearded man showed up next to me. "Hey Jules, it's Jim and with a beard."

"Of course Jim, I remember the beard from your visit to the funeral home."

Jim shook hands with the Thompsons as well. "Are your parents here, Jim?" I asked.

"Yes, they're in the house. I'm not sure if they'll make it down the steps to the dock. They did say that they were hoping the Thompsons would be here since they haven't seen you all in ages." Jim nodded toward the Thompsons. Jim's younger sister was approximately the same age as the Thompson boys so I assumed that the parents had been in touch through children.

Mr. Thompson said, "Oh, how great. We'll go up and say hi while you two catch up."

"I was over at Mom and Dad's house when they got your invitation. I couldn't believe you ended up back on the cove. And Siobhan too. It's a regular reunion."

"Where are you living?" I inquired.

"I'm over closer to Annapolis renting a townhouse. I got divorced a few years ago, and I rented a place until I decided what I wanted to do. I can't say this in front of them, but the house is getting to be too much for Mom and Dad, so I want to see where things are headed with them before I make any real estate investments of my own."

"Are your parents looking at any senior communities? My Grandmom chose one of those a few years before she died, and she swore it was one of the best decisions she ever made. She had more friends than most school kids do."

"We've tried to convince them of that, but absolutely no takers there. Dad says outright the only way he's leaving his house is in a box feet first. My sister is tied up with her kids, so it may be me moving in with them. I'm not 100% keen on that idea, and neither are my parents. They're offended that we think they need help.

Right now, I'm spending more and more time on the weekends with them."

"I'm sorry they're not doing well."

"It's all right. Besides, I'll use it as an excuse to get a Jet Ski or something, and then you can try and cadge rides out of me again." Jim smiled remembering that I had wheedled, cajoled and pleaded at any opportunity for a Jet Ski ride.

"You never know, I might get my own now." I teased back. "I should go in and say hi to your parents."

"Of course. Did Siobhan come? "

"She did, but she has to work some weird shift this evening so she wasn't able to stay very long."

I walked up the dock and found Jim's parents. They had settled on the sofa with the Thompsons. I perched on the arm of the sofa and greeted them.

Caitlin brought the kids over the day after the open house. Her oldest, Katie, was right about the age Caitlin had been when I started bringing her over to the Owens' to swim in the creek. I wanted Caitlin's kids to have the same chance to love life on the water that I had tried to give my kids. Caitlin showed up with water shirts, water shoes, and life jackets for both Katie and Mike, who had just turned five.

The water was still a little cool, but substantially warmer than when the poor men putting in my new riprap had been standing thigh deep in it. I had known the water was warm enough for swimming when I had seen some of the teenagers across the creek out swimming after school earlier in the week.

I climbed down my new dock ladder and stood by the dock to lift the kids down. Caitlin was a little too far along in her pregnancy to be clambering up and down ladders, although she looked mournfully at the water as she had always been a fish herself.

I shivered a little bit. I was a lot wimpier than I used to be. Siobhan and I never wore water shoes or aqua shirts as kids. We lived with bathing suits on under our clothes most of the summer and would leap in the water no matter how cold as soon as we were allowed.

The tide was out far enough that even Mike had no problem walking around. The water shoes saved the kids from having to get used to the silty bottom that used to ooze up between our toes as we were kids. We threw a small bright orange ball around until the kids got bored with it. Katie wasn't quite brave enough to try swimming yet, although I stroked out past the end of the dock and then back in to show her the water was quite swimmable. Mike had just started swimming lessons. He was more fascinated with the way the waves splashed into the holes in the riprap. He wanted to move the rocks and stick his hands in the holes, but I told him that he shouldn't stick his hands in because snakes sometimes lived in those holes. Katie shrieked then, "What do you mean snakes? They don't come in the water do they Gramma?"

"Yes, of course they do, dear. I don't like them anymore than you do, but that's part of swimming here." I of course was not going to tell her about the visceral squeals that I let out whenever I saw one swimming in the water. And, in fact, since the shy skinny river otters that also played in the cove made sinuous movements as well, I tended to squeal whenever I saw a long slender creature. Which was too bad because the otters were rather cute, but they were so skittish that the slightest noise out of place would send them running, and I would usually squeal first and then realize it wasn't a snake second.

Once the kids had had enough, I lifted them back up onto the dock where Caitlin dried them off. I climbed up the ladder and toweled off. We went into the house and got everyone changed. I took the tray of snacks I had made earlier, leftovers from yesterday's event, and we all went back down to the dock to nibble.

"So, Grandmom's house isn't too far from here, is it?" Caitlin queried. I realized that she had never played in the neighborhood itself or gone out on the canoe independently to see how close we actually were.

"It's closer by water than road. On the road, you turn off two streets back. On the water, you can be there in under 10 minutes by kayak."

"No kidding, it's that close?"

"Yes, honey, all of us kids played together. During the summer, we spent as much time in the water as we did on land. Siobhan's brother Brian and Bobby were practically best friends, so they were always going back and forth, up until they went on that stupid canoe ride."

I didn't even realize I'd used the word "they" but Caitlin pounced on it right away.

"What do you mean 'they' went on a canoe ride? Are you saying that Dad was with Siobhan's brother when the accident happened?"

I cursed myself for my slip of the tongue. I hadn't wanted her to have a reason to judge Bobby when he wasn't here anymore to defend himself or for the knowledge to taint her memory of her dad. "Yes, honey. Brian, your dad and this guy Jim whose parents are still right over there." I pointed to Jim's parents' dock. "Going out on the river on a canoe on the Fourth of July was an incredibly stupid thing to do and all three of them knew it, but being teenaged boys they decided they had to have a great view for the fireworks. By the time I told you about the accident, your dad was already gone and I didn't want you to think badly of him. What happened to Brian after the boat flipped wasn't your dad's fault."

"But then, what happened? Where was Dad when Brian got hurt?" Caitlin nibbled on a leftover madeleine while she waited for me to share my recollections.

I told her about how the canoe had flipped and when the three boys weren't successful in getting it flipped back over, they had all agreed to swim to shore. No one could ever be sure of the reason

Brian had gone back and tried to tow the canoe after him, although maybe he did because it was his family's canoe and he didn't want to get in trouble for losing it. I then went on to explain how Bobby and Jim had reached shore and were surprised to find out that Brian wasn't right there with them. I told her how men from the neighborhood had taken out boats to try to find Brian but it was too dark, and that they didn't find Brian until the next afternoon. Even reliving the memory by telling Caitlin was awful, remembering how I cried all night long not stopping until Grandmom and I went over to Siobhan's house in the morning to wait for someone to find Brian.

I could tell that Caitlin wasn't fully satisfied with my explanation about why I hadn't told her and her siblings about all this, but recalling the accident still upsets me, and I was saved from further questioning by some roughhousing between Katie and Mike that required parental intervention.

Katie was slated to spend at least a week with me when Caitlin had the baby. Mike would stay with Caitlin's brother-in-law, who had a little boy who was almost the exact same age as Mike. We all wanted to give Caitlin and her husband a little bit of time to get the new one into a routine. Unlike when I'd had the kids and Bobby had to keep working the same insane hours he always did, Kevin's job allowed him paternity leave giving them some time together with the newborn. Otherwise I might have offered to stay with Caitlin at the house, but with her husband home I felt like I'd be in their way.

That first summer that my parents had both been working and traveling, I was furious at having to leave my perfect room to go spend the whole summer at Grandmom's. Before that summer, Grandmom had done a fair amount of babysitting in my parents' house, but I learned later from Grandmom that she had told my parents in no uncertain terms that she was not abandoning her own house for a whole summer because they had taken on jobs that didn't allow them to raise their child. The spare bedroom at Grandmom's house with its wood paneling and gold shag carpet at the time had been unspeakably ugly and utterly uncool as far as I was concerned. The bed was the small twin Ethan Allen bed my mother had used growing up, with its small matching desk and dresser. The bedspread was scratchy with a yellow and brown weave pattern.

One thing I can say about my mother is that she was vain about her house, and that meant that I had had the perfect princess bedroom. I had a white canopy double bed with a lavender fabric canopy and a matching bedspread and dust ruffle. All the furniture was white. I had a collection of plastic horses, brown and black with black manes on one of the bookshelves, many years before every little girl had a My Little Pony collection. My stuffed animal collection was piled on a big pink bean bag in the corner.

When Mom told me that I'd be spending the summer with Grandmom, I had raged at Mom about having to leave my room to go to Grandmom's ugly spare bedroom. When Grandmom came to pick me up I overheard Mom telling her that I had thrown a hissy fit about wanting my purple bedroom. Grandmom at least had the good sense to grab a plastic trash bag and help me load all my stuffed animals for the summer. The room at her house was still hopelessly brown but I covered as many surfaces as possible with stuffed animals. Also, as my "artwork" collection grew, Grandmom would let me tape the pieces of construction paper to the wood paneling, something Mom would never have tolerated. She never insisted that I keep the room perfectly clean either, like Mom did because she wanted to show off the house if anyone happened to come through. As long as I didn't leave food in the room to attract bugs, I could leave it a mess. She warned me though that she had no intention of digging through my mess to find my laundry so if I wanted clean clothes, I had to put them in a basket where she could find them. Over the years, although I still found the room unattractive, I felt more at home there where I had put my own personal stamp on everything.

Although Katie would only stay with me for a week or so, I didn't want her to feel the same resentment that I had. I wanted her to view staying with me as an adventure. I had checked with Caitlin about what Katie's favorite color was in order to buy a bedspread or something she would like. Caitlin had informed me that Katie was still infatuated with the *Frozen* movie, and I was able to enrich the Disney coffers by purchasing a set of their bed linens.

When we were heading back up to the house from the dock, I leaned over and told Katie I had a surprise for her. I led her upstairs to the spare bedroom and showed her the huge clear plastic bag with the *Frozen* princess bedroom set. Her eyes grew wide.

I questioned her, "You know how you're going to come stay with me for a little while when your mommy has the new baby?"

She nodded yes.

"Well, the first thing we'll do when you get here is decorate this room for you. Would you like that?

She asked, "Can't we do it now?"

"I think your mom's about ready to head home. Besides, won't it be more fun to decorate when you're actually here?"

"But can I take it home until then?" she persisted.

I hadn't thought about that wrinkle, but I deflected, "Well, then staying here wouldn't be as special if you take it home."

Caitlin teased me a bit as well. "Thanks, Mom. You know that means that all I'm going to be hearing about is the *Frozen* bed set and how come she can't have one at the house and when is she going to be at Grandma's to use it."

"That's the privilege of being a grandmother, dear, spoiling them rotten and leaving the parents to deal with it."

CHAPTER EIGHTEEN

I was reading on the dock after work when a snowy white egret landed at the small beachy area exposed by the low tide in front of the next door neighbor's house, the neighbor I had started to refer to in my head as the mad piano player. The egret unfurled one wing and ducked his head under. When he stood up again he surveyed the water in front of him. With surprisingly efficient movements, he began to run along the shore, his bright yellow feet disproportionately large for the toothpick thin legs. He stopped and then began bobbing his head in the water, coming up with something I couldn't make out.

I trailed my eyes along the water back to my dock and noticed dozens if not hundreds of consecutive circles in the water. I stood up and took my sunglasses off for a better view. Hundreds if not thousands of tiny little fish were right at the surface, each one of them responsible for a little circle in the water that beat up against the circles made by all the other fish in the school. No wonder the egret had decided on supper at Cecil Cove.

The egret took off suddenly with a few graceful flaps and flew down a couple houses. I was still leaning over looking at the water and damn near fell in when a male voice behind me yelled, "Permission to come aboard." The head of a sandy-bearded man was out at the edge of my dock near the ladder. "Hey Siobhan, how are you? It's Jim."

I looked closer and realized that it was in fact Jim. Jim's parents were still right across the cove so I saw him over there occasionally, and I had seen him from a distance at Julie's party right as I was leaving, but he looked a bit different dripping wet.

"Of course you can come up. Even if you did scare my egret off." I walked to the end of the dock. I tilted the aluminum stairs of the dock ladder forward releasing them from the lip that caught them and then slid the steps down into the water for him. Jim pulled himself up and shook off.

"Sorry I don't have any towels down here," I said.

"No worries. I was visiting Mom and Dad, but they both fell asleep in front of the TV so I decided to get in a swim."

"How are they doing?" I asked.

"Slowing down. Dad fell last week. Mom didn't call either me or Laura for about three hours until she finally realized she couldn't get him up on her own. The house is way too much for them. It's more and more likely that I'll have to move in with them than that I'll get them out of there to someplace else."

"Sorry to hear that. If it makes you feel better, that's what I did when Mom got sick."

"Yeah, we all take our parents' houses in this neighborhood. I'm hoping one of the MacArthur kids takes over next door to us soon. The sailboat they had back when we were kids is still there rotting. The cover's all torn, the raccoons live in it, and it looks like it's taking on water. Looks like you've got new neighbors on at least one side these days that are going to keep things in better shape."

The piano player was drilling away at a series of arpeggios. "Yes, don't tell anyone else but I refer to that as the mad piano player's house. I secretly think it's some poor teenaged girl whose parents force her to practice a hundred hours a week."

"Surprised they keep the windows open then."

"Oh, maybe the girl is hoping someone will call the police to complain about excessive noise so she can get out of practicing." I said this with a grin. "Just kidding, I really have no idea."

"And on your other side you've got the standard family takeover. I heard old Bill had passed away, but didn't know it was Julie moving in until Mom and Dad got the flyer for her open house. The open house was a great idea, get the neighborhood gathered together. I hadn't known where that house would go once Bill died." Jim said.

"No one knew the house was going to Julie. As I understand the story, her grandmother had only left Bill the right to live in the house as long as he wanted to, but after he passed away, the house went to Julie."

He nodded, "I was still kind of surprised that Julie moved here. I didn't want to pry too much at the open house, but I assumed she'd stay in the ritzy Chevy Chase neighborhood"

"Yes, she said she couldn't stand to be in their big house where they'd raised the kids, so she fixed this place up. One of her kids and some grandkids are living in Julie's old house."

"Well, it sounds like you and Julie have had some civilized conversations, and I don't see any artillery placements on the dock. If I have to move back here with Mom and Dad, I'd rather not have you two still hating each other." Jim delivered these statements in a joking manner to cover up the obvious awkwardness of bringing up our rift.

"We're actually doing well. I still have some issues with her parents, but I know I shouldn't have gotten mad at Julie back then. Apparently ditto for her toward me."

"I'm glad to hear that. It feels like we all come full circle and land right back here at Cecil Cove. I should swim back over now. If Mom and Dad wake up and don't find my note, they'll flip out."

He did a shallow dive off the end of my pier and headed back across the cove with a good strong crawl. I yelled after him for diving. I know there's nothing in the water at the end of my pier, but diving into shallow bodies of natural water is foolish. Our little cove only averages about four to six feet deep at an average low tide, not even enough water to support a fixed keel sailboat.

About two weeks later Jim did end up moving in with this parents. Jim's dad fell yet again. Jim's sister Laura is about 10 years younger than Jim and her three kids are still at home and in school. Jim was therefore the obvious choice to take care of their parents because he was only renting a small house closer to Annapolis following his divorce.

SIOBHAN JUNE 2015

"Bobby was the one who saved me, you know. I was so angry at everyone, absolutely everyone. He was the first person who had the nerve to tell me to suck it up and stop blaming everyone else. I mean, I can't say I was all better after that night at the frat party. I needed the counselor, but that night was a breakthrough for me." Julie finished up the story of how she and Bobby got together following a College Park frat party.

"I can't say I ever had a breakthrough in getting over Brian's death. There was no one a-ha moment. For me, getting better was like an ice cube melting, one drip at a time. More like an iceBERG melting. It took a long time. I felt bad for being such a shit to Mom, she lost so much more than me. I tried to apologize once I moved back here but Mom could never talk about the accident. She would just blow me off if I brought it up."

"Yeah, Bobby and I barely talked about it either. Although it was funny, after one of the counseling sessions, after I'd been going for quite some time, the counselor told me that I should try to find some way to make something positive out of what happened, you know, view it as a growth experience or some such nonsense. I went home and vented a little bit on Bobby, telling him I thought the counselor was falling off her rocker trying to make out that the accident and the aftermath could be positive. But then Bobby responded that he could sort of see that, and I was about to backslide and lay into him. But he told me after the accident his parents let him have it, telling him if he kept acting like a screw off and making such ridiculously bad decisions he would never make it through college, let alone get into law school or get a job at a big firm. He had assumed all his life he was going to be a lawyer in a big firm just like his dad. But when his dad informed Bobby that if he didn't start growing up he could forget about having dear old dad's help getting into law school or into a law firm, Bobby said that scared him, saying it was the first time he realized his big firm lawyer job might not just get handed to him."

We were both getting a little too serious, so I tried to make a joke. "Well, I'm glad someone got a growth experience out of the accident, but I'm with you, the counselor was full of it."

We both laughed a bit and then sat silently on the dock for a few minutes. A large boat roared toward Lord's Creek, not obeying the no wake buoy and only slowing down when not doing so would have endangered the bottom of the boat. I started counting alligators like Dad had taught me to do as a kid. One alligator, two alligator, three alligator..... until the wake from the boat reached the shore of the cove, and the swells of water falling in between the rocks in the riprap created an almost musical swoosh. From the creek to my dock was usually about a minute.

Our conversations since Christmas Eve seemed to turn out this way. We would start innocuously talking about the dogs or her kids or some shared childhood memory, and then we'd end up twisting it into a far more serious conversation than either of us wanted at the moment; then one of us would try to make a joke or change the subject to get ourselves out of it.

"Oh, shit, there's a snake." Julie exclaimed right on cue. "Look, look, look, seeing him swimming there right at the end of the dock. Oh crap, I hope Guilty doesn't see him." Julie had knocked her chair over in her haste to stand up once she saw the snake.

I stood up more slowly and walked down to where I could look at the offending reptile. "Oh, please, it's just a plain old northern water snake. No need for a panic attack, and he's going to slither himself away as soon as he sees us. The dogs are over swimming by your dock anyway." As predicted, the snake had noticed the commotion above him, literally turned tail and started moving away from us as quickly as possible in a typical serpentine swirl.

CHAPTER NINETEEN

SIOBHAN JULY 4, 2015

A mother mallard was floating by the dock with her five little ones at low tide. The babies were still all fuzz, and I had never figured out a way to distinguish the baby males from the baby females. Momma was ducking her head under the water and coming up with mouthfuls of the sea grass that flourished in the early summer. Later in the summer, the grass would break apart and get washed to shore with the tides. Right now though, the ducks found the grass a perfect lunch. The little ones quickly got the hang of sticking their heads under to get the mouthfuls. The male mallard was further out in the cove, obviously in a protective mode. Turtles can sneak up underwater on baby ducks and yank them beneath the surface even despite the parental protective circling, sadly leaving many a momma duck shepherding a dwindling flock as June wears on.

I was absentmindedly pulling crab grass and the occasional oyster shell out of my petunias right above the dock while I watched the ducks. Godiva and Hershey were in the fenced part of the yard, pushing their noses through the gaps in the fencing, hoping I'd take pity and release them to go swimming. After I had finished the gardening I wanted to do, I did free the dogs, and all three of us refreshed ourselves in the cove.

Later in the afternoon, Jim, Julie and I started drinking Dark 'n' Stormys on Julie's dock. I was telling a story about the 83-year old man at the nursing home who made his way from his room to the pharmacy and demanded that I get him some medical marijuana. I tried to explain to him that Maryland had not yet reached the enlightened state of allowing medical marijuana, even though I knew that draft legislation had been introduced. He was irate, yelling at me, screaming about how his children dumped him in a Maryland nursing home because they didn't want to be bothered with traveling out to Colorado but that he'd been out in Colorado smoking pot for the last 60 years of his life and he was damned if he was going to stop now. I had to call security.

Jim laughingly said, "You can only expect more of the same as the hippies and the stoners generation ages."

Julie responded somewhat stiffly, "Bobby and I just never did any of that stuff, even as kids. I just can't imagine what's so compelling about pot that you can't give it up by the time you get to the nursing home."

Right at that moment, Julie's phone rang with some rap ring tone. She jumped up, saying, "It's Bobby Jr. Excuse me while I run up and talk to him."

Jim exhaled. "Oh good, I wasn't going to be able to take the Saint Bobby stuff. Oh please, Bobby Owen never smoked pot. If he didn't, then neither did Bill Clinton."

"I wouldn't know one way or the other, but I guess you'd know if anyone would."

Jim looked at me with a little surprise. "Oh, I'm not the only one who would know. Bobby's uncle who was in Vietnam was a big time dealer, and that's where Bobby got his stuff. All of us kids got ours from Bobby. I'm not saying Bobby was a big time dealer or anything. He always had a joint or two to sell to a friend though."

JIM JULY 4, 1979

The light was just starting to fade on the cove. Brian, Bobby and I were on Bobby's parents' dock because his parents were at a barbecue somewhere further down the peninsula. Bobby was urging Brian, "C'mon man, let's take the canoe out to the duck blind. I left all the weed hidden there."

The duck blind was a structure built out in the river consisting of six pilings driven into the river bed. The whole structure was roofed over. Half of the structure had a crude plywood floor. During hunting season, the whole structure would be covered with new cornstalks or dried rushes or any sort of thatch that hunters believed ducks would find innocuous. The county had some sort of lottery and permit process, and during the late fall, the lucky hunters would pull their small usually camouflaged boat under the roof of the blind in the half without the floor. They and their dogs would crawl into the part of the blind with the floor and wait for the ducks, often floating fairly elaborate decoys in the water near them.

Outside of hunting season, adventurous teenagers would use the blinds as hangouts despite the "No trespassing" signs that were posted all over them. Kids knew, however, that as long as no one's parents were out on a nearby dock, and you weren't stupid enough to crawl in when a Coast Guard or Natural Resources Police boat was going by, you could hang out in there for hours. During the day you had to swim there from one of the houses fronting the river or else someone would come check out the boat tied up next to the blind, but all of us that grew up on the water were good enough swimmers for that. You had to be awful careful smoking in there to make sure the dried cornstalks didn't go up in flames, but many the teenager had swum over with a few joints in a plastic bag and a six pack of beer.

Bobby had made a little hidden compartment up near the roof covered by cornstalks where he hid joints in a plastic bag. He was afraid his parents would find them if he left them in their house. He had planned to swim out earlier in the day and grab a few to have during the fireworks. Too many parents and small kids were splashing in the water and chilling on the docks during the holiday day though, and he wasn't able to get out there without someone noticing.

He had been trying for at least an hour to convince Brian to paddle out there in the canoe as it got dark. Brian was putting in his application to the Naval Academy that year, and he wanted nothing to do with weed. Not that Brian hadn't tried pot a little earlier on as a teenager, but he didn't want to blow his chances at the Academy by getting caught with drugs.

Bobby was absolutely relentless though. "We've been out there a hundred times. We can even bring the canoe right up against the duck blind so that we're stable in the water. If the police come up to us, we just say that we got a little spooked by the size of the waves and decided to use the pilings for stability."

Maybe that argument was what convinced Brian even though he knew better. Maybe he was sick of Bobby bugging him about it. Maybe Brian really wanted to see the fireworks from the river. All I know is that eventually Brian agreed, "All right, already. Let's go."

People watching from their power boats usually anchored closer to the mouth of the river or closer to Annapolis, so not many boats were anchored around the duck blind. Still, the river around the blind was majorly choppy from all the boat traffic that had gone past. We got to the duck blind safely, although we had to repeatedly zig zag the nose of the canoe into passing boat wakes. We had barely enough light going out to see the waves and keep from getting hit broadside and capsizing. Bobby climbed up into the blind and pulled down his stash. He must have been a little spooked though because he didn't even talk about lighting up in the canoe. We watched the fireworks as Bobby had suggested, with lines thrown around two of the pilings for stability.

When the fireworks were over, we started back and that's when we knew we were in trouble. The water wasn't any smoother and we couldn't see a thing. The moon was waxing gibbous, but the clouds were covering it most of the time.

We all knew we were going to capsize at some point. Bobby was no help with the boat though because he was so busy trying to find some way to stash the little plastic bag of joints in his clothes to keep them from getting smashed and to have both hands free for swimming. I remember my oar hitting something plastic in the water, probably a bleach bottle someone was using to mark the location of their crab pot. Then we were in the water and the canoe was upside down. Once I got my head above water, I stretched down with my toes, but couldn't feel bottom. Brian was at the stern of the canoe yelling at us to get ready to flip her back over. I know I had to flip a canoe back over in deep water for a Boy Scout merit badge, but in Scouts we didn't do it at night with waves slapping us in the face. The three of us tried but couldn't get the canoe right side up again. I heard Brian saying something about the line being caught on something, and I suspected we'd gotten caught up in whatever I'd hit my paddle on right before we capsized.

After three or four times, Bobby told Brian to scrap it and swim to shore. Brian was pissed, and he didn't lose his temper that easily. "You bitched at me for over an hour to bring you out here to get your damn weed. Now when we've flipped…" A wave must have slapped Brian in the face because he spluttered a bit before continuing. "Now that we've flipped, you want to leave the canoe, and I'll be the one who has to explain to my Dad where the hell it is. Asshole."

Bobby didn't say anything, but he did get back in position next to the canoe. We still couldn't do it, and we were all getting a little tired. I knew Bobby wouldn't speak up again since Brian had unloaded on him, so I did. "Bri, this is not safe, man. I'll go with you to explain to your dad about the canoe, but we gotta get ourselves back on shore before we're too tired to swim in." I thought I heard him agree, and Bobby swore later that Brian had said OK. With some relief, Bobby and I started stroking toward shore, never doubting that Brian was right there with us.

When we got back on shore and realized that Brian wasn't with us, Bobby begged me not to say anything about the weed. "We're going to be in enough trouble as it is going out on the river in a canoe without adding the weed to the story."

After Brian's body was found, I was a nervous wreck. "Bobby, man, we went out to that duck blind to get weed that Brian didn't even want and now he's dead."

"Are you saying it's my fault, man?" Bobby's face was flushing red and his voice was raised. "Brian took that canoe out in the river dozens of times. If he didn't want to go, he wouldn't have gone. We weren't even smoking the weed. The weed didn't make any damned difference as to whether he got hit. It's bad enough that my parents have been all over my case telling me if I keep doing stupid shit like going out in canoes at night I don't have a prayer of getting into law school or my Dad's firm, no less if I tell them I had weed on me."

Julie still wasn't back when Jim finished his story, which obviously was news to me. The story from Bobby and Jim back then had only been that they went out into the river to watch the fireworks. Besides, once Brian was found with the blood all over the back of his head, no one was focused on Bobby and Jim anymore.

"I was never square with how Bobby kept his mouth shut. After I found out that he'd proposed to Julie, I tried to bring it up again. He lit into me with, 'Julie doesn't need to know anything about that. Her life has been fucked up enough because her parents were driving the boat. It's not like we were stoned out there, man. We just made a stupid decision to go out in the river. That's all I'm ever gonna tell Julie, you got that man.' That was about the end of our friendship."

I replied eventually, still trying to digest this new twist on the story of the night Brian died, "Well, it's not exactly on the up and up, but Bobby was right that the weed itself didn't make any difference to what happened to Brian. Even if Bobby was pushing Brian to go out, Brian should have had enough sense to know that going on the river in a canoe in the dark on Fourth of July was stupid. I can't pretend Brian wasn't at least partially responsible for what happened to him solely because Bobby was being pushy."

"Yeah, I know," sighed Jim, "but it bugged the hell out of me when he lit into me about never telling Julie what happened. Didn't she deserve to know that Brian might not have been out in that river for her parents to hit if Bobby hadn't wanted his weed?"

I drank a fair amount of my Dark 'n' Stormy while I deliberated.

Finally I said, "You know what, I think enough people's lives got screwed up by that accident. Julie is just pulling her life together after losing her husband of thirty years, and she was in counseling for years after the accident trying to deal with what her parents did. Would telling her something bad about Bobby after he's dead and not able to tell his side of the story help anything? Maybe he did feel guilty, maybe he was scared that he wouldn't get into law school if anything about the weed got into some record. Look at what Julie's parents did because they were afraid of losing their security clearances. But maybe instead of telling her about it, he made it up to Julie by being a great husband to her, a great provider for their family, and a great father to their kids. I think I'd like to let his record as a man for thirty years stand for the sort of person he was rather than an accident that happened when he was still a kid."

Jim nodded. "I hadn't thought of it that way. But if you of all people can let how he acted go, then I'm certainly not going to bring it up."

"Good, because she's heading back," I said. Then in a louder voice that would reach Julie I shouted, "and hallelujah, she's brought a fresh round of drinks."

Julie came out on to the dock carrying a tray with another round of Dark 'n' Stormys. "Sorry to abandon you all for so long, but Bobby Jr was telling me about his clerkship this summer with the LA office of Bobby's old firm. They have some BIG clients in the music business, and one of the partners took Bobby along to a meeting with them. He couldn't tell me who the client was due to client confidentiality, but he was super excited."

We congratulated her. I ran over to my place and got some guacamole and chips so we wouldn't be totally wasted by the time the fireworks started.

Large firework displays are no longer the purview of just the surrounding municipalities, although I'm not sure what the legalities are. Across the creek and out in the river, several people were clearly launching them off their boats. Over the trees to the right, the fireworks set off at the community beach lit up that part of the sky. The big show at Annapolis went on for at least fifteen minutes. For 270 degrees we were surrounded by colored rain.

"There's nothing like watching fireworks over the water," Julie remarked. "One year, Bobby and I were stupid enough to try to take the kids down to the National Mall in D.C. Crowds don't normally bother me but I was terrified that one of the kids was going to get trampled, and I couldn't even pay attention to how spectacular the show was. We got about two square feet on the mall for all five of us. I swore I'd never go back, and that I didn't care if I ever saw another fireworks display in my life. I forgot how great they are here."

SIOBHAN JULY 5TH, 2015

Julie is floating in a neon green river raft, sangria in hand. I'm in a pink raft with a craft beer in a plastic cup. Jim went back to his house to check on his parents. We adults got our exercise earlier in the day swimming back and forth across the cove a couple times. The dogs had by this point given up on swimming; all of them were sound asleep on the dock, still dripping wet, not even having had the energy to spray the water off their coats all over the humans before lying down.

Now, only Jim's teenagers and Julie's grandkids are splashing around us, periodically climbing the ladder back onto the dock, only to jump right back in again. Pink and purple foam water noodles float aimlessly, waiting for someone to claim them. The mother mallard keeps nudging her still fluffy little ones away from the hustle surrounding our docks.

The teenagers three docks down are playing some horrible modern music, daring one another to climb up on the pilings and jump in from there. A disembodied mother's voice yells down "No diving, only jumping" at the teenagers. They mostly obey, but every now and then one of them sneaks in a shallow water dive.

Katie squeals as her head pops up above the surface, "Mike pushed me and I can't find my goggles."

Caitlin, who looks like she is about to pop, yells at Mike who is still standing on the dock trying to look innocent. "No pushing or you can't swim anymore."

A heron circles over the cove, grunting as it surveys all the activity below and finally chooses a high pine tree on the far side of the cove as a landing spot. Aside from the style of the bathing suits, the snapshot of the cove I'm seeing right now could have been taken forty years ago. I lean my head back against the raft and take in the sounds of the cove. The tide is coming in, and my raft is slowly brought to my shore on the incoming waters.

ABOUT THE AUTHOR

Ms. Sausville earned her B.A. from Cornell University, her M.P.H. from the Johns Hopkins University School of Hygiene and Public Health, and her J.D. from the University of Maryland School of Law. She lives near fictional Cecil Cove with her husband and two cats.

Made in the USA
Lexington, KY
23 July 2018